A WAR

A putrid, poison-green mist rolled out from behind the pool, concealing the belly and feet of the great serpent slithering around the overhang. The serpent dipped a tongue the size of a pitchfork into the pool for a long drink, then let its glowing green eyes sweep the area. I cringed back into my hiding place, away from those eyes, but they did not look at me then. Instead, the monster spotted my jalapeños, flicked them into its mouth with one deft snap of its tongue, and incinerated my sombrero on the next exhalation.

Seeing the dragon was like seeing the queen of England. I did not think either of them would care to chat with me, though of the two I'd have preferred the queen. Though I had never cared for her politics, she was at least a human being with no known tendencies toward pyromania. . . .

THE DRASTIC DRAGON OF DRACO, TEXAS

Elizabeth Scarborough

BANTAM BOOKS
TORONTO • NEW YORK • LONDON • SYDNEY • AUCKLAND

THE DRASTIC DRAGON OF DRACO, TEXAS

A Bantam Spectra Book / June 1986

ISBN 0-553-25887-7

Published simultaneously in the United States and Canada

This book is for the people who gave me a love for western story telling—Grandma Gladys Scarborough, my Dad, Don Scarborough, and my friend, Allen Damron. Also for the memory of my cowboy Grandpa Scarborough, Great Uncle Hap Scarborough, who roamed Oklahoma with Quanah Parker's kids, Great Aunt Virginia, who loved beadwork and Navajo silver, and Great Uncle Noah Piersee on my mother's side, who introduced me to Marty Robbins and Zane Grey.

In addition I have to thank about half of the folk music and fantasy-loving element in Texas for their help in researching this book. Allen Damron, Mack Partain, Art Eatman, Bennie and Danna Garcia, Rittie Ward, Tom Knowles, Warren Norwood, Lillian Stewart Carl, Sue D'Artez and Tim and Marian Henderson for rides, lectures, inspiration, reference material, and in Bennie Garcia's case, a family tree of Spanish names. Also particular thanks to Elena (Wuggins) Damron for playing dragon real estate lady and helping me find various places in the Big Bend where my characters would feel at home. Grateful acknowledgment to the Third Annual Cookie Chill-Off staff at Terlingua, Texas, and Uncle Joe, the Panhandle Plains Museum, and the staff at the Lajitas Museum and Desert Gardens. Anyone wanting the real folklore of the Big Bend should consult, among others, the writings of J. Frank Dobie, whose *Tongues of the Monte* was of tremendous assistance, and those of W. D. Smithers, to whom I am indebted for the contents and results of Mariquilla's burn cure, though to the best of my knowledge Mr. Smithers never had the opportunity to test the concoction to the extent that my characters did. Folk tales of the Big Bend were gleaned from several accounts, including *Tales of the Big Bend* by Elton Miles. Thanks also to Professor John Whitehead and Professor Carol Gold of the University of Alaska, Fairbanks, for their assistance in researching the lives of western women. And last but not least, many thanks to Lillian Hassler, Robin Russell, and Jerry Steen for taking the time to listen to the story in progress.

THE DRASTIC
DRAGON
OF
DRACO, TEXAS

1

Paladins of the Prairie may very well exist on the prairie, but they have clearly drawn the line at carrying the Code of the West into the Texas desert. I know for a fact that muleskinners bear no resemblance whatsoever to either Saint George or to any of those other gallant knights who traipsed about rescuing damsels in distress. When *I* was abducted by wild Indians and subsequently menaced by a dragon, none of the fifty teamsters with whom I was traveling lifted a finger to rescue me.

Of course, forty-nine of them weren't aware I needed rescuing, since the wagon in which I was riding had bogged down behind the others just before midday siesta and of *course* the mules had to be rested before we were dislodged and reunited with the rest of the train.

Not that my traveling companions were being intentionally neglectful. They were simply more accustomed to dealing with mules than with ladies. Had it occurred to them that I might be in some danger, one of them would undoubtedly have insisted that I join a wagon further up the trail in a more protected position. But, as usual, they were so intent upon their own routine they forgot my presence. I believe that they did so not so much because I am unmemorable as because my presence presented them with something of a dilemma. A frontiersman curses in front of a lady only at peril to his life and immortal soul. Unfortunately, cursing is an absolute requirement in the practice of the muleskinning profession.

Since my objective was to sample the true flavor of the wild west, I willingly accommodated myself to this benign neglect. Though but three days away from the cavalry outpost, I had already grown accustomed to the teamsters' priorities. First animals, then equipment, and then people were tended to. When I inquired of Mr. Jones, the driver of my wagon, what might be a human ailment sufficiently severe to halt the caravan, he gave the various personal insects inhabiting his chin whiskers an affectionate scratch and replied, "Oh, I don't know, ma'am. Indians—though there ain't been that many bad raids since the menfolk got back from the War. But if there was, we'd stop, I reckon. Indians steal mules. And mebbe a panther"—(he said "painter")—"that'd be bad for the mules too. But strictly human—I don't know, a bullet in the belly maybe, specially if a fella was bleedin' real messy."

I remained skeptical about the negligibility of the dangers of the *despoblado*, the great Texas desert. The cavalry wives at Fort Davis were also less blasé than the muleskinners, especially regarding Indians. The tenth night I stayed at the fort, a minor earthquake shook the ground. While the men ran to their soldierly duties and the comfort of their horses, the women clustered together in one room and talked of how the earthquake had to be a sign from God that no decent person should live out here among the heathen, after which the conversation degenerated into morbidly grisly and graphic descriptions of past Indian raids.

Current style dictates that I should claim I was gathering wildflowers or something equally genteelly frivolous when the Indians captured me. Nonsense. I had awakened from my siesta half-melted despite the shade of the wagon above me, nauseated by the stench of mules and Mr. Jones and, by now, myself, begrimed and annoyed to

2

have to stray from my nest even as far as the closest cactus large enough to provide a modest concealment. I scanned the ground for snakes, not wildflowers, of which there are none in the middle of the desert in late September. Finishing my necessary errand behind the only sort of greenery around—the prickly kind—I stood, adjusted my skirts, and was about to return to the wagon when I saw the Indians.

I cannot report that I was instantly terrified. My first instinct was to shoo them away. There were only three of them, riding around our disabled wagon, poking through the canvas, and pawing through the contents. Earlier in my journeys I had encountered several members of the pacified tribes around Tombstone and Santa Fe, folk with a distressing penchant for examining other people's property and begging a portion of it, when possible. My brain was still so befuddled with sleep and heat that I failed to make the distinction between those curiosity-seekers and the three painted, armed, and mounted warriors before me.

Therefore, I felt less alarm than vexation at Mr. Jones for being remiss about guarding his cargo. I fancied he was still enjoying his afternoon nap beneath the wagon. Though several hours past noon, the day was still far too hot to travel. At least for civilized folk. The Indians didn't seem to mind, having adjusted themselves to the climate by wearing very little but scraps of skin, beads, and eagle feathers.

While I was fuming over Mr. Jones's supposed laziness and contemplating native haberdashery, one of the braves rounded the wagon and spotted me. Those who fancy that Indians have no sense of humor should have seen the delighted grin on his face as he galloped his horse straight toward me. I had never heard of Indians killing victims by simply trampling them, but evidence seemed immediately forthcoming.

I would like to testify that it is not necessarily one's life that flashes before one when death seems imminent. I saw nothing of my previous pallid existence. Neither my childhood nor the most stimulating of the duties I performed while making sure that our newspaper functioned when my father did not intruded on my consciousness at that time. What I saw were the gruesome mental pictures my fertile brain had conceived while the cavalry wives were scaring each other silly with the histories of literally hair-raising Indian savagery.

I stood frozen for a moment, then flung myself down to one side, twisting to avoid a nasty patch of Spanish dagger. The grinning savage scooped me up beside him, clasping his hand over my mouth so that I could not scream and alert the wagons in the mule train preceding us. My middle did not take kindly to being scooped. The air went out of me and my limbs flailed so that I bore some resemblance to a landed fish as I was hauled onto the horse. I squirmed in my captor's grasp enough to straddle the animal—backwards, as it turned out, my seat facing the horse's neck, my face buried in the Indian's breathtaking chest, which reeked of rancid something or other and dead something else besides the natural odor of a very active man on a very warm day.

My new position amused the Indian further, for he now could gag and strangle me at the same time simply by holding my face against him with the crook of one arm. Only my eyes were free to stare across his shoulder as he and his fellows plundered the packs, extracted as many as they could carry of the whiskey bottles comprising a large portion of our cargo, and galloped back into the desert. As I was spirited away I saw the craven Mr. Jones, who had saved his own neck by feigning his absence while huddled between the wagon wheels. Now he peered out from beneath the wagon, his mouth working silently. I almost forgave him, knowing that I probably would have hidden too. As soon as we were far enough away that he could run to the other wagons, I prayed that he would engineer my rescue in time to save me from death and whatever it was that was supposed to be worse. Meanwhile, of course, I had this splendid opportunity to apply my ability as a trained journalist and learn all I could of Indian ways.

Sad to say, the only Indian ways I was able to observe from my unusual vantage point were entirely too similar to the white men's ways with which I was already more familiar than I wished to be. My captors broke the necks of the whiskey bottles on convenient boulders and proceeded to get very drunk.

My riding companion prodded me in what he seemed to feel was a jocular manner, and sloshed whiskey over my head. As he made laughing comments to his fellows in what must have been a highly slurred version of his native language, the cowardly part of me was grateful for two things. One was that my hair is of a nondescript dark brown of no particular beauty or luxuriance. The other was that I am not versed in the Indian languages. The little bit of Chinese that our printer, Wy Mi, imparted with his native myths of fox women and wind dragons and the wee bit of Gaelic sung to me by my father while in his cups is the sum of my linguistic expertise. I could not understand a single word that passed between my captors but I had the clearest impression that I would not like what was being said. This was no time for an interview.

The drunker my brave became, the funnier he seemed to consider his antics, and he refined them a bit, carefully smothering me in his armpit before pulling my head back by the hair and pouring whiskey across my face, then repeating the process. Although I am as a rule a teetotaler, I used part of my gasping breath to lick in the whiskey, reckoning it would make the experiences to come easier to endure by dulling the sharp edge of my perception.

The other braves began remonstrating with him about wasting the whiskey, I suppose, and rode in close to pinch and pull at me. For the first half-hour or so I listened for hoofbeats behind us, but heard none. After that, we passed by means of a shallow cavern hidden behind some brush through what looked like a sheer cliff face. I stopped listening and tried to remember what James Fenimore

Cooper had written of the noble savage. My captors did not look especially noble. They were squat, with round faces, eyes a little glazed, and mouths wet and slack from drink. When they looked at each other their expressions were little more fearsome than those of any group of drunken miners just in from the creeks. When they looked at me, they seemed to be doing their best to scare the wits out of me. They did an excellent job, but I couldn't think what would be the best way to respond. Some stories indicated that because Indians prized courage, they would prolong tormenting a cowardly prisoner just to hear him (or, lamentably, her) scream. Other stories claimed that because Indians prized courage, they would increase the nastiness of the torture until the prisoner, no matter how stalwart, did finally scream. As I was rather short of breath at the moment, I decided to save my screams for later.

Sunset is no gradual affair in the *despoblado*. One moment the sun was hovering on the horizon, the next it sank with an almost audible clunk behind the mountains. The thumbnail moon rose just as quickly, popping up ahead of us. Its light was frequently obscured by flying tatters of cloud, so we rode in relative darkness down the steeply winding pass, hugging a cliffside beneath a rocky overhang. Seven out of ten whiskey bottles were now emptied and tossed aside. So much for wily trail covering. If those fool muleskinners ever got past that false wall and failed to follow this trail, they should move to Philadelphia and take up garbage collecting.

Something sharp struck my knee. I jumped, suddenly afraid the other braves had now resorted to knives. But they were nowhere near me. They rode ahead of us, slightly swaying on the naked backs of their horses as the shoeless hooves quietly plopped on the sand between the boulders. More sharpnesses fell then, spattering all of us, and above us something trembled, rumbling. Another earthquake, I thought, as first dirt and small rocks, then larger stones showered down. My brave dug his moccasined heels into his horse's flanks and we sprinted behind the others, trying to outrun the slide.

The pony whinned, his sides heaving beneath me as flying rocks and dust struck him. My captor stopped and clung against the wall. Overhead, something else roared. Not rocks this time. Something with a voice that was at once a cry, a howl, and a hiss. An animal, but what animal? A panther? Perhaps the rocks magnified the sound, but even accounting for that, it had to be a very large panther.

A very large fire-breathing panther with wings, I thought, stupidly trying to assemble my first surmise with the new information that rapidly assembled as a great winged shape outlined in glowing mist swooped toward us. Eyes as big as croquet balls burned no less brightly than the bloom of intense green fire licking toward us from its gaping maw.

I screamed, but I was the only one facing the apparition. My captors had their faces inward, toward the cliff. When I shrieked, the brave who held me turned and stared straight into the monster's unblinking eyes. The vein in his throat throbbed against the top of my head for exactly three heartbeats before the green fire flared upward like a shooting star reversing its course and the dragon vanished over the rim of the cliff wall. A final spattering of stones curtained its flight.

My captor's arms hung slackly around me as his companions trotted cautiously out onto the trail. One of them prodded a dark heap with his rifle barrel. Something glistened briefly, and against the dark gray night a paler gray wisp of smoke wafted, bearing the stench of burned, rotten meat.

The brave holding me called to his brethren, his voice a weak but urgent grunt. They stared silently back at him, their eyes reflecting the sickle moon and flickering from me to each other. He in turn stared from them to me with what I can only describe as horrified awe and attempted to slide backward on the horse in an effort to put as much distance between us as possible. The horse pranced sideways, sniffing skittishly at the putrid odor pervading the night. In its prancings it stumbled into the thing the beast had thrown down before us like a gauntlet, the dismembered midsection of an animal of some sort—a steer or a horse—the front legs and head, the back legs and tail missing, the raw ends streaming half-bleeding, half-cauterized mess on each side. The stumbling pony screamed and reared, scrambled away from the carrion. My companion, his grip loosened by drink and terror, slipped and would have unseated us both had I not caught him.

One of his fellows grabbed our mount's mane and urged the horse forward until we were well past the smoking carcass. Beyond sight and smell of it, and with many glances back in its direction, the two of them wrestled me down from the pony and thrust me up behind their friend, tying my wrists around his chest and to the horse's neck. They took one last drink from the whiskey bottles, then deliberately threw them away. With a jerk on the rope, the shorter and calmer of the two warriors tugged us forward. Once on flat ground again, he pulled us behind them at a dead run.

I clung for dear life to the warrior and the horse, slippery with our mutual perspiration. Now I feared my ultimate fate far less desperately than I feared to lose my grip and fall dangling between the hooves, to tear my head and upper body on the cacti flashing past us at such an alarming speed. Exhaustion soon pierced my limbs with jabbing pains. My whole skull throbbed with the bounce and pound of hoofbeats. The horse's ragged breath blended with the wind of its passing into one continuous roar. Tears flew from my burning eyes and my mind grew numb as the part of me that thought, felt, and feared was outdistanced by the headlong dash of my body. The arroyos yawning and contracting beneath me, the thorned arms of cacti outstretched, and all the perils of the treacherous trail snaking through the jagged hills blurred into random dapples, solid shadow, blinding moonlight, and, abruptly, gloriously, a thousand points of light that I saw were the stars glittering just beyond my *wingtips*.

The roaring subsides into sweet peace as the layers of desert horizon stretch deep purple to black. Far below, three of the animals the Spaniards introduced to this desolate northern corner of our domain crawl across the desert floor, falling behind us as they run with their human burdens to do our bidding. Now the inhabitants will realize that the pattern of their lives needs order, their violence constructive direction. We disapprove of random raiding. Our own raids at this time are deliberate and necessary. Our sleep has been long and we are weak. Also, we have a mission, a prayer to answer at the behest of the supplicant who has awakened us from our long sleep. We are not normally a glutton but from time immemorial there has been but one way to demonstrate to the presumptuous kings of earth the error of their ways, and that is to eat them out of castle and kingdom.

I revived from my shock-induced dream hungry enough to eat a horse, or a whole herd of them. The one upon which I was riding walked a few halting steps inside a huge cottonwood gate and stopped on the packed earthen floor of a corral surrounded by a vast adobe compound. A grizzled man in a sombrero and proper trousers loped forward, motioning to two armed Mexican men who pointed rifles at the Indians. Then the grizzled man and the Indians argued while my poor mount sank slowly and exhaustedly to its knees, dumping the brave to whom I was bound forward over its neck. I too began to fall, but I never quite felt myself land. I am grateful that only strangers witnessed that ignominious entrance into the heart of the wild west, that Papa was not there to see his daughter, the dauntless would-be frontierswoman, swoon. He would have died laughing.

2

Even before I opened my eyes, the condition of my backside assisted me in sorting reality from dream. The part about riding a horse all night strapped to an unconscious Indian, which should certainly have been a nightmare, was decidedly real, as the evidence of my stinging saddle sores clearly testified. The part about flying through the air in control of all I (we?) surveyed had been nothing but a sanity-saving figment of my imagination. Regarding the part about seeing a dragon, my saddle sores were stubbornly silent and my mind skipped skittishly past. Perhaps I had absorbed more whiskey through my skin than I realized. Perhaps I had been in a state of shock. Yes. Almost certainly I had been. Never mind that I distinctly recalled every detail of seeing the creature and that I have a very good memory. The unlikelihood of my having done so at that time seemed to preclude the possibility that I had. So I ignored the whole matter and began reorienting myself. It was a daunting process. Lying on my side with my limbs scissored into the only comfortable position I could find, I reflected sadly that my new career as a chronicler of the romance of the western frontier did not seem to be beginning auspiciously.

I could not honestly say, however, as do the characters in some popular novels, that had I but known of the dangers awaiting me I would have arranged my affairs any differently. I knew well when I embarked upon my flight from San Francisco that the raw wildernesses lying between California and the Mississippi River were filled with natural and manmade catastrophes, bloodthirsty savages, and uncouth desperados.

My father's financée, Mrs. Higgenbotham, was very fond of telling me of the hardships and horrors of her trip west with the late Mr. Higgenbotham and never tired of pointing out that only her stern adherence to Virtue and her Moral Standards had seen her through. "Pelagia," she would say, "I see from that smirk on your face that you doubt me, but when Mr. Harper and I are married you shall learn the value of Christian charity and moral virtue or you'll find yourself out on the streets, my girl." Mr. Higgenbotham had not been so virtuous or moral as his wife, apparently, since he failed to survive their journey. He had, however, been very wealthy, thus the widow Hig's attraction for my father, who had for some years been on the verge of drinking away our livelihood.

Papa did it charmingly enough that Mrs. Higgenbotham had thus far failed to discern the source of the moral deterioration she sniffed around our newspaper office. She assumed that source was me, and took it upon herself to correct my sinful ways. To this end she regaled me with cautionary tales plucked from her own bitter experiences— all of which had been caused by the carelessness and moral turpitude of others. The more she talked, the more she inflamed my desire to be punished for my sins by having a few adventures myself. Whatever Mrs. Hig was against, I was pretty sure I'd find agreeable.

The journalism trade was getting less attractive all the time as her presence around the office became more pervasive. I took to closeting myself with penny dreadfuls and decided I could write one just as well as Mr. Buntline and all I needed were a few lurid experiences to fill in where my imagination failed me.

Thus when at last I set out, I expected, even hoped, to encounter hostile Indians, prairie fires, runaway horses, stampeding cattle, bandits, perhaps a touch of cholera, which I would, of course, survive while valiantly nursing others through. On a more mundane level not nearly so attractive as wild Indians but nonetheless necessary to attain the requisite amount of local color, I anticipated meeting a few reptiles. I had in mind loathsome lizards and hissing snakes, which I would endure bravely. Encountering something on the scale (if you'll pardon the expression) of the creature of the night before was far beyond the bounds of even Mrs. Higgenbotham's cautionary tales. I firmly directed my mind away from that topic, disciplining myself to adhere to the journalist's litany of the "where, when, why, who, how," and most of all the "*what*" that had brought me to this desolate country.

I was born of originally poor but honest parents, but as soon as my mother died, when I was about six years of age, that all changed. My father began drinking, which contributed little to his character but much to the floridity of his prose and thus to the popularity of the newspaper he and my mother had published together. No longer bound by my stolid Cornish mother's ethics and her inhibiting adherence to truth that had formerly cramped his literary style, Father found new freedom to express his natural Irish aptitude for embellishment of lackluster facts and events.

Little wonder, then, that I had less taste for straight reporting and more of a mind to try my hand at the sensational frontier chronicles that had made Mr. Buntline rich and famous. That sort of story was not so very different, after all, from my father's heavily varnished truth. And I had always loved tales of distant places and strange customs.

I spent hours listening to the printer, Wy Mi, telling of his homeland and the stories people told there. I picked up a few words in the Chinese tongue in this fashion, since Wy Mi, seldom soberer than my father, tended to forget himself when especially deep in story or bottle. He frequently attempted to deliver his homilies on proper attitudes in dealing with pesky girl-children (he favored exposure to the elements at birth) in his native tongue.

I received my education in female matters from another source. My father's seemingly unceasing supply of what may be loosely referred to as lady companions often assumed the appearance of motherliness toward me to impress my parent. The few of these female persons who actually were ladies were my least favorites. They prodded me into church, attempted to wean me from the mug from which I preferred to drink my tea and replace that sturdy vessel with dainty china cups whose handles were not large enough to accommodate one's pinky finger. They sometimes went so far as to try to dress me in the prevailing confining fashion. Overall, I much preferred Papa's more flamboyant friends. The incomparable Sasha Divine, a star of the local opera house, was a particular idol of mine. She wore a lot of curls and a great many jewels, furs, and ruffles and her sweetness and light were so fleeting that I felt no need to take serious notice of them. Her example provided me with the only practical instruction I received from any of my father's conquests. She served as my inspiration when I needed to cajole, persuade, bully, flatter, and dicker with the rugged males with whom the frontier abounded. Dealing with them was essential if I was to go where I wished and acquire other necessary services for personal survival and comfort. Though I did not possess Sasha's beauty, my imitation of her graces stood me in far better stead than my own oft-lamented straightforwardness, which had seldom been successful at winning me more than grudging cooperation. With great interest I studied Sasha's manipulative techniques, with great glee I employed them, and with great amazement I observed how often even the most transparent ruses enjoyed the most astounding success.

Still, charm can do only so much to improve what are essentially limited circumstances.

The sooty and deafening train ride from San Francisco was soothing compared to the bone-jarring mail coach I commandeered in Santa Fe. Santa Fe was my original destination, and I wandered around for a day or two hoping to run into Kit Carson or at least hear from someone who had news of Billy the Kid. I was disappointed, however, and felt increasingly restless as I strolled through the colorful but well-populated plaza. Though more isolated than San Francisco, Santa Fe seemed to me far more civilized than what I had in mind. It had already been written of exhaustively. I wanted territory of my own. Something new and original, more desolate and dangerous than anything described by others. The luck of the Irish, or perhaps the Cornish, was with me. On my third day at the hotel, just when I was despairing over the inroads the cost of my lodgings was making in my research fund, I overheard the desk clerk commiserating with the driver of a mail coach. The men were discussing the rugged trip the driver was about to embark upon to deliver the mail to a cavalry post in what the men referred to as the *despoblado*.

"Ought to just let the Indians have it," the mail driver grumbled. "Nothin' but snakes, rocks, and greasewood out there anyway."

"*Sí*," the clerk agreed. "As you say, nothing but those things and the Indians and *bandidos*. Unless you count the comancheros. My uncle, he used to be a comanchero in the old days, but now he says the new ones, since the wars, are worse than the Indians and the bandits combined. Comanche over in Tejas stole my cousin's wife's sister, you know? Our whole family ate our tortillas with no frijoles for a year to ransom her from the comancheros. Otherwise, they would have let the Indians keep her. And then, my cousin says she is not much good now anyway."

"Yeah, well, I know what you mean. It's a shame when those bastards get rich off other folks' grief. Still, I suppose a man's gotta make a livin', and out there when it's too dry to run cattle, tradin' with the Indians beats farmin' cactus. And havin' a few of 'em out there, like that

14

Drake character, at least gives the mule trains a fifty-fifty chance of makin' it through to San Antone."

That was my cue. The *despoblado* sounded exciting enough and wild enough to provide me with an entire series of thrillers. I would have an exclusive. I began to wonder whether one of my father's competitors wouldn't pay dearly to run a serial. "Excuse me, sir," I said with just a hint of tremor in my voice. "Did you say San Antonio? I am trying desperately to find my way there. It's my mother, you see. She's very ill . . ."

By the time we arrived at Fort Davis any fears I had entertained that some other author would infringe upon my exclusive right to explore my chosen territory evaporated, both literally and figuratively. No one else was likely to brave the appalling heat. And the country was so sparsely settled that the most imaginative writer would have difficulty finding someone to tell a story about. The landscape is stark as a beggar's plate, although I suppose if one is in a positive and charitable frame of mind, it could be described as dramatic. Bare mountains fold up from the desert floor, shading from tawniness to gray and mauve at the skyline. Hills bulge out of nowhere, their slopes strewn with great boulders. Cliffs built of thin slices of stacked rock permit passage into sheltering canyons. The dust and sand give way suddenly to arroyos deep enough to hide livestock. The gray-gold land with its yucca and barrel cactus, its greasewood and prickly pear, has a whiskery appearance, like a man gone three days without a shave.

The two weeks I spent at the cavalry post waiting for the mule train to San Antonio were interminable. I told the commanding officer about my ailing mother and added that I intended to find a teaching position to support us both while I cared for her. I was hoping for some offer of employment, writing letters home for the troops, perhaps. I reckoned without taking into account the impact of my newfound feminine charm, much enhanced by the scarcity of other females. Immediately several of the single cavalry personnel attempted to persuade me to remain, with unalluring offers of marriage. I received other sorts of proposals from a few of the married personnel as well. So for three weeks I dodged suitors, studied cacti, doodled in my notebook, and listened to the talk of the half-dozen wives in residence. The women wore a pinched and put-upon look as uniform as the blue suits of their husbands. Though at least two of them were younger than I was, they were careworn and nervous and yelled at their children a great deal, trying to prevent the poor little things from various enterprises devised by childish minds to make life more interesting. Initially, the ladies had been friendly and curious about my trip, but when my imagination eventually failed to provide me with suitable background about my fictional past, I lapsed into silence and soon they reverted to talking among themselves. Their conversations consisted mainly of babies and shortages and a hushed sprinkling of atrocity stories. It was unclear to me who they considered to be responsible for the most atrocities in their lives, the Indians or the army. Or perhaps the commanding officer's lady, when she wasn't present. I welcomed the frightening diversion of the earthquake for I feared I would succumb to madness before the mule train at last arrived.

I was beginning to wonder now if it hadn't been too late after all. Certainly I was not the self I had imagined myself to be when I left San Francisco. I was a total failure as an Indian captive. I had not fought bravely when captured, nor resisted even mild torment with any degree of spunk. Furthermore, upon finding myself spared all but inconvenience by a fictional hero's standards, I dreamed up outlandish creatures more suitable to opium hallucinations than to proper western adventures. Now I, the heroine who had so intrepidly set forth to learn all she could of this allegedly thrilling country, was loathing the thought of opening my eyes to see what fate held in store for me. Partly my reluctance was to move any part of my person, since that portion that had been intimately connected with the horse burned me ferociously.

Shame pried open one eye. Since it was the one pressed against the straw mattress, I saw very little, so I had to open the other as well. I lay on a proper bed in a small dim room with white walls and a built-in fireplace. A stiff hand-woven blanket of blue and brown stripes covered me to the waist. High overhead stretched a ceiling of cottonwood timbers with shingles layered in a chevron pattern across them. Very fancy. The window bore a lattice of wooden bars, which cast ominous shadows across my bed.

Before I could make any further discoveries the door banged open, a swath of pure hot sunlight blinding me so that I closed my eyes again. When I opened them, I was trapped in the keen scrutiny of a short Mexican woman wearing a gray-gilded black braid, silver hoop earrings, and a voluminous black fringed shawl. Only the cornshuck cigar dangling from the corner of her mouth contradicted the impression her bearing and expression gave that she was a member of the not-so-minor nobility.

"Ah, so you live," she announced, though I couldn't tell whether or not she was pleased about it. "But you are dry from the desert, no? Drink." She extended a netted gourd stoppered with a small piece of corncob, which she removed. I obeyed her with alacrity.

"*Bueno,*" she said, and that was all, for I accidentally leaned back and touched the wall. The pain made my eyes swim and my gorge rise. She was as swift as a foreclosing banker in whipping forth a tin pail with which she intercepted my illness.

"Sorry," I said, wiping my mouth and feeling more than a little mortified. She set the pail outside the door.

"*De nada.*"

"Pardon?"

"It is nothing."

"Thank you so much. You've been so very kind. I don't know how I can ever repay you."

"Roll over," she commanded.

"Eh?"

"Roll over. I have here a remedy for your incapacity to repay your debt, but you must roll over so I can apply it."

She produced a small earthenware jar of rancid-smelling salve which I eyed dubiously. She puffed her cigar twice without lifting her hand to it or removing it from her mouth. I decided anyone who could do that was competent enough to tend my backside, so I rolled over.

"Since we're on such personal terms already," I said, lifting my skirt, "I suppose introductions are in order. I presume you're the lady of the house?"

Her fingers stopped halfway between her jar and me and she hastily removed the cigar from her mouth before she choked on it. "No, not I," she answered, her voice still a bit hoarse from the smoke she had accidentally swallowed. "I am Mariquilla. I am the cook and *curandera* and am far more *importante* to *el patrón* than my poor Doña Seferina ever was, for I am also his *cigarrera*."

"His what?"

"I make his cigars. And you, *señorita*, what do you do? I suppose you are a fine lady who knows only a few embroidery stitches?"

Her fingers moved in smooth circular motions and everywhere they touched, the burning miraculously subsided. "Hardly," I answered, so relieved I was feeling quite relaxed and chatty. "I was never any good at sewing of any kind."

"You cook then?" She sounded hopeful.

"No. Not much." My father was far fonder of drinking than eating any day, and Wy Mi's sister not only supplied laundry service but also sent over meals large enough for all of us. She'd begun the custom when I was too small to cook and continued to do so as I grew older and became too preoccupied with chasing stories and subscribers to learn.

"You must have a very rich husband," she said.

18

"Not at all. I am a writer," I informed her with all the dignity I could muster in such an undignified position. "I am composing a novel about the West. And I must say, you certainly have a wealth of material here. I saw something very strange I was wondering if you—"

"*Ay yi!*" she said, sounding far more impressed than I expected or intended. She flipped my skirt back down with the reverence due my exalted person.

"Is something wrong?" I asked.

"Oh, no, *señorita*. But Don Francisco must meet you immediately. He asked that I heal you in order that you might work off your bond—"

"My bond?"

"*Sí, señorita*. For the three horses El Caballerango paid *los indios* for you. An outrageous price."

"Handling charges," I told her. "The Indians ruined their mounts in their haste to rid themselves of me. After we saw the strange thing I mentioned."

Her left eyebrow climbed toward her widow's peak, and she took three deep puffs on her cigar. She looked as if she wanted to say more, but instead stoppered her salve jar and buried it somewhere in the depths of her shawl. "More and more I think you are one *el patrón* must speak with himself, *señorita*," she said, and departed.

"Now, then, little lady, Mariquilla says you're somethin' pretty special," the *patrón* said as he entered my room. When both my eyes and his adjusted to the light, I could see from his expression that my appearance did not persuade him to share his cook's opinion.

His appearance, on the other hand, certainly impressed me. He was the embodiment of the western hero I had imagined—tall, his stance easy and graceful, his voice deep and softened with an ear-caressing drawl. Like the man in the corral, he wore a wide Mexican sombrero which he pushed back until it hung against the back of his neck, secured by a thong. The eyes that assessed me were pale and surrounded by leathery tanned squint lines. A ring of golden sunlight haloed the crown of his sandy-blond hair, making him look for a moment like a particularly shrewd archangel trying to decide what to do with a troublesome sinner. A Mexican archangel, with flattened silver coins trimming his trousers.

"I . . . I beg your pardon?" I said rather stupidly. I was too preoccupied with memorizing the details of his entrance to be sure how to answer his opening remarks.

He stuck out his hand. "I just came to welcome you to Fort Draco. I'm Frank Drake. I own this place."

"Drake?" I asked. "The comanchero Drake the men in Santa Fe were talking about?" What luck! A real live comanchero suited my purposes much better than an archangel.

"Indian trader, ma'am," he corrected me stiffly.

"Oh, of course," I said. "But . . . er . . . is that the same thing?"

"Some folks are too narrow-minded to see that all of us need to get along out here. They object to some of us doin' business with our Indian brothers. They slap that name on us to make it sound like we're just a little worse than the Comanche, when all we're doin' is makin' a livin'."

"I *do* beg your pardon. But it sounded like such a romantic term to me that I immediately latched onto it and hoped to use it in my novel."

"Then it's true? Mariquilla didn't get it mixed up? You really do write books?" His grin was so delighted that had I been illiterate I would have been tempted to say yes anyway. "Don't that beat all. I sure am glad you said somethin'. I never would have taken you for a lady author."

"Nevertheless, I am. I was researching a book on the American West in the style of Ned Buntline when the Indians captured me."

"You *know* the celebrated Mr. Buntline?" he asked, and slapped his knee with his fist. "Why, I've read everything Mr. Buntline ever wrote. I s'pect I didn't realize

20

who you were because I don't read all that many lady authors, though I have a fine library with books and rare papers from both sides of the border—"

"Perfectly all right, Mr. Drake. I didn't realize who you are because I've read so little about men engaged in slave trade with the Indians—"

"Whoa there, little lady. You've got me wrong. 'Course you haven't read anything about men like me. For a start, there aren't all that many. Besides that, Mr. Buntline, fine writer that he is, doesn't seem to think a man is a hero unless he's shootin' off a gun or his mouth, neither of which is a good way to live very long around here. I am not a slave trader. I buy folks from the Indians, that's true, just like I bought you, to save 'em from what my redskin customers might dream up for 'em. But as far as *sellin'* anybody goes, the only thing I do is try to get in touch with their relatives and ask 'em to reimburse me for the money I spent rescuin' their kinfolks and a little extra to pay for the food and lodgin' I provide while I'm waitin' for my guests to get themselves collected. I'd do it all out of the goodness of my heart, you understand, but I'm a businessman and this spread takes a heap o' wampum to run. As a matter of fact, if you'll be so kind as to tell me who I have the pleasure and honor of addressin' and where I might reach your folks, I'll try to get you back to civilization as soon as possible."

Not if I could help it, he wouldn't. I had not traveled so far and endured so much to be shipped home again. And though Papa ordinarily would never have been able to ransom so much as a watch chain from a pawnshop, I was pretty sure Mrs. Hig would buy me back just to spite me.

"That's very considerate of you, Mr. Drake," I said with my best Sasha Divine flutter, "but this is civilization enough for me. Your explanation of your mission here among the heathen of the desert fascinates me. In fact, several aspects of this country are, shall we say, unusual enough to excite my interest."

"Why, that's mighty kind of you, Miss . . ."

I feared that if I gave him my real name he'd find me out. And at any rate, it was high time I invented a *nom de plume*. I considered the most literary names I could think of, but I could hardly call myself Nathaniel Hawthorne or Fenimore Cooper. My mind harkened instead to another branch of the arts, the one particularly favored by my father. "Lovelace," I said, giving the last name of one of Sasha Divine's cronies. "Valentine Lovelace," I added, because it sounded right.

He stuck out his hand again, but this time when I put mine in it, he raised it to his lips. "Miss Lovelace, darlin', you have no idea what a pleasure it is to meet a fine lady like yourself. I do believe Providence must have sent you to us. You said it all just now when you were talkin' about my mission here at Fort Draco, because, dear lady, I do feel I'm here for a purpose. I have been tryin' and tryin' to convince the army to build their main road right through here so that I can help the settlers as they travel west through this great land of ours, but I must tell you, the army is as prejudiced against me as those fellas you heard talkin' in Santa Fe. They seem to think the Indians would all be peaceable as sheep if I didn't sell 'em a little hooch and a few huntin' rifles. That just shows you what Washington knows about Indians. Most of them bluecoat boys never saw an Indian before they came out here. Why, if I didn't sell the guns and whiskey, the redskins would have to get it from somewhere else, and where do you think that would be? Raidin' and killin' folks worse than they do now. Probably even overrun the fort. I try to run things so that everybody gets a little somethin' they want. I have my home and business, the Indians get the goods they want, the Mexicans get jobs and doctorin', and we none of us nose around in the other man's business. I think I can truthfully say that Fort Draco does more than any other single thing in the entire *despoblado* to make peace for everybody. But do I get any thanks? They call

me 'comanchero.' If they had any sense, they'd be callin'
me 'governor.' "

"Perhaps your viewpoint has simply never been properly presented to the public before, Mr. Drake."

"No perhaps about it, ma'am," he said, and then
dropped his crusading pose to wink at me conspiratorially.
"I bet a famous lady writer like yourself could explain it to
folks better than an old *vaquero* like me, now, ain't that
the truth?"

"My very thought, Mr. Drake!" I said. "And I can
repay your kindness once I have obtained the proceeds
from the book. I fear the Indians stole all the cash I had on
me." Letting the Indians take the blame seemed a good
way to explain why a woman as successful as I pretended
to be was too broke to pay her own ransom.

He grinned most attractively and patted my knee.
"Don't you worry your pretty little head about that, honey.
You just tell people about all the good work you see goin'
on here in that book of yours and you'll have more than
paid me back. I want you to feel free to use my library as
if it were your own and to ask any questions your little
heart desires."

I could not resist such open magnanimity. My curiosity was too great, and besides, if I was to remain in this
country I needed to ask. "Mr. Drake, I don't want you to
think my experience with the savages unhinged my reason, but I must ask you—are you by any chance raising
dragons on your property?" I described to him the events
of the previous night as I recalled them, though I declined
to mention that at one point I had imagined myself to be
flying.

Drake threw back his head and laughed until the
tears rolled down his ruggedly handsome face. "Oh, Miss
Valentine, you beat anythin' I ever seen. You're gonna fit
right in here, gal. That's the best whopper I've heard
since I was up to Denver for the Trappers' Rondyvoo
when I was a boy. I can see now why you chose your

profession instead of a husband and children like most women. You have got yourself one fine imagination."

My tentativeness on the subject disappeared, replaced by somewhat unreasonable indignation. I believe it was the slur on my marital status rather than his understandable doubts about my already compromised veracity that triggered my pique. "Oh? I suppose it was my imagination that impressed the Indians too, despite the fact that they spoke no English, I spoke no Indian, and we were not exactly on storytelling terms. Really, Mr. Drake! I assure you, my powers of observation are most acute. I know what I saw and heard. The streak of fire, the horribly mutilated animal, and that fearsome roar were unmistakable."

"Now, now, no need to get huffy. I apologize for laughin' at you, honey, but you're new out here. I bet I can tell you what you saw."

"Pray do."

"Well, you see, we've had us a dry spell lately and there's no water on the back range. The Rio's been gettin' lower faster than anyone can ever recollect. When things get like this, one of the more agreeable chores the *vaqueros* get stuck with is burnin' prickles off the prickly pear so's my cows can eat 'em without gettin' a mouthful of thorns. I'll lay you odds we'll have one of the boys in here in a day or two laughin' about how he spooked them Indians by lightin' his torch and hollerin', tryin' to scare them away from you. Worked, too, didn't it?"

Exhaustion overwhelmed me suddenly, muddling everything. Perhaps Drake was right and both the Indians and I had been tricked. The explanation did not jibe with my memory of the incident, but I could hardly risk my host thinking I was insane, as he might have. "Very well," I said, "you're probably right about the fire and the roar. But judging from that carcass, your *vaqueros* must have some peculiar dietary habits."

"You can judge that for yourself real soon, darlin'," he said. "Ledbetter heard from the Comanche that they took you from the mule train. It should be here in a day or so, and when it comes, we'll be havin' a little play-party and a dance, what we call a *baile* around here."

"But, Mr. Drake, if your water supply is low, won't a party be a strain on your resources?"

He laughed again. I began to feel he'd keep me around for amusement, if nothing else. "Shoot, Miss Valentine, you are really somethin'. Water a problem? At a *baile*? No, ma'am. Only time water comes into the deal is when the animals go to the river to wet their whistles, and they'd have to do that whether we had a party or not. Otherwise, there's no problem. Nobody drinks *water* at a fandango."

I slept clear through the evening and into the night, dreamed and half-wakened only to sleep again throughout the rest of that day. My dreams were confused, full of images like those of the previous night of the earth gliding past beneath me, and also of mutilated animal bodies, flashes of light flaring suddenly in front of my face, hundreds of pairs of terrified animal eyes dancing before me like fireflies. Hills and mountains became towers and pyramids, the desert blossomed into a lush pastureland, certain cliffsides thinned to transparency and I clearly saw caches of precious gems within. Sometimes when I woke, I saw, or thought I saw, faces at my window.

One in particular seemed to actually pull me from my dreams on several occasions. I tried to speak, but before I roused sufficiently to do so, she vanished. I remembered her in the twilight wakefulness between dreams. Something about the shape of her face, the stormy play of expression across its surface, a fey, feline quality in its beauty, made me think of Wy Mi's fox women or perhaps a Mexican version of one of the Little People. I knew that I urgently wished to communicate with her, but when I finally truly awakened, I couldn't imagine why. No one was at the window. My blanket was tangled around my legs and my hair and clothing were soaked with perspira-

tion. I had rubbed and sweated most of my salve off and
my sores burned again. I rolled to my side and stood
painfully, still half-caught by my dreams. I wondered briefly
if it was possible that I turned into a dragon when I slept.
But as my brain cleared, I realized that that was unlikely,
since the room would in that case surely be in much worse
shape than it was. Also, if I were to credit any of my
perceptions about the dragon, I had to allow that I had
definitely seen it from the outside. It was all too confus-
ing, and the longer I stood there, the more thoughts of
food and a bath prevailed over my dreams.

I smelled coffee brewing and bacon frying and heard
voices and movement nearby. Holding onto the wall, I
ventured as far as the door, which I pushed open. I dared
go no further, for my clothing had been torn beyond the
boundaries of decency.

The rising sun probed only one corner of the patio—
the rest was still shrouded in shadow. A valkyrie of a
woman in a faded checked dress and a stained white apron
strode forth from a doorway on the far side. I hailed her.

"Howdy," she greeted me. "How you feelin'?" She
was as dark as Mariquilla, but her hair was yellow blond
where it was not gray. She stood probably an inch or two
taller than Drake. Her arms looked strong enough to fell
an ox.

"Better, thanks," I said.

"Still walk like you got a corncob up your rear, but I
reckon a few saddle sores never killed anyone."

"I was hoping I might beat the mules to the bathwater
and perhaps wash my hair," I said. "Mr. Drake informed
me there was to be a party after the mule train arrives. I
would think they should be here sometime today."

"You figured that pretty handy. Dolores is boilin' up
some yucca suds for hair-washin' this very minute. You
can be second in line after Widow Jenkins, if you like, you
bein' the honored guest and all. Boss gave orders. Says
you're special." Her expression let me know she was doing
the Christian thing and giving me the benefit of the doubt.

"Mr. Drake is too kind," I replied.

The valkyrie stifled a good-natured snort and pumped my hand so hard I almost fell off my shaky feet. "I'm Hulda Ledbetter. Mrs. E. F. I'm housekeeper. E.F. is Mr. Drake's head wrangler. He told me about having to untie you from a drunk Indian and pull you off a dead horse. Matter of fact, you smell a mite of strong spirits yourself."

There was indeed a stench about me that would have made my father proud. After decorously draping me in my blanket, Mrs. Ledbetter led me straightaway to the hair-washing area, where the other women were already gathering. The laughter and bilingual chattering carried across the corral and working courtyard as we approached.

Fort Draco covered more ground than most of the army posts I had been on, parade grounds and all. The entire area, larger than two square blocks of choice real estate in San Francisco, was totally surrounded by a high adobe wall. The room I had been assigned, the office, and the family living quarters were centered around a patio with double doors wide enough to drive a wagon through, leading down to the river in the front, and another set of doors, usually left open, leading back into a corridor. On one side of this corridor the pantry and kitchen were situated. Opposite it was another room dominated by a large fireplace where a whole beef roasted on a spit. Beyond the corridor a waist-high wall of adobe separated living quarters and work space for the servants from the corral. An area wide enough for two horsemen to ride abreast had been allowed between the rooms on the inside wall and the corral. The back of the baking stove bellied into the corral on the southeast side. Extending from the tiled roof on every side was a thatch of bound sotol stalks about a yard and a half wide, the edges supported by cottonwood poles. This shade constituted a sort of porch. At the far end of the working courtyard a section of this awning had been screened with blankets.

"There they are, yonder under the *ramada*," Mrs.

Ledbetter informed me, unnecessarily since from the feminine commotion it was quite clear that some sort of gathering was taking place behind those blankets. "I reckon I better give another speech on etiquette to the Fort Draco Ladies' Aid Society," Mrs. Ledbetter said, shaking her head. "They're louder than the blamed goats and chickens."

"Ladies' Aid Society?" I asked. "Out here?"

"Sure. We made bandages during the war, just like other ladies. 'Course, I s'pect most other societies don't feature quite so many *señoritas* and squaws among their membership, but we contributed more *jalapeños* and *tortillas* to the war effort than any of them other clubs, I'll bet you. For both sides, too. That was Mr. Drake's idea. He's a southern gentleman, himself, mind you, but he wanted to stay in good with the Union just in case the cavalry post was reoccupied by Yanks and might have a mind to put the main road alongside Fort Draco.

"I understand you're gonna write a book that'll help 'em see things his way," she continued with a sidelong inquisitive glance at me. "The army gets an honest trader and frontier hero such as himself confused with the common riffraffy type of profiteering border trash. Can't imagine why." Her tone told me that she was being modest about the breadth of her imagination. "Anyhow, it's a right good thing for both of you that he thinks you writin' about him will do him some good."

I stammered a little disclaimer and she clapped me on the shoulder, all but knocking me down.

"There I go again, talkin' out of turn. Gets me in trouble every time. But don't mind me, honey. It's just good to have another lady here who's seen somethin' besides greasewood and tumbleweed lately. Nice to have someone who won't slip into swearin' at me in Spanish if she gets riled, too. But I'll be hanged if I can recall what he said your name was."

"Valentine Lovelace."

"No foolin'?" She looked dubious and held onto me a shade less comfortingly.

Outside the blanketed enclosure Mariquilla sat munching a *tortilla*. When we reached her she flipped the fringed end of a shawl around her and flicked the cigar ash in our direction in greeting.

"That Mariquilla," Mrs. Ledbetter said, shaking her head. I took it the two did not always get along. In a stage whisper Mrs. Ledbetter told me, "Some people would be better off forgettin' sins they committed above their station when they were young and foolish and should have known better anyway. Doña Seferina would have turned over in her grave if she'd known. Mariquilla was her lady's maid then and she still thinks the sun don't shine without her even though she cooks now, works same as the rest of us, and the only thing the boss wants her for is to feed him and roll his cigars. Would have made my life easier if he'd stuck to that to begin with."

I felt it best not to encourage her in her gossip with the object of it so close. I needed no enemies my first day at the fort. "Was she Mrs. Drake, the lady you're talking about?" I asked, unwilling to try pronouncing the name when I'd have to scream over the squeals and splashing water to make myself heard.

"Yes, ma'am, and a fine lady she was, too. A proper *patrona*. Claytie seems to take more after her pa's side—when she's not imitating that rascal Felipa. Looks like her ma, though. See there?"

She nodded toward a child whose lank pale hair looked much in need of washing. From the expression the girl wore as she regarded the suds, however, they might have been boiling oil in which she was about to be deep-fried.

"Both of 'em blond as me. Wouldn't think so, would you? Claytie jabbers Spanish fast as a Mexican and if you didn't see her you wouldn't know but what she wasn't dark as little ol' Felipa there." She nodded that time to a very swarthy young girl about the same age as the blond.

I shrugged and tried not to look too stupid. The Mexican folk I had met here and in Santa Fe were the first Spanish-speaking people of any complexion I had ever met. In San Francisco, those who spoke Spanish were transplanted Spaniards, true aristocrats, the descendants of the grandees who used to own the place. They lived in a much better neighborhood than Papa and I did, and didn't rub elbows with the press.

The blanket flap drew back and a gauntly pretty woman in an orchid wrapper trimmed with lace joined us. For a moment I stared rudely past her at the dark maid accompanying her. The lovely, tragic eyes met mine briefly and slipped away. I let them. I could not for the life of me think what to say to her, since my dream had blown away like morning fog as soon as I stepped into the sunlight.

" 'Mornin' Miz Jenkins," the Ladies' Aid Society greeted the American lady—with varying degrees of Spanish variations and accents.

The lady nodded in a queenly fashion. "Good morning, girls, Mrs. Ledbetter. Ah, Miss Lovelace, we finally meet. I trust you"—her eyes ran down my blanket to the remnants of my skirt—"are bein' made comfortable after your horrifyin' ordeal?"

"Mariquilla practically saved my life with that salve," I said gratefully.

"Stuff and nonsense, sugar. Nobody dies of saddle sores. I do hope that's the *only* indignity you suffered at the hands of those savages."

"I think the water is just right now, *señora*," the sad-faced girl said in quick-paced but quite intelligible English.

"Thank you, Dolores." Over the iron pot where the Widow Jenkins ducked her strawberry-blond curls, Dolores shot me another look, the sadness mingled with sympathy and a disturbed sort of curiosity.

When I too had been properly shampooed and had taken as much of a bath as anyone was allowed, Mrs. Ledbetter accompanied me back to my room.

" 'Scuse the widow, will you, honey? Can't believe that woman's been here purt' near twelve years and still hasn't taken up any of our ways. She just doesn't understand that there are things a body doesn't ask another person. Because she's the boss's sister, nobody's put an end to her yet, but between you and me, she wouldn't be here at all if her husband hadn't used the war as an excuse to get away from her. She's been plaguin' us since just after Doña Seferina died. Thinks she's teachin' Claytie and Felipa how to be ladies, but I vow and declare, she has some of the peculiarest notions."

Mrs. Ledbetter had not been gone five minutes when a servant girl ran up with an armful of lacy froth. "From Señora Jenkins," she said, handing me the garment on top. Beneath it were two less ornamental items, a skirt and a blouse. These the girl presented with a slightly apologetic air. "The skirt is Merenciana's. She sends it to you to wear when you would not wear your best. Mariquilla sends also this blouse. You see the birds she sewed there?"

"Lovely," I said. "Thank you, uh . . . *gracias*. I appreciate these loans. My own clothing should be here when the mule train arrives."

Claytie and Felipa, their wet hair streaming down their loose Mexican shifts, barged through my open door without ceremony. "The lookout has spotted the train, Paquita. Mrs. Ledbetter says everyone must hurry to prepare for them," the Indian girl, Felipa, told the maid.

"I . . . *Por favor, señorita, excusa*—"

"In English, Paquita," Felipa said with mock sternness. "If Señora Jenkins hears you talk Spanish—" She ran a finger across her throat in a graphic gesture.

Her playmate slapped at her and said something in a guttural and clicking tongue which made both girls laugh, and then said seriously to me, "My aunt just thinks it's so much easier if everyone who works for my pa talks civilized so she can understand them. She says it's part of the white woman's burden to bring the Christian benefits of the English language to the heathen and the Roman Catholics."

Well-bred Irish colleen that I was, I kept my tongue

and resolved to say a rosary and pray for the soul of Mrs. Jenkins—in Spanish or Comanche, if necessary.

The great cottonwood gates groaned as mules clomped into the corral with a veritable symphony of creaking leather and jingling harness. My youthful admirers immediately deserted me for newer and more entertaining strangers.

I turned back to my bed and was occupying myself with the difficult task of realigning my battered limbs when Dolores slipped into the room and braced herself against the wall between door and window where she would not be seen.

"*Señorita,* I must speak to you."

"Oh?" I was at a loss for something to say. Could this pretty but, in broad daylight, prosaic serving maid have read my dreams? I hoped so. Maybe she would be able to explain them to me.

"*Sí. Señorita,* I beg of you, you must leave with the mules when they go." Her hands ceaselessly fingered the rosary she had half-pulled from her pocket, and the rest of her looked as if it would jump straight up in the air and never come down if someone were to touch her on the shoulder from behind.

"Really?"

"*Sí.* You are in great danger. I cannot explain. You would not understand, but—"

"Try me. Please." However great the danger, I was sure I couldn't sit a horse or a wagon seat, but I hoped her explanation would answer some of my own questions.

"I can only tell you that terrible things will happen here. Things that no one can stop. And you, you must not be here then."

"Dolores—" I almost started to tell her about the dreams.

"Please. I need you to do a thing for me, and in order to do this thing, you must be alive."

Before I could learn more, however, Mariquilla entered, cigar hanging from the side of her mouth, ladle in hand.

"Dolores, make haste. We have a *baile* to prepare."

The girl fled with a backward, pleading look, resembling in that instant a trapped rabbit more than a fox or a cat.

3

Perched, like the prospective bride from the fairy tale about the princess and the pea, atop a pile of mattresses provided by Mrs. Ledbetter in deference to my wounds, I surveyed the swirl of color and activity that was the *baile*. Bright blankets and candles set along the top edges of the walls transformed the patio. Long wooden tables groaned with every imaginable good-smelling food—the beef I'd seen roasting earlier, platters of hot *tortillas*, bowls of beans, jug after jug of drink. The central table was dominated by a fanciful spray of fuchsia and turquoise fish surrounded by purple roses with lime-green leaves. The whole thing covered about a yard in the center of the table, and as I learned from Claytie and Felipa during the early portion of the festivities, was made by the baker Merenciana from bread dough and animal glue. I should see her creations for the Day of the Dead, the girls told me. She made skulls from which one could drink and skeletons larger than life. The technique was a specialty of the fishing village from which she had come as a bride. I agreed with them that truly the baker was an artist as fine as any we had in San Francisco, and we talked about that for some time before they wandered off to see the musicians, or mariachis, tune up.

Mrs. Jenkins passed me with a slight superior smile. After trying on the gown she loaned me, I had reluctantly decided that neither the fit—lacking three inches of meeting at my waist—nor the color, a grayed-down lavender not flattering to sallow skin, suited me. I was comfortably attired therefore in the artistic baker's best skirt and Mariquilla's bird-embroidered blouse. Far from seeming offended, Mrs. Jenkins had raised widened eyes and smiled sweetly, spreading her fingers at her own pinched-in waist. "Don't you worry, sugar. You're probably just a teensy bit bloated from your harrowin' experience."

I forgot all about my waistline as food passed under my nose. Bowie knives flashed to spear meat which was genteelly sawed up before being gnawed as a concession to company table manners. Most of the men supplied their own tin drinking mugs. Just as I was about to risk hopping to the ground and waddling to the table, I spied Mrs. Ledbetter's blond braided corona nodding in my direction. Seconds later an Indian brave clad in ill-cured antelope hide delivered a full plate and a red clay mug of what smelled like apple cider. The Indian nodded gravely at the mug. "From Saint Louis, Missourah," he informed me in a singsong voice redolent of recitation.

Before I could regain my composure sufficiently to thank him, the Indian blended back into the crowd.

"'Evenin', ma'am." E. F. Ledbetter tipped his sombrero and leaned against my mattresses. I had been introduced to the wrangler earlier by his wife, when she supervised him in transporting the mattresses. "I see you just made the acquaintance of one of our best customers."

His eyes twinkled at my discomfiture. With his sharp eyes and beakish nose, he resembled a hawk at a convention of blue jays and parakeets. His drawl had been scoured to a soft growl.

"Some customers," I said. "How Mr. Drake can have built this place with the proceeds of Indian rai . . . trading is absolutely miraculous."

"Marryin' a rich widah was a help, I'll grant you," E.F. said.

I spotted my unconventional waiter again. He stood by the gate, near a Mexican man with a rifle slung over his shoulder. At the other gate was another armed *vaquero*, carefully supervised, as it appeared, by another Indian. "Does Mr. Drake employ his customers as gatekeepers?"

Ledbetter coughed. "Not exactly, ma'am. The Indians do that as a token of respect for Mr. Drake, I reckon you might say."

"Indeed?" I said.

"Yes'm."

"They just stand guard like that because they respect him? That's remarkable."

The old wrangler grinned at me. I had taken the bait. "Well, he had to earn it, natcherly. Indians ain't much for your basic business etiquette, as a rule. Right after he built this place, Drake wanted to show his goodwill, so he threw 'em a party and gave his speech about how they'd all get somethin' outta the arrangement."

"Yes, I believe I heard that particular speech."

"He'd been out here awhile but in the line of work he'd been in before, he hadn't had much call to actually talk to the Comanch. Mistook what literal sorta critters they are. The next mornin' after his party when he woke up, what do you think he saw?"

I shrugged.

"Well, actually, it's more what he didn't see. And that was cattle and horses. Seems like his guests took every head of stock he owned home with 'em as party favors."

"But that's terrible. The poor man. He was wiped out. What did he do?"

"He bought more stock, told the Indians it had been a good joke, and threw another party." With admirable expertise, Mr. Ledbetter spat a wad of chewing tobacco into the ornamental cactus beside us. After another few chews he continued, "What he didn't tell 'em was he

36

bought more'n livestock in Mexico. He brought back that little ol' cannon you see up there on the roof, yonder. See it?"

"You mean that thing covered in canvas?"

"That's the one. Once the party got goin' good, he climbed up on the roof and aimed that thing down. That was the signal for the boys to hotfoot it out to the corral and close the doors behind 'em. Only one that survived was Felipa, Claytie's friend. She was five, six years old and wandered away before the grown folks got set down. Missus Drake, the Doña, found her wanderin' in the desert and took her in to raise with her own youngun."

I blinked stupidly, absorbing the story. I had not realized that Indian massacres worked both ways. "I am surprised that Mr. Drake allowed his wife to do such a thing," I ventured finally, my voice heavily laced with irony.

Mr. Ledbetter spat again and gave me a sly sidelong glance from shrewd blue eyes. "Yep, well, Drake's known for his soft heart," he said, lengthening his drawl and his face into an exaggerated appearance of solemnity. I choked on my Missouri cider and sprayed it halfway across the courtyard.

"Miz Harper, oh, Miz Harper!" A familiar voice hailed me from across the patio and the wiry figure of Mr. Jones bounded toward me, relief and guilt having a tug-of-war with his face. "You pore little thing. I never thought to see you again, ma'am, and that's a fact."

Mr. Ledbetter tipped his sombrero and drifted away toward the table.

"Nevertheless, here I am," I said coldly. Jones flushed clear back into his well-used cavalry hat, having no hair to impede the evidence of his embarrassment. Captain Cramer, the leader of the mule train, stalked up behind him.

"You ain't heard the most of it, Jones," the captain said, eyeing me with the same favor with which he might regard a mule thief. "Miz Harper here, or is it Miz Lovelace, is a lady bookwriter. Understand you're stayin' around to write somethin' for Drake. What about your dyin' mama in San Antone?"

"Oh, that," I said. "That was very sad. She died."

"Sudden, weren't it?"

"Not really. As I mentioned, she had been ailing for some time. One of Mr. Drake's employees recently returned from San Antonio and brought a copy of the newspaper, which I read as I recovered from my ordeal. You can imagine my chagrin on reading her obituary."

"Yes, ma'am, I reckon I can imagine that," the captain replied. "But leastways she was spared hearin' about you gettin' run off with by Comanche. Tell me, though, ma'am, was your dear departed mama Mrs. Harper or Mrs. Lovelace?"

Oh dear. The captain was one of those factual types Papa had always abhorred, the sort who preferred to believe truth was limited to one version, usually the one they first encountered. "Mrs. Lovelace," I fluttered with a sweetly dismayed expression that would have done Sasha Divine proud. "I can understand your confusion about my name, gentlemen, but I often find it necessary to travel incognito so that my subjects will not recognize themselves and their associates in my books. Mr. Drake naturally required my true identity—"

Mr. Jones nodded earnestly. "I reckon he would, to know who to sell you back to. You surely were lucky them Indians brought you straight here instead of . . . Well, I confess, I was sort of wonderin'—"

"That makes two of us, Mr. Jones," I responded with acid sweetness. "Perhaps they feared the swift reprisal you were no doubt prepared to launch on my behalf."

"I would have, too, Miz Harp . . . Miz Lovelace, I mean, we all would have, and we started to, but when we went to fetch the fresh mules, what do you think?"

I shrugged.

"They were gone. The lines busted and all of 'em scattered—six of 'em we never did find—they just disap-

38

peared with nary a bray. And them only a few feet away from the wagons. We figured that was a mighty big, mighty mean bunch of Indians and we'd best get help. Besides, by the time we finished puzzlin' over the mules, you were long gone."

"You are to be commended for your dedication to your primary purpose and your prudence in refusing to be drawn into rash action," I said, my voice still sweet. "And I do understand perfectly that my safety is less important than that of your mules. I'll have you know, however, that Mr. Drake paid three horses to the Indians to ransom me."

"Worth every one of 'em, too," Drake said from my left side, and laid his hand lightly on my shoulder. Mariquilla sauntered up beside him and hunkered down against the mattresses, blowing long clouds from the cornhusk cigar that matched the one Drake held elegantly between thumb and forefinger. "Gonna make me famous, this lady is," he said.

"Wouldn't hold my breath on that, Drake, any more'n I'd hold it till the rain comes a pitty-pattin' down," Cramer said. He started to spit for emphasis, glanced at his host, who was glaring in return, and reconsidered. He barely managed to mosey rather than slink back into the crowd.

"Not in a party mood, is he?" I asked, my gaiety marred by a degree of nervousness for fear Drake would heed his reservations about my self-proclaimed and vastly overstated fame and talent.

"It's just his way, ma'am," Jones said, twisting his hat between his hands and actually wringing a few drops of sweat from it. "He don't mean nothin'. Man's been around mules long as he has starts to act like 'em."

"Cramer never did like you, Frank," a new voice said. Its owner did not so much join us as insinuate himself between Jones and Drake. "Never wished either of us well since that time in Presidio. I told you what we should have done."

"John, you musta ridden straight through since yesterday to get here from Chihuahua so fast. You always could smell a free drink. I want you to meet this young lady. Miss Valentine Lovelace, Mr. John Kruger, a former partner and sometime business associate of mine."

It was all I could do to shake hands with Kruger. Though his features were not irregular and might have been attractive with a less malevolent spirit to animate them, his eye bore a wild and vicious glitter and his mouth seemed to water excessively, causing him to lick at its corners, his tongue flickering in and out like a snake's. I knew without asking that what he felt he and Drake should have done in Presidio would have been extremely unpleasant for Captain Cramer. His proximity almost made me nostalgic for my Indian captors.

"It's a party, John," Drake said, as if soothing a feral animal. "Let's forget our differences and enjoy ourselves. The good old days are gone. We gotta move with the times. You can't change the mind of every man who disagrees with you by liftin' his hair."

Kruger paid no attention to him. His attention was fixed on me in a manner that I found insolent. "You're the one Cramer insulted, ma'am. Say the word and I'll—"

Drake cut him off smoothly. "Mariquilla, Mr. Kruger looks a mite dry to me. Why don't you take him and get him a drink?"

Mariquilla dropped her cigar, rose, and ground it under the ball of her bare foot. She jerked her head toward the table, and Kruger, with a backward glance at me which caused me to abruptly avert my face, followed her.

Jones swilled a long drink from his tin cup, shutting his eyes tightly as he gulped. Drake sipped from a fluted crystal goblet, his eyes smiling at me over the rim. I emptied my cider.

The mariachis, their instruments finally playing more or less together, struck up a dance tune. Mrs. Ledbetter tripped forth with her lanky husband.

Kruger and Mariquilla reappeared, whirling around

40

the older couple. Mariquilla looked pained, as well she might, since Kruger had her wedged against him in a stranglehold. The music bounced along in a kind of Mexican polka. I watched the musicians, since none of the conversation was particularly edifying. There were three of them: two *campesinos*, hailed with staccato handclaps as Pedro and Arturo; and one of the few gringo *vaqueros* in the employ of Fort Draco, Drake whispered to me in an aside, a fellow named Delbridge. Delbridge, who played a sort of miniature guitar made from the shell of an armadillo, and Arturo, on the concertina, paced happily in time with their music, but Pedro strummed his guitar as seriously as if he were weighing gold. Claytie and Felipa hopped into the crowd like a pair of jackrabbits, dancing together until each was claimed by an itchy-footed *vaquero*. Jones set his cup on the edge of my mattress, eyed me nervously, and started to open his mouth.

"What wonderful music!" I cried effusively in Drake's general direction. "I am so distressed that my injuries prevent me from joining the merriment."

Jones's mouth shut again, then dropped open once more in pure wonderment. Mrs. Jenkins, who had disappeared to "freshen up," at last made her grand entrance. She swept onto the patio like a cross between a parrot and a wedding cake, clad in green-and-yellow-striped taffeta tucked into a polonaise composed of white lace tiers, her hair an intricate series of twists and curls topped with a tiny hat crammed full of daisies, green-and-yellow-striped bows, and a baby dove no doubt mourned by its mother.

This finery won her immediate admirers. Kruger abruptly turned Mariquilla loose and bowed himself low in front of the widow. Drake quickly excused himself.

"You plan to stay here, do you, missy?" Jones asked me.

"I have accepted Mr. Drake's commission."

"How long you reckon it'll take you to write about him?"

"A month or two, I should think."

"There'll be another train through in three. If I was you, I'd come on along with this one."

"How odd that you should say so. That's the second time today I've had such advice. I appreciate your concern, however belated, Mr. Jones, but I have no intention of leaving yet."

"Miz Harper, that feller over there dancin' with Missus Jenkins? Kruger? He scalps people for a livin'. Not just Indians, mind you, but Mexicans and purt' near anybody else gets in his way. He and Mr. Drake are old workin' buddies."

"Thank you, Mr. Jones. I was looking for local color."

Jones gave me the same sort of look with which he might favor one of his characteristically obstinate charges, drained his tin cup, tipped his hat, and grabbed Captain Cramer for the next dance.

Like my dear papa, the more inebriated Drake became, the more conscientiously chivalrous he grew. Flying to the side of his sister in an attempt to shield her from Mr. Kruger's terpsichorean advances, he met with rebuff. Mrs. Jenkins clung shamefully to the odious man, drinking to him only with her eyes but looking as if she was well prepared to go further.

Drake then decided to deliver me from my isolated perch and volunteered to carry me to the roof over his office, the same roof where the cannon reposed, for a gander at the view. I declined to be carried. He was a romantic figure but the steps were steep, I am no featherweight, and he walked like a sailor who has not yet found his land legs.

Nevertheless, I was hard put to remember that I was to be the chronicler of his story, not the heroine, and leaned more heavily on his arm than was strictly necessary. The waxing moon, the stars sparkling on the puddles and rivulets of the Rio, the mountains rolling back like the ragged tiers of a Gypsy's skirts, the sharp clean scent of the desert coupled with the rosewater cologne favored by the manly presence at my side made a compelling combination.

"My domain, Miss Lovelace," Drake said, sloshing his wineglass at the countryside. "I built it myself, with little more than grit, brains, and courage." Self-deprecation was not his style. "It's in my blood to break new ground, I reckon. I don't believe I mentioned that my family is kin on my paternal grandfather's side to Sir Francis Drake, famed explorer of Queen Elizabeth's court?"

"Really?" My ancestors were kin on my paternal grandmother's side to Seamus O'Reilly, famed liar and pickpocket of the County Cork pubs.

"Yep, we're plumb historical, we Drakes. I reckon that's why I like readin' and hearin' all the old stories about this country. You know, I been studyin' on it. Maybe what you saw back there was the ghost lights. We got plenty of them out here. S'posed to be some old Indian chief lookin' for his lost people. Kept lookin' after he died, which is how come they're still around."

"Is the chief prone to roaring?" I asked innocently.

"Not anymore, he ain't, but the hills up there are full of hoodoos and if there was any wind at all—and you gotta admit you might not have noticed it right then—you might have been hearing one of them. Hoodoos are funny-shaped rocks sittin' up on the mountains, and when the wind blows through 'em they make a noise that's a cross between a wolf, a cryin' child, and a panther in heat. Even if there wasn't any wind, could be that earthquake you said you felt touched it off. Or maybe you heard La Llorona weepin' for her baby—the *campesinos* say she wanders anywhere there's a river. That's where she was supposed to have drowned it. Listen, I think the boys are startin' up her song—"

The musicians were indeed wailing a mournful ballad, but frankly, I wasn't listening. I was seething. "Mr. Drake, if you can believe I saw ghost lights and heard dead ghost women crying for dead ghost babies, why can't you believe I might have seen a dragon?"

43

"It's not that I can't believe in dragons, darlin'," he said patiently. "I've read as much about dragons as anybody, I reckon, and I'll allow they might be true in some places. But they got nothin' to do with the Indian-tradin' and ranch business. Dragons are one thing. Runnin' cattle is a whole nother can of worms." He gazed bemusedly down onto the patio, where a resentful elfin face raised to stare into his. He extracted a cigar from his breast pocket without removing his eyes from hers and took a long and thoughtful pull. "After you been here for a while, little lady, you'll understand these people like I do. They're not like you and me—you know they have a day here, right around Halloween, when they go to the graveyards and have parties and eat candy skeletons? And that's just one of the Christian customs. There's things in them old Aztec records I got from the missions that would curdle your ink."

"I'm a journalist, Mr. Drake. I have schooled myself to avoid oversensi—" My words died in the rising of the lament from below. I bit my lip and turned away from Drake in a fit of vexation—just in time to see a flash of green light disappear between two mountains. "Mr. Drake, I . . ."

But it was no use. The light was gone and Drake would never believe me. I wasn't sure I had seen it, in fact. Perhaps I just had green light on the brain. Drake certainly had Dolores on his. She held his complete attention as the song finished, when she whirled away toward the band, clapping her hands to indicate a new beat. She turned slowly from them, circling, her arms above her head, throwing it back to reveal a length of slender golden throat. We were down those stairs and I was redeposited on my mattress pile so fast it nearly took my breath away. Drake planted himself right in front of the band, puffing his cigar rhythmically as they played and Dolores swirled, stomped her dusty little bare feet, and snapped her fingers, her face like Christ's on the cross. Her costume was dark, a black skirt, her white blouse covered with a black fringed shawl similar to Mariquilla's.

She flung herself about with abandon, her dancing a sort of exorcism, a draining of some intense emotion, her black hair falling behind her like a waterfall, then whipping forward to veil her face and shoulders. She was all pantherlike grace and sinuous movement. I don't think any man on the premises took a breath for a quarter of an hour while she danced and the musicians played, as enthralled by her as the rest of the audience.

I kept watching the sky for more of the green flashes, annoyed that I had allowed myself to be so easily led away from my vantage point. I still was not fully recovered from the shock of my encounter with the Indians, I suppose, for my reactions are normally much quicker and more forcible. The shock no doubt also accounted for my looking for invisible dragons while everyone else watched Dolores.

Well, not quite everyone. Mariquilla leaned against my mattresses, smoking her cigar, her head tilted and her expression critical during the first five minutes or so the girl danced.

Slowly the cook shook her head and disappeared beyond the corral gate. She returned a moment later. The situation on the ground started interesting me almost as much as the one in the sky. Perhaps we would now witness the passionate duel between rivals for the affections of the *patrón*. The old mistress, cast aside, and the new flame, burning so brightly amid her master's guests. But Mariquilla merely whistled sharply, caught Dolores' attention, and tossed her two sets of wooden shells. Then, draping herself against my mattresses again and flipping the corner of her fringed shawl back across my feet, Mariquilla resumed her role as observer.

Dolores missed but a step or two as she tucked the castanets into her fingers and clicked her rhythm to complement that of the musicians.

Chewing her cigar, Mariquilla grumbled, "Ah, the

young. I keep telling that girl it's in the ankles, the down down of the heels, not the hips."

"No one seems to mind," I pointed out.

"Yes, because they are all horny bastards who care nothing for the dance. But I know. See, it goes like this," and abruptly she threw her arms above her head and faced me, stamping her heels in time, twirling and subtly swaying, snapping her fingers with the clack of the castanets. Soon Dolores gracefully dropped away, leaving the floor to the older woman.

Drake brushed past me, stopping for a word with E.F., who stood nearby. "I'm turnin' in now. Keep an eye on Kruger, will you? You know how he is, not too particular about which black hair he lifts. Wouldn't want him to scalp any of the staff."

Despite the best effort of E.F. and several of Drake's other more responsible employees, the party degenerated after that. I could not regain the roof alone, and to venture from my perch was to invite trouble, so with the assistance of Felipa and Claytie I retired among much hollering and ungentlemanly language.

Sleep eluded me, for I kept replaying my conversations with Drake, my encounter with the Indians, their facial expressions, the dragonish outline I had seen, the dream fragments I remembered. Drake was absolutely right. Dragons did not belong on ranches. Seeing them there was madness. But I did not feel like a madwoman. I felt highly confused. The more I thought about what had happened, the more it refused to make sense. I tossed and turned, but my sores hurt and my limbs were numb from lack of exercise. At last the night grew quiet. I rose carefully and left my room, holding onto the walls of the littered courtyard, stepping with difficulty across the men who lay sprawled there. Both Mexican and Indian guards dozed at their posts, while beyond the open gate, what was left of the river glistened in the pallid moonlight.

The owls and the coyotes, quite vocal earlier in the evening, had ceased their cries. Something just beyond the corner of my vision shifted. When I turned to look, a shadow I had assumed was another bush suddenly rose and glided along the riverbed, wailing softly. My hair roots prickled and I stood as still as the shadow previously had been.

4

Winglike appendages unfolded from the central shaft of shadow, the edges feathers of blackness. I inched forward, trying to make out some other detail. A cry burst forth from the shadow, initially in Spanish but breaking into another tongue I had never heard before. A pebble slid beneath my foot and I caught my breath. The blackness whirled toward me, wings raised high, and flung itself upon me. Its sudden weight knocked me from my unsteady stance and we both collapsed onto the mud of the riverbank, me cursing and my assailant sobbing.

"Ah, *señorita*, you come to comfort me. I knew when first I saw you you are one with the second sight. But, alas, it is too late. I am lost. We are all lost. I gave him everything—everything—and still he would not heed me. Now the doom must certainly fall."

"Everything?" I muttered, disentangling myself from her. "Everything? Oh, dear. I understand that's never wise." I quoted the wit and wisdom of Sasha Divine, somewhat belatedly to be of use to the girl. "I wish you would not talk in riddles all the time, Dolores. And this creeping around in the middle of the night moaning about doom falling—I mistook you for a ghost."

"I am distraught, *señorita*. I have nowhere to turn.

That is why I tried to bespeak you earlier. And then, when I saw Don Francisco with you, I thought—"

"You had only to come to my room again if you wished to confide in me. As for Mr. Drake, I only just met the man. While your jealousy is very flattering, it is also very mistaken. Mr. Drake is not at all my type."

"Those were the same words he spoke of you, *señorita*, tonight, after my dance." Did he? The cad! Dolores stared at me trustingly. I was not flattered. Beautiful young women never trust Sasha Divine. Or confide in her. Or expect her assistance. But then, Sasha and I were in different businesses, and on the whole, looking like a trustworthy schoolmarm would probably be more of an aid to me than looking like Sasha.

"What was it you wanted to ask me earlier tonight, Dolores?"

Tears welled up and dropped from her tilted eyes and she began trembling pitiably. Her English waned as she spoke ever faster, "My *niños, señorita,* my children, the Indians stole. Don Francisco will not have them returned to me. They are so little—please, take a message to my uncle in San Antonio. Tell him . . ." What I was to tell him was in fast and incoherent Spanish punctuated with sobs and tears.

I was about to break in on her bilingual hysterics when a horrible bawling scream cut across our conversation. It echoed from far out in the desert night. A flash of green streaked across the sky and three quick flares of orange blazed in its wake.

Dolores' large dark irises were completely surrounded by white as she stared up at me. "Alas! Too late! It has come!" While I was crowing with delight that someone, someone at Fort Draco, understood the significance of what I was beginning to *believe* was my imagination, Dolores, looking more guilt-stricken than frightened, fled for the hacienda gates.

Perplexed as much by the girl's behavior as by the fires, my dreams, and my memories, I watched the distant orange blazes flicker until they burned themselves out. Then, resolving to speak again with Dolores in the morning, I returned to my room.

Even had my sores not been so painful, it was unfeasible to consider leaving right away in order to perform Dolores' errand. She could give one of the muleskinners a bribe and the name of her uncle. Probably her original purpose in directing the plea at me was to get me out of the way so that she could have a clear field where Drake was concerned. That thought stayed with me as I drifted into sleep, peeving me far more than it should have.

The colossal impudence of these barbarians! The discourtesy, not to say irreverence, with which our warnings are disregarded, our omens and portents ignored. Even our own supplicant has not had the manners to include us in the celebration, to offer a token in our honor, to thank us for our beneficent interference. Surely she is much degenerated from her ancestors, our own chosen jaguar people. We suppose that is the fault of our nemesis, our downfall, the one who has wreaked havoc from our order while we repaired and regenerated ourselves. We must therefore exercise our sublime, well-known, and much-exploited patience, recalling that we are not of these barbarians, merely among them.

Do they fail to see how low they have fallen? Very well, they will fall lower still, until they seek the true way, see the light, and beseech us once more with prayers and sacrifice, as in times past, when all affairs were conducted properly according to our dictates. Those who stole the maiden begin to understand even now as they discover that we have extracted a tithe of beasts from their herd. How we suffer for their sake! Even their beasts are contrary, causing us excessive digestive indisposition before we wisely deduced that the necessary nourishing gases are more readily released into our system if the beasts are allowed to decompose somewhat prior to ingestion.

As for the king who has offended us in spite of our gracious and subtle announcement that he is in dishar-

mony with us, our retribution is swift, its warning implicit. Below, the horned herds scatter bawling from our claws, but we catch the beasts one by one, granting them obliteration from this life and the joy of the next. We strike again and again, our mind filled with bestial terror, our claws slick with the by-products of death. At last we complete our task, our inner workings rasping with our exertions. We are too fatigued to return to our personal source of moisture, that clear pool that pleases us so well. What is left of this begrimed stream must suffice. Alighting gracefully near our night's work, we lower our muzzle to the first of the remaining channels and, unsatisfied, progress to the next, and the next, all along the length of the riverbed.

The horrible caterwauling of the butchered steers continued to ring in *my* head even as the "we" of the dream congratulated themselves. I struggled to wake for what seemed hours, my eyelids stubbornly sticking together. Several times I dreamed that I rose, opened my eyes, climbed out of bed, and flew away—and each time I knew that I was still asleep and had to start all over again trying to wake myself, to loosen the hold the "we" had on me. For whoever "we" were, they were in no part Pelagia Harper or Valentine Lovelace. I was sure of that now. Though their voice had spoken to and within me, it was not my voice. I have never been known, even in my most imperious moments as an assistant editor, to refer to myself in the plural.

At last I felt the burn of my sores and smelled the ghost of the breakfast I feared I would miss entirely if I did not bestir myself at once. Somewhere distant the caterwauling continued at a lower pitch, but otherwise the compound was oddly quiet. No jingle of harness. No stamp of hooves. No rough masculine voices. The last was not too surprising, as the men would be nursing massive hangovers. But the horses and mules?

I ventured forth, feeling quite cheerful in spite of an

exceptionally active night. Once I shed the cobwebs of the dream, my head was clear.

"Good morning, Mariquilla," I called, waddling past the kitchen. Mariquilla did not so much as look up from the peppers she chopped, whacking her vicious-looking knife down upon the hapless vegetables with grim ruthlessness.

Inside an empty corral, Mrs. Ledbetter busied herself with a shovel and the leavings of the animals. She answered my greeting shortly. "You look too chipper to be decent," she complained.

"I must," I said. "Mariquilla snubbed me."

"She's just riled 'cause Kruger got liquored up and ruined the cockfight. She had a hefty sum bet on that red of Manuel's. She'll get over it."

"Has the mule train departed so soon?" I asked.

"You don't see it, do you? The fools lit outta here like someone'd set fire to their tails," she replied scornfully. "Them and all the other men, after usin' up or carryin' off durn near ever' drop of water on the place. The well's about give up the ghost, the mules drank the storage tank dry this mornin', and the Rio's been down to an extra-wet mud puddle for days." She wiped her forehead with the side of her arm. "We don't get some rain pretty soon, we'll have to take to haulin' from the spring, and that's a pain in the rear."

"Why? Is it very far?"

"About eight miles, but half of one of 'em is straight up. There's a little wagon road but it won't go all the way into the canyon and the spring is about a quarter-mile inside. It isn't all that big, but it's never been known to give out."

"A pity it's so inconvenient," I commiserated. "One would think water would have the sense to flow downhill where a person could get at it."

"Good Lord doesn't always arrange things to suit us, does he? If you want a nice bit of timber hereabouts, you dig up roots—poor little ol' plants got to sink deep to get a drink. And the water gets caught up in the hills, where the rock catches it from runoff and whatnot. So you gotta dig for wood and climb for water."

"Oh, I wish I had my notepad. I want to write that down."

She stuck her shovel hilt deep in the odoriferous pile she had collected. "Shucks, honey, don't get your knickers in a twist. I can say it again later. You really want to write down somethin' *I* said for your book?"

"Most certainly. Your remark was eloquently put."

"Well," she said in a pleased way. "I vow and declare. By the way, might that notepad of yours be with the bundle of goods you got in the storeroom? Millard Jones heaved it in there when they took on provisions this mornin'. I meant to fetch it in here for you, but then all this ruckus broke loose with old Benito, and Cap'n Cramer and Mr. Drake havin' words about it, and that polecat Kruger bustin' in with his two cents' worth. The cap'n didn't take to Mr. Drake lockin' up El Mellado, and dumped his boys out of their bedrolls before first light so's they could take off three days ahead of schedule. I don't much blame him. Kruger's got a nasty streak as wide as he is, and Mr. Drake was pretty hard on El Mellado. That's the nickname they give old Benito, the shepherd. Poor old fellow's a harmless soul, and if he had a little celebration of his own out there . . ." She stopped with a sigh that was more like a stiff breeze. "Still and all, I suppose Mr. Drake's right. A body can't have some damn fool settin' fire to the whole range and then claimin' he's seen a giant fire-breathin' gila monster. I swear, the stories people won't tell to keep themselves out of trouble."

"When did all this happen?"

"Oh, bright and early, honey. Before the chickens was up. El Mellado come barrelin' in here like greased lightnin', his eyes big as milk pails, babblin' in Mezcan about this big gila monster. Boss was hung-over somethin' fierce and not in the mood for it *a*-tall, as were none of the rest of us. He stuck the old man in the pokey to sober up."

From the look on her face, she considered El Mellado's story considerably more odoriferous than the task in which her shovel reposed. I was so excited to think that the dragon had appeared to someone else that I could hardly contain myself enough to preserve what I fondly hoped was Mrs. Ledbetter's good opinion of me.

"Extraordinary!" I said. "The story sounds like the folk tales Mr. Drake was telling me last night. I must interview this man at once. You say he's in the pokey. You don't mean you have a jail here, inside the fort?"

"We sure do. Right behind my pantry. Fair makes my hair raise when Mr. Drake has to hang somebody in there. Don't seem sanitary, somehow."

"They *hang* people in there?" I asked, taking more quick notes.

"Just your criminals and common filth."

"I'd think that would be up to the army."

"The army is here to fight Indians and keep an eye out to make sure the South don't rise again, startin' here. They don't give doodly about much else, or so Drake says. Between you and me, E.F. doesn't exactly hold with that opinion, but then, Mr. Drake is boss."

"Yes, indeed. And a good one, I'm sure. Did you say he has gone for the day?"

She nodded. "He rode out right after the muleskinners. See, old Benito claimed, besides seein' the lizard, that he'd found part of the missing mules and a passel of our steers, off in the left-hand shut-up. What the devil he was doin' up there, I don't know—"

"I intend to find out," I said. "May I talk to him?"

"Sure, but he won't understand you, 'less you talk Mezcan. Better go along with Dolores there. She's fetchin' his breakfast to him now. Here, take the keys and let yourself into the storeroom to collect your kit. Dolores can show you where that is too. I'm gonna haul this out to the compost pile."

Dolores strode by with her head so high I thought she'd put a crick in her neck. I had to call to her three times before she acknowledged my greeting. I thought she might be embarrassed about her disclosures of the night before, or possibly angry that I had not complied with her request.

"I'm sorry, Dolores, but the mule train got away before I could speak with them," I said.

"Already last night it was too late, *señorita*," she responded in a low and wispy voice.

"So you said. I merely meant that perhaps you could have sent the message to your uncle in San Antonio with one of the muleskinners. Is he your only nearby relative?"

"*Sí*, he is of my father's people, who have lived here since the *conquistadores*. My mother's people came from the jungles. Those who are left live near what you would call Mexico City. We are a very old family on both sides. I myself was raised in a convent."

"Is that where you learned English?"

"*Sí*. And many other things."

"But not dancing?" I asked facetiously. I too had been to convent school from time to time. I knew better.

"No. The dancing I learned from my husband's sister. And Mariquilla—she shows me a thing now and then to cheer me. I had not danced since my first baby was born. After the birth of my second, my husband decided we should move here, find land, but then we were attacked, he was killed, and we . . . my *niños* . . . I came to live here." Her voice faded away.

"I am sorry about your family. Perhaps we still have time to save them. But right now I must talk to the prisoner, old Benito, or El Mellon, or whatever it was Mrs. Ledbetter called him."

"El Mellado, the toothless one. But he is so old he is *loco*, *señorita*. You can believe nothing he says to you." She sounded guilty and frightened, like an errant school-girl hiding something from an all-seeing nun.

"Nevertheless, he has a story I need to hear. If you will be so kind as to translate."

We talked to him through the head-high bars of the

cell door, though I had a key on my ring to fit the lock. El Mellado did not want to come out of his cell, Dolores said. When I quite naturally took the lead and asked her to inquire why he did not, she paused, then asked my question in rapid-fire Spanish. The old man responded quickly and loudly, spraying spittle through his unadorned gums. Dolores paused again. Her mouth was pressed tight and she looked a little pale.

"What did he say?" I prompted.

She shrugged with unconvincing disinterest and answered haltingly, "Nonsense, *señorita*. Only nonsense. He talks of a great lizard-bird who breathes fire and sets aflame what it eats. But how can that be?" Her voice rose from a wisp to a mousy squeak and she would not look at me when she spoke.

"Where did he see the creature?" I asked.

Spanish volleyed between the two of them, the old man at one point opening his mouth and emitting a breathy "Haaah." He ended by saying, *"No. Muerte."*

"By the line camp, *señorita*, many hours' ride from here. In the left-hand branch of a very old canyon where sometimes a creek runs. He went up there to get brush to start his fire and found the bodies of the beasts—what had been left of them. He says they were burned. He says he was afraid when he saw them and clung to the canyon wall. The beast swooped down from the same side of the canyon where he was and did not see him. It carried a live and bawling steer, and as he watched, it dropped the animal and haaaah"—she imitated the old man imitating the monstrous beast—"it cooked it before it hit the ground. I asked El Mellado if any of the other animals were alive or if they were all dead, and he said no, all dead."

I had been taking notes. When I finished I said, "Ask him again what this beast looked like."

El Mellado took several steps backward and threw his arms wide, jumped up, and tried to touch the air above his head, all the time talking excitedly to Dolores. He pointed to his own gums and drew his hands apart a good six inches, turned his side to us, and with the edge of a gnarled hand indicated spinal ridges, and finally broke into a birdish whistle.

But she had had enough. She shoved the breakfast *tortilla* quickly through the bars and retreated.

I limped after her. "Wait," I said. "What else did he say? Was it too horrible to repeat? I beg you not to spare my sensibilities. As a journalist I have both seen and heard of many gruesome creatures." Indeed, I had. Many of them held political office.

She ignored me, but outside the guardroom she paused, leaning against the wall and taking deep deliberate breaths. She looked ill and panic-stricken.

"I beg your pardon, Dolores," I said. "Perhaps I'm the one who should watch out for other people's sensibilities. Forgive me." I fingered the keys in my hand, then regarded them with dismay. "Bother. Mrs. Ledbetter showed me the proper key to the storeroom and now I can't remember which it was." I held them out to her. "Can you point out the correct key? I have to fetch my bundle from the storeroom. Mrs. Ledbetter suggested you could show me where that was as well."

She took the keys from me. They jingled like Christmas bells in her trembling hands. Without another word she led me down the working courtyard, through the outer gate, along the wall toward the broad and nearly dry riverbed, to a pair of great wooden doors bound with huge iron hinges and a locking latch. Outside of the cool adobe walls and the shade of the *ramada*, the morning was far too warm for comfort. The beads of perspiration I had already generated flowed into runnels. Dolores selected the proper key, and with the accompaniment of a lot more jingling, and one final decisive clank, the lock sprang. Heat swelled the wood of the heavy doors and they stuck. Both of us tugged on them to wedge them open.

Blackness swallowed all but a thin slice of light pouring through the open doors. I could see nothing for several moments. In contrast to the outside, the storeroom was almost icy. After a time, I began to notice a grayness high above me and to the left. Drake's idea of a storeroom differed considerably from mine. I had been expecting, perhaps, a building of smokehouse or root-cellar proportions. I might have known better. As the only purveyor of goods for so many people so far from all other trade centers, Drake would naturally need a space on the order of an attached warehouse. He had it. The storeroom was a vast cavernous chamber, perhaps a fourth of the size of the entire fort, its roof supported by great square pillars wider than two arms could span. Tidy stacks of cloth, bags of grain, hides, new harnesses, and barrels piled upon barrels lined the walls. I mention only those items near the door. I did not care to explore the far corners.

On the hard mud floor in an untidy pile half-leaning against the nearest pillar were my belongings. I knelt and started gathering them. Dolores' shadow fell across the streak of sunlight. She chanted in a soft familiar cadence and I heard the click and whisper of rosary beads. With an armload of clothing I joined her. The two of us had to lean on the doors to shut them.

I spent the rest of the morning puzzling over what I had learned and what I hadn't. My legs hurt again. I stayed in my room and sorted my clothing, folding the garments in a neat pile and laying them by the cold hearth. Greeting my beloved notebook enthusiastically, I wrote detailed descriptions of occurrences to date since the last entry I made under the muleskinners' wagon. I also jotted down as much as I could recall of my dreams. My fingers were cramped and my mind muddled with questions by the time I finished, and I decided I needed something to distract me until Drake and his men returned and I could learn more. I wandered as casually into the courtyard as I could while walking like a cowboy who has had too close and long a relationship with his horse.

Mrs. Jenkins stood in the middle of the patio, clapping her hands together and shouting, "Claytie Jane! Claytie Jane. Felipa, you little heathen. You girls come out now, wherever you are, and tend to your lessons or Mr. Drake will hear of your behavior."

A cough, a giggle, and Claytie stumbled forward, pushed along by a disgusted-looking Felipa.

"Aunt Lovanche, it's siesta time," Claytie whined.

"Claytie Jane Drake, that is a decadent native custom as you *well* know, invented by the lazy people who populate this disagreeably torrid land. Vigorous folks who get places do not sleep half the day away. They do their studies."

"What are you studying?" I asked, as much to get the girls off the hook as because I really wanted to know.

"History," Felipa said, her lip curling. "And exposition. That's writing."

"Say," Claytie said. "That *is* writing. Didn't I hear Pa say you are a real live author?"

Mrs. Jenkins, recognizing her own deliverence when she saw it, developed a convenient headache and took herself off to rest her eyes, a process which involved reclining for several hours but which was, of course, quite distinct from taking a siesta. From Drake's library I gleaned another piece of the mystery and further insight into my host's character. From my pupils I gleaned the more unsavory aspects of other characters. On the whole I received rather more instruction than I gave that afternoon.

5

The dragon was right there in Drake's library. *El patrón* had not been exaggerating about the size and eclectic composition of his collection. For much of it, "eclectic" was too narrow a term—a better one was "haphazard," many selections obviously booty from Indian raids. About a quarter of the books were Bibles, everything from New Testaments to monstrous family Bibles whose previous custodians were now receiving their religious instruction firsthand, having traded their scalps for halos. There was also—hurrah!—a collection of Fenimore Cooper's work, one or two of Mr. Twain's stories, and in one corner quite a few of Ned Buntline's dime novels. I found histories of England, the United States, and Mexico in English. Many other volumes were in Spanish.

I prowled through the books while the girls completed the writing exercises I assigned them.

"How do you spell 'annihilate'?" Felipa asked.

"Use the dictionary."

"Yes, ma'am. Only you're standin' in front of the shelf it's on. Would you hand it to me, please?"

I tugged on a volume three times the size of the largest of the Bibles. When it pulled free, a handful of unbound papers slumped down on the shelf, a few drifting onto the floor. I bent to gather them and saw that they were in Latin. No doubt plundered from some mission. I handed Felipa the dictionary and was about to replace the papers when an illustration, a simple line drawing, caught my eye. It was labeled "Stone Carving of a Jaguar Priestess." It bore an uncanny resemblance to Dolores, had she been wearing a Sunday hat as feathery and ridiculous as one of Mrs. Jenkins'. I would never have noticed it had not the delicate old parchment been defaced with a penciled circle around the picture. Further on, more of the text was underlined in the same pencil. I shuffled a few more pages and found drawings of temple etchings, hard to make out in places. One of these, of a snaky monster with feathers like those on the jaguar woman's hat, was captioned "Kukulkan, or Quetzalcoatl, the Plumed Serpent."

"Aha!" I said triumphantly to the picture. To the girls I said, "You may resume your studies tomorrow, ladies," and tucked the papers under my arm. I had found studies of my own to pursue.

That afternoon I sorely wished I had gone to church more regularly. I could decipher the archaic Latin texts, but only just. I read through until early evening, too excited to rest my eyes, which burned from the strain of reading the faded ink by the barred light falling across my blanket. When Mariquilla rang the dinner bell, I stowed the manuscripts carefully between my straw mattress and the ropes that held it to the wooden bed frame.

After dinner I did not feel like returning immediately to my room. Mariquilla sat outside the kitchen on the ground, her back against the wall, her eyes watching the sky as she offered up her own cloudy contributions.

"May I join you?" I asked, leaning very carefully beside her.

"Sí," she said. "You are walking better, no?"

"I am walking *much* better, yes, thank you, but I could still use some more of your salve. I fear I overextended myself this morning, running errands with Dolores. How is she, by the way?" I finished innocently.

"Eh?"

"Dolores appeared to be ill this morning when I left her."

Mariquilla shrugged noncommittally.

"I do hope I didn't say anything to upset her," I babbled on. "It is so difficult to be thrust without introduction among strangers. One doesn't know enough of their histories to know what to say to them. Dolores appears so sad."

"The *patrón* bought her in July from the Comanche, but her children they kept to raise. Naturally, she grieves. But it is no assured thing, to be a mother in this land. Children are lost to sickness, to snakes, to many things as well as Indians. I myself had only one baby who lived, and she died before the end of her first year. My other children never got both feet out of heaven. I light candles. Dolores would be smart to do the same and try to have more babies."

"You're right, of course, but I'm sure it isn't easy for her, losing her whole family like that. And no one to help her."

Mariquilla rolled her eyes and said sourly, "Yes, she is all alone and helpless, that one."

"You sound as if you don't like her very much."

"I neither like nor dislike her, *señorita*. I tried to aid her when first she came here, and for a time she seemed to take my advice. But then the *patrón* began to hang around the kitchen and she stopped speaking to me. Now she smiles too much sometimes and otherwise always has the sad face. I think she needs to see a priest. It is unfortunate that Don Francisco will not allow one to stay here, as Padre Alfonso did in the time of La Doña."

"Wouldn't he send for one if everyone asked him to?"

"*Sí*, but only for Mass. He does not want someone else to advise his people. He felt Padre Alfonso turned Doña Seferina against him. That was not so. La Doña knew right from wrong without the advice of her priest. She left her husband's bed after he killed Felipa's people, and would not hear him when he told her it was a necessary thing. Her father was a gentleman who governed all of his people with kindness, according to her. Of course, a papa's shortcomings are harder to see than a husband's."

"I have heard that there were others nearby who were more tolerant of Drake's shortcomings."

She grinned rakishly and puffed a reproving billow up at me. "My English is not so good, perhaps, but I think 'tolerant' is not the word telling why I took over certain of La Doña's duties. I was healthy and not ugly and he is *muy hombre, el patrón*. That is how it started. Then after a while I am no longer so what you call 'tolerant.' A young *vaquero, muy bonito*, who values the refinement of an experienced woman, begins for my sake putting himself in danger of growing no older. But God is good and sent at the same time a lady missionary, who arrives with her *estúpido* husband, and suddenly I am the cook and the *cigarrera* again, nothing more, and my little *vaquero* is even today making someone happy with what he learned at my bosom." She sighed, her eyes as smoky as her breath. "Dolores need not be alone and unaided. Many of the *vaqueros* admired her, many of the American soldiers from the fort. One among them would help her in finding her little ones if she asked, and help her make more if she failed. Instead, she is like the lamb who flies to the *lobo* for protection. Not wise. But also, I think Don Francisco will find, not tolerant."

A door banged somewhere behind us, and like a gingham tornado, Mrs. Ledbetter stormed past us and through the unbolted front gate.

"Paquita! Dolores! Where in tarnation is that river water I told you to fetch me? The well's plumb dry and the animals won't take kindly to cider for supper."

"If you can find water in this river, *señora*, I will bring it to you in a golden bucket," Paquita called back.

We followed the housekeeper to the riverbed, now dry enough to walk across without muddying one's feet. In a single shallow puddle, barely enough water remained to fill a demitasse cup.

"Shoot," Mrs. Ledbetter said. "Guess they'll have to drink cider after all. I never have seen the like of this. Hot and dry is one thing, but this is like the desert all of a sudden sprouted a gullet and drunk the river down its own self."

"Perhaps it did," I muttered. Dolores shot me an unfathomable look.

I don't believe anyone got very much sleep that night. The men should have been back long ago, and we had only a few of the more elderly and infirm *campesinos* and firearms of low caliber with which to defend ourselves. The able-bodied *vaqueros* had ridden with Drake and Kruger. The lookout paced the rooftop above me, a new and dire sign. When the night guard was too nervous to sleep on duty, the rest of us had good reason to worry.

I lay on my bed and studied the manuscripts by candlelight, until slumber overtook me. I dreamt of lambs leaping over winking wolves, only to be snatched out of the dream by some invisible something I could not manage to look up far enough to see. The durable candle made locally of candelilla wax was still burning when I awoke, my cheek creased from the papers beneath it. When the sentry shouted again, I realized what had roused me.

The shout degenerated into a cry and a whimpering prayer. I limped from my room, staring upward. The guard sat on the rooftop, a shaking arm extended, jibbering to himself. The ladder leading to the roof leaned against the wall next to my doorway, and I was up it in a trice, my wounds forgotten. Mrs. Ledbetter ran out in her nightgown and mobcap, followed by a throng, but I paid no attention. I was watching the shooting star as it pierced a mountainside, burning brilliant and green, hovering in the sky just above the sentry's pointing finger before delving deeper into the distant slope. It hurt the eyes to watch for long. When I glanced away, Mariquilla and Paquita knelt on either side of the guard, crossing themselves. Dolores stood behind them with closed eyes, her rosary beads clicking like crickets. When I looked back, the light in the sky had disappeared. I too crossed myself and descended the ladder.

The courtyard exploded with bursts of Spanish. Mrs. Jenkins, who had stood on the ground as the rest of us watched from the rooftop, demanded to know what had happened. When told, she pretended it was all a conspiracy to keep her awake and demanded that we all "quieten down" and return to bed. Claytie and Felipa remained on the roof, bugging their eyes at the horizon, searching for more mysterious light. Mrs. Ledbetter allowed as how, since we were all up anyway, we'd best start the day's chores. Mariquilla prepared the breakfast *tortillas* alone. Dolores was nowhere in sight.

We were just starting to eat when Felipa let out an adolescent girl's version of a war whoop. The sentry who was supposed to be on the roof polished off his *tortilla* and climbed the ladder to reassert his authority. He regretted it at once. "*Ay yi*, Señora Ledbetter," he cried.

"It's Five Horses Running, Missis Hulda," Felipa said, "with Dry Cloud and Wounded Hawk and a war band. Apache and Comanche *together*?"

"Looks like they're draggin' somethin' behind them," Claytie added.

"Lord in heaven," Hulda gasped, and ran for the ladder. It took no mind reader to know she feared the worst for her husband and the rest of Drake's party.

I followed her in spite of myself. Though I'm not normally a coward, I didn't relish a meeting with authentic savages nearly as much as I had before being abducted by them. I hunkered behind one of the adobe crenellations trimming the outer wall. The guard and Mrs. Ledbetter crouched behind two of the others. The Indians reined in to form three long rows covering the front of the building all along the riverbank.

Felipa squatted beside me.

Mrs. Ledbetter told her to ask Five Horses Running what he wanted.

Felipa added a few amenities, from the sound of it. Five Horses Running looked not a whit more amenable. He shouted back something guttural and angry, then raised his lance.

Felipa turned back to Mrs. Ledbetter. "He says he wants to see Buzzard-Who-Lives-Within-Walls. The Comanche and the Apache have joined together this one time to do business with him."

Five Horses shouted something else and his back ranks split in half, the riders galloping around their comrades, dragging dusty cargoes at the end of ropes behind them. When within plain view of the roof, the riders dismounted in a unanimous flurry. Blades flashed and the warriors sprang once more onto their mounts and galloped back where they had come from. Carcasses such as that I had seen the night of my abduction now lined the riverbank. Except that these carcasses were of sheep and horses. Cooked sheep and horses. Spotted horses, white horses, blacks, grays, chestnuts, roans. Some heads were intact, some tails, but all were missing parts.

Hulda let out a low whistle of dismay. "Tell 'em Mr. Drake may be a spell," she said. "Tell 'em I'll be glad to give him the message but they should just go make camp somewhere and he'll come talk to 'em about all this."

Felipa duly began to translate, but Five Horses Running barked back an immediate response. "He says that's okay, missis, they'll wait."

6

The fact that E.F. was not at the end of one of the Indians' ropes had a calming effect on Mrs. Ledbetter, but her mood was far grimmer than previously. She watched the Indians with a baleful eye and clenched her jaw as they began splitting off to ride around the fort peering into windows along the outside walls. "That fool Drake," she hissed as a screech issued from the vicinity of the bakery. "He should have known better than to build a fort with windows on the outside. But no, this was a tradin' post. Wouldn't need windowless walls to conduct business. Derned idiot."

We stayed where we were, fighting down the urge to track the progress of the braves encircling us by something other than the thud of horses' hooves. If we showed ourselves, they might guess how few men guarded the fort. For medicinal reasons, we preferred to keep that information to ourselves.

The general cacophony created by our uninvited guests prevented us from hearing the approach of the riders at our back gate until a familiarly imperious voice called, "Open up, Manuel. Can't you see us comin'?"

Felipa and I scurried to the ladder just in time to see the gates swing open, Drake and his horsemen sprint inside, and the gates slam shut again before the Indians caught wind of what was happening.

Mrs. Jenkins flew into the corral, tastefully attired in her orchid wrapper, her strawberry hair floating behind her, and threw herself upon her brother. "Oh, Bubba. You're here! We're all gonna be murdered in our beds."

"Ever'body but you's been up for hours and you know it," Mrs. Ledbetter said sourly. Then she, Manuel, and Felipa all tried at once to explain to Drake what had transpired, while outside the Indians whooped and shouted.

Drake, Felipa, and two armed guards climbed to the roof again for Drake's conference with Five Horses and his allies. With all of the Indians watching the roof, I felt it safe to watch from the window in Drake's office. Claytie squirmed in beside me. It wasn't especially interesting hearing a conversation in a language I couldn't understand, but I did note the two strange-looking green plumes curling high above the eagle feathers fringing Five Horses' lance.

Drake did not need Felipa's help except in the initial explanation, for he spoke both Indian languages fluently, so she soon climbed down and joined us at our window. She looked up at me rather coyly as the Indian pointed at the fort and at the sky and at the horses. Drake argued in return.

I thought I was starting to make something out when Mrs. Jenkins swept through the doorway to the office, hands on hips, crying, "Girls, come along. Miss Lovelace, honey, if you had a lick of sense you would have learned your lesson about those redskins by now. It is simply not fittin' for decent females to stand there in plain sight of those savages. It inflames their baser instincts and makes them more difficult for Bubba to deal with."

She shepherded the girls away, but the Indians were leaving too, though they did not appear satisfied. Drake climbed down the ladder as I entered the courtyard.

"You saw all of that?" he asked me.

"I did," I said. "They seem to be in a dangerous frame of mind. Will they attack us?"

His laugh was reassuringly unpleasant. "Not likely. They thought they could cheat me out of a few head of stock. Claim you sicced your fire-breathin' lizard on 'em, and since you're my property, they figure I oughta pay them damages. Five Horses must be gettin' soft in the head to think I'd fall for somethin' as *loco* as that. Did you see those green plumes he carried on his lance?"

"Yes, I wondered—"

"Well, take a gander at these." He pulled two more from inside his jacket and shoved them at me. What I had taken to be feathers were actually resilient pieces of some spined, leathery substance, with an armor of hard scales covering all surfaces and needle-sharp points to its spines.

"Ramón found that up above where we found what was left of about half my herd." His voice wavered and he blinked before he continued, his tone brittle and bitter, "Whoever it was killed my animals is either just tryin' to ruin me or sure likes their meat well-cured. Musta taken blow torches to the cows, the ground, everythin'. There's scorch marks all over."

"Well, there you have it. The old man saw the same thing I did, and you have the evidence to prove it."

"What I have is some barbecued beef and a couple of overgrown turkey feathers, plus a wild story or two. What I need is to make sense of it. Claytie Jane tells me you been readin' those old mission manuscripts of mine. You reckon anybody else could have read 'em too? Somebody smart enough to set this up and dumb enough to mistake my interest in a good yarn for superstition? Maybe some old Mexican livin' with the Indians told 'em about that old dragon story and put 'em up to it. Maybe it's a band of extra-smart renegades. What do you think?"

"I think there certainly must be a reason for the dragon to appear now, and that if it isn't the feathered serpent of the manuscripts, it's a close relation. But the only thing I can tell you about a person or persons behind it is that whoever it is, it is not I. I have no motive for trying to ruin you. I would lose a good story and gain nothing. But surely there are others—how good a friend of yours is Mr. Kruger, anyway?"

We adjourned to the library to discuss it while Drake ate his breakfast. By discuss I mean that I listened to him expound on various theories explaining how Kruger could have engineered the lights, the burnings, the eerie sounds, in order to gain control of Fort Draco. "I reckon he could be doin' it. Be the likeliest person. Not a bad idea, neither. Set yourself up as some make-believe critter and kill off enough animals at one place or another to make people scared enough to do whatever you wanted, if you put it to 'em right. Wish I'd thought of it, to work on somebody I wanted to get rid of. But John's not especially interested in gettin' rid of me that I know of—we always have worked pretty well together. And as far as studyin' Latin manuscripts, well, all I can say is, even if John were a studious man, he's a lot more interested in Mexican scalps than Mexican stories. But then, that notion's no harder to swallow than yours, I reckon. So who knows but what you might be right? Maybe there's some redskin out in the brush cuttin' up virgins, tellin' some big horny toad he can have his fill of Drake's cattle."

I squirmed uncomfortably, remembering the pencil underlinings in the manuscripts indicating an unwholesome interest in the parts about cutting up virgins. Had I but known how close he was to the truth at that moment, I would have been even more uncomfortable. It was my turn to play the skeptic. "You said yourself, sir, that what I saw the night of my capture was a product of my imagination."

"All I can say then is your imagination packs quite a wallop."

"So does Mr. Kruger, sir. And one wouldn't have to know Latin to make sense of the pictures. Some of the illustrations bear close resemblance to people and things I've seen since I've been here."

"Now, that's a thought. I bet that picture of the jaguar lady reminded you of our little Dolores, too, didn't it?"

I nodded, disturbed by his sudden relish of our topic and far less relieved than I expected to be by his sudden willingness to entertain the possibility of a dragon on the premises. He finished his bacon, wiped his hands on a napkin, and leaned back with a new cigar and a cup of coffee. "She put me in mind of that picture the minute I laid eyes on her. Thought I'd rescued me a genuine Mayan princess. I'm a touch of a romantic, if you want to know the truth, Miss Valentine. But I've wished ever' once in a while since I made that deal that I'd kept the rifle I bought her for. Just when I'm thinkin' she's real sweet, she starts naggin' me about buyin' her brats back. Shoot! The Indians never let on if she was part of a package deal. All the kids there at the time looked Comanche to me. And Dolores, she was lucky I was even interested in her. She was pretty beat-up then, half-dead. Had been drug some through the cactus. Nearly spoiled her looks. She kept clawin' her free hand in the general direction of that pen full of Indian kids but I never did know what she was fussin' about until . . . You want another cup of coffee?"

"Thank you," I said.

". . . until finally she settled down and got well enough and calm enough to talk sensible. She was just makin' sounds before that. Not even Spanish. Mariquilla'll tell you even she had trouble understandin' the girl."

If he thought that lame excuse was ample justification to me, he was mistaken. I could see it clearly, the mother hysterical with grief, clutching for her sobbing babes. He would have had to be blind not to see what she was getting at, and heartless not to help her. Nevertheless, I held my tongue. But not, unfortunately, my expression.

"Coffee that bitter, Miss Lovelace? No, no, I know what's eatin' you. You're like all the ladies when it comes to kids. You think I should search high and low to find those poor little children and bring 'em back to their mama. Well, I'll tell you. If they were your children, I might. Or Hulda Ledbetter's, or my sister's. They'd have different colorin', you see, and I could tell they didn't belong with the Indians right off. But short of puttin' Dolores on a horse and takin' her with me, I'd never have any chance of identifyin' those kids now. The Comanch would give me any pair of kids the same age and sex and claim it was them. If they gave me any kids. Which would be real unlikely. They keep the younguns to raise up to be Indians, which is why they steal 'em instead of kill 'em most times. I doubt Dolores'd want 'em back by the time we found 'em."

"It *is* a little late now, isn't it?" I agreed. But I am not as good an actress as Sasha. His eyes struck sparks from the flint in my voice.

"Yes, and that's too bad. But I won't tolerate mutiny from anyone. I make the decisions here. This fort of mine can be a major landmark in the growth and development of Texas, ma'am. That's what I want you to tell people. Not kitchen maid's gossip."

"Nor would readers be interested in such gossip, Mr. Drake," I replied evenly. "In establishing your character, however, it is necessary that I understand your viewpoint on these matters."

He blew a smoke ring at the ceiling and said quietly, "And I want you to know I understand *your* viewpoint, Miss Valentine. Yours are natural and womanly sentiments and I revere and respect you for them. But you see, this ain't women's country. It's too hard, too desolate, and too isolated. The Mexican women here know that, and however much they may gripe about their little problems, they understand there's not a whole lot can be done about 'em, and if there was, there'd probably be more important things to tend to anyway. Dolores really doesn't want me to give in to her. It would worry her, because if I did what she wanted, I wouldn't be boss, and if there was no boss, all these folks would be out of work and out of a home.

72

"Dolores was lucky I could save her, and deep down, she knows it. She's just a little shy about showin' her gratitude if she thinks she can twist me around her finger by poutin'. Don't you trouble your head about her anymore now, you hear? Just get to writin' that book for me, and in your spare time, try to talk to that monster thing of yours, huh? And, seriously, try to think about how Indians or outlaws could butcher my cattle and make it look like somethin' out of a Mexican fairy tale did it."

" 'Scuse me, Mr. Drake," Hulda Ledbetter said from the doorway, "but speakin' of outlaws and butchers in general, Mr. Kruger in particular is waitin' in your office to speak to you." Drake glared hard at her as he marched by her. She reciprocated with an expression of pure and untroubled innocence.

"Have a nice chat, honey?" she asked me when he had gone. The question was ingenuous but her calculating glance was not.

I growled low in my throat, and pretended to be clearing it.

She grinned. "The *patrón* has that effect on a lot of people. See you're gettin' to know each other."

"He's insufferable! How can you continue to work for such a person?"

"You see any other places to work around here?" she asked. "Besides, once you been here awhile, you can't afford to leave. You buy everything you use from Drake, and we're four of E.F.'s paychecks and two of mine behind now. I raised my younguns years ago, honey. Drake's got to raise himself. Once in a while, when captives are bein' traded and His Highness doesn't want to go make the deal personally or isn't interested in buyin', E.F. has a chance to do a little barterin' on the side and get a baby bought back or some poor woman. He has better luck when they've sold Drake somethin' else already. Once an Indian has a little of Drake's trade hooch for some of his goods, he'll sell his own grandma for a tad more."

I returned to my room and removed the papers from

under my mattress. I sat under the *ramada* and read all morning. During siesta I wrote, not the sanitized version of events Drake had ordered me to write, but my own account, for the *Crier*, for my novel, for posterity, but not for Drake.

About two hours before dinner, the drums began.

7

Boom boom boom boom *boom* boom boom boom. A good ten or twenty tom-toms pounded in unison, and I would have pledged my byline that if I stepped outside the front gate I could count them in person and watch a war dance. I bolted for the patio to investigate.

The unmelodious sound of Kruger's voice, rasping over the drums, stopped me before I pulled my door open. "Aw, hell, Drake. I told you there'd be trouble. Give 'em the woman. You can send to San Antonio and get somebody better than a dried-up Yankee spinster to do what you want."

"They wouldn't have her, Kruger. She's bad medicine. Think she's got some connection with this bogeyman everybody is so damn ready to blame all my troubles on. You sure you don't know anything about this, *amigo*? Sort of in your line—"

"I don't care much about *cattle*, Drake," the scalp-hunter replied, offended.

"Well, I'm here to tell you somethin' sure as hell does. What do you reckon the savages are up to now?"

"I don't know. But if I was you I'd send that woman out of here fast. You're gonna lose business keepin' her here."

"I respect your kindly advice, John, but did it ever occur to you that if they think she runs this thing it *could* give us a certain advantage? If we could just find out who *is* behind it and *how*, we could rebuild my herd and get you all the scalps you want pronto by goin' into the dragon business ourselves. The Indians'd do damn near anythin' we said and the army boys would find it mighty expedient to cooperate with us. No, I'm inclined to keep Miss Valentine around just in case she comes in handy. Five Horses doesn't need her scalp any more than you do."

I thought Drake was dreaming, conjuring illusions that would snatch his fortune away from certain disaster, but if the reasons he gave were sufficient to keep Kruger away, I was not about to fault the purity of his motives for championing me. I stayed inside until the men's voices receded toward the back of the compound.

Two of the *vaqueros* did not return from their chores for the evening meal that day. Drake posted extra guards after dinner. We retired to the thump of the drums. Far out in the desert, fires burned brightly, overshadowing the pearly glow of the rising moon.

I was still awake with a throbbing headache when I heard the scream and the crash and felt the very floor tremble beneath me. Another earthquake, I thought. The horses whinnied shrilly and a rifle shot cracked like a tree struck by lightning.

I forsook both caution and all thoughts of modesty or consideration for my wounds. By running to the far side of the patio, nearest Drake's office, I could discern in the moonlight the top half of sentries' bobbing heads and here and there the glint of metal on the far side of the flat storeroom roof. Screams still resounded, and soon curses joined them.

Finally Drake's voice rang through the night. "Saddle up," he commanded.

In the corral, almost before I could get there, horses were saddled and every available man mounted.

Mrs. Ledbetter, Mariquilla, and the maids scurried

about to provide food and drink for the men to take with them.

"You're leaving us?" I asked, not, of course, out of trepidation, but incredulity, since it seemed to me that in the face of Indian attack the proper course of action was for the men to remain to guard the fort.

E.F. Ledbetter misunderstood my concern. "Got to, ma'am. They broke in the storeroom and run off with the extra rifles, busted up whole bottles of Drake's prize booze, and run off the outside stock."

A warm wind whipped my nightgown tail around my legs as I watched them leave. In the void of silence left in the wake of so much frantic activity, a hoarse old voice sobbed its fright and recited prayers.

"My stars!" Mrs. Ledbetter said. "It's pore old Benito! The pokey's right next to the storeroom. When he heard them Indians, he musta been the one screamed and give the alarm."

El Mellado, when released from captivity for a hero's predawn welcome, was vastly relieved to learn that we had been visited by mere Indians. He thought his flying friend had attacked us.

No cooking or cleaning got done that day. Mrs. Ledbetter armed the maids and me, at my request, and we kept watch from the rooftop. Up until then my stay had been uneventful and comfortable. Now, as the sun blazed down upon me, I began to wonder why adventures seemed necessarily to entail *dis*comfort. We spent a long day with no water, hastily cooked food, and direct exposure to the insufferable heat and dust. We also had to forgo siestas for fear that the Indians might have led the men off in one direction while circling around to attack our undefended haven from another.

At sunset I learned the meaning of the saying that one's heart catches in one's throat, when Felipa's coppery arm shot forth, pointing at dust in the distance, which gradually became riders. With considerable relief we made out the sombreros of the returning searchers.

"Gone," Drake said. "Pulled up stakes and lit out, with *my* guns and livestock. This time it's not just war parties gone across the river. It's women and children, the whole kit and caboodle, picked up and headed for New Mexico, from the look of it."

The men stayed only long enough to thoroughly provision themselves before riding out again. This time Drake left no men to protect those who remained at the fort, including his own daughter. Unless one counted old Benito, who slept off his fright while the other men came and went.

"I s'pect Drake figgers that with the Indians all gone, we don't have anything to be protected from. Since he took Kruger, he's probably right," Mrs. Ledbetter replied reasonably when I expressed my indignation to her. "It's just as well he took as many as he did. With them gone, maybe the little water I stowed in kettles and washpans'll last until we can fetch more. I just wish he'd asked me before he took all the horses and the wagon. The Indians took the rest of the stock. Come on along, honey, and make yourself useful. We need to find out if there's any drinkables left in the storeroom."

Mrs. Jenkins beat us to it and stood clucking over the obstacle course of broken glass and rubbish. Bolts of cloth were tangled among the wreckage of barrels and soaked up creeks of fine wine. Small hills of flour and sugar drew flies and ants. Mrs. Jenkins and the very pregnant laundress Manuela tripped through the ruins, Mrs. Jenkins cradling a ledger book on her arm. Now and then Drake's sister would point and Manuela would wrestle herself down far enough to pick up whatever it was that was being pointed at, and Mrs. Jenkins would check something off in her book.

"This is my brother's business, Mrs. Ledbetter, not a household matter. I will attend to it," the self-styled lady of the house declared.

"I shoulda known if it involved money she'd be right there in the middle of things," Mrs. Ledbetter whispered to me. To the widow she said, "That's real fine, Lovanche. I was just lookin' to see if there was anything left for drinkin'. Water's all gone."

"Then by all means, fetch some," Mrs. Jenkins said graciously.

"I intend to, but it's goin' to be about eight hours' worth of fetch, the way I reckon it. We'll need somethin' for the girls to drink along the way."

"Can't they cut cacti or something? I don't know how I'm supposed to keep track of my brother's belongin's if you intend to haul things away for the use of the servants."

Mrs. Ledbetter had already spotted some untouched jugs buried under a tent of gaudily striped and wine-soaked yard goods.

"I didn't say you could take those, madam. They must be accounted for."

"Then account for 'em and shut up," Mrs. Ledbetter replied, hoisting a jug in her hand as she used the back of the same arm to wipe sweat and flies from her face. "Maids can't any more go without somethin' to drink in the desert than society ladies."

8

We began walking as soon as we had gathered the necessary supplies and personnel—namely those who were the strongest, most able-bodied, and who wanted the most to avoid staying at the fort with Mrs. Jenkins in charge. With us came Dolores, Felipa, Merenciana the baker, Paquita, two other maids, and El Mellado. Mariquilla and Claytie were forced to remain behind, at Mrs. Jenkins' insistence, with the remaining staff members, Manuela and a seamstress named Innocencia. Like Manuela, Innocencia was too large with child to be of much use. The fort's extra children all remained behind as well, under Claytie's grudging administration. Getting the children to stay at the fort, their mothers to consent to leave them, and Claytie to watch them were all herculean feats that attested to the respect and esteem in which all concerned held Mrs. Ledbetter and to the statesmanlike manner with which she wielded her authority. "It is *so* fair, Claytie Jane," she'd insisted with a snap in her voice that silenced Claytie's whining. "Felipa is comin' along to watch the goats. You stay behind to watch the younguns. I don't know what could be more evenhanded than that."

Though still somewhat disabled, I managed with the help of my papa's pilfered britches to join the water-bearing expedition. Mrs. Ledbetter tied on her sunbonnet and the others their sombreros. I borrowed an ill-fitting straw sombrero from Mariquilla, though Mrs. Jenkins assured me it was infested. My sunbonnet looked entirely too ridiculous with the britches, even if there were no gentlemen present to observe the effect.

The morning was fine, the air clear, the jackrabbits hopping, and the hawks soaring above the prickly desert face. The goats were not amenable to work on such a pleasant day and paused frequently to graze and relieve themselves. The cart, burdened with three barrels, often mired in the drifts of sand and dust. Felipa could not loose the cart alone, so the rest of us needed to set aside our own burdens and assist her. This was inconvenient, since we were each paired off with another and dragged behind us a makeshift travois, a device borrowed from the Indians. On each travois lolled a barrel. El Mellado and Mrs. Ledbetter made up one team, Paquita and Dolores another. I assisted Josefita, while the remaining pair, Merenciana, and Natividad, hauled the last of our burdens.

We would have made poor time had we all proceeded thus the entire way to the spring, but with the threat of the Indians considerably diminished by the abrupt departure of Mr. Drake's former customers, we decided to risk splitting up, each pair retaining a weapon for defense. Mrs. Ledbetter carried E.F.'s deer rifle, Dolores a dagger, and Natividad the machete with which she had in her youth attacked jungles. El Mellado also carried a machete. Not to be left out, I armed myself with one of the cavalry sabers I had earlier spotted crossed with its mate on the library wall. I can understand why it was a cavalry saber. Certainly the infantry never could have walked very far with the wretched things banging against their legs all the time, the handles jabbing them in the ribs.

When we had walked approximately two miles, which took us a full two hours, encumbered as we were, Merenciana and Natividad stopped and set down their barrel. They would have the longest vigil of any, but would have occasion to return to the fort briefly while the rest of us spent the day in the desert. They found themselves a sheltering clump of mesquite and settled down to await the first relay. Before we reached the next two-mile landmark, El Mellado began puffing and panting, his age apparently telling against him. *"Pobrecito!"* cried Josefita, the mother of four and wife, presently, of none, with whom I was in harness. "He is so tired. He must remain here in my place—"

"Then I would appreciate it if you would stay here in mine," I told her. "I would be of little reassurance to him since my Spanish is so poor. And I am closer to Mrs. Ledbetter's size than you are. The load would be better balanced between the two of us." I didn't need the rest of the argument, actually, since Josefita said, *"sí, señorita,"* after my initial offer, which was the end of it as far as she was concerned. I had presented my case mainly for Mrs. Ledbetter's sake, so that she would not take offense at my usurping her authority by changing the order in which we proceeded. I had no wish to miss seeing the water hole.

We made the six-mile stop in about the same time as the others, for though there were fewer of us, we were wearying and the land took an upward turn. On every side of us now ridges hemmed us in, their slopes full of randomly scattered boulders and curious long scorch marks on earth denuded of vegetation.

"Hmph," Mrs. Ledbetter said. "Looks like this might have been where some of the spotty little fires that we've been seein' were. There was a cottonwood over yonder last time I was up here."

Nothing stood in the place she indicated now, and we kept walking until we located a shallow cave where Paquita and Dolores could wait and rest at the base of a hill. Caves penetrated certain of these hills all along the way. A very good thing if one were fortunate enough to require shelter from the rain. Not so fortunate if the caves already sheltered something else.

The three of us, the goats, and the barrels clattered up the protected valley lying loosely between the disorderly ranks of hills. The path took a sharp turn and we found ourselves facing a small rectangular adobe structure, somewhat less commodious than the average hotel room in San Francisco.

"A sheepherder's jacal," Mrs. Ledbetter said in answer to my curious expression. "No one lives there now. When Mr. Drake took over this country, he forced all the sheepherders who didn't work for him to the other side of the Rio."

The rocks above us were layered like plates stacked high after a parish banquet. We labored up a rocky incline, turned another corner, and encountered an entirely different sort of terrain.

A narrow canyon, its walls also layered in places, rose perhaps eighty feet above us. From shoulder height, however, the rock was smooth wall-to-wall, as if poured in liquid form and molded. The goat cart rumbled like thunder as it passed over the first section of the canyon, but soon the floor flowed so erratically that though the sure-footed beasts could have negotiated the terrain without difficulty, their cargo could not. At that point Felipa tethered the goats to a defiant bush thrusting its way from a narrow ledge created by the meeting of the layered and flowing rock formations. Mrs. Ledbetter picked up a barrel and Felipa and I hefted another, sharing the relatively light weight but considerable awkwardness between us.

I staggered along, not because the barrel unduly taxed me, but because I could not hold it in place and twist my head to see all that I wished to see. The smooth floor was a creamy beige, but its bumpy prominences were ringed twice and sometimes thrice with beautiful red-clay markings. Along one side, the wall cut away to a small green place with cacti and even little yellow flowers, a veritable garden in the desert. A few yards farther and we stopped at the gem worthy of the splendid setting. Sheltered by a curve of smooth rock arching above it and sweeping down

83

to hold it in an oblong cup was a pool of brilliant emerald-green water, so clean and clear that one could see plainly the details of the rock underlying it.

"Here we are, girls. Set yourselves down and rest a spell. You'll need it. Felipa, you didn't let them goats eat up lunch, did you?"

"No'm," Felipa said, her mouth already stuffed with *tortilla*. Belatedly she distributed cloth-wrapped packages to Mrs. Ledbetter and me and we sat there by the pool in the shade of the twin cliffs, eating slowly and drinking in the exhilaratingly moist air which smelled, almost, of greenery.

"Ah," I said, surreptitiously hiding my share of the *jalapeño* peppers, which were much too hot for me, under the lip of a rocky outgrowth. For some reason, admitting that a food is too hot is admitting to unforgivable weakness. "What a lovely spot. Smell the fragrance of that air!"

Mrs. Ledbetter sniffed critically. "Smells like snakes to me, honey. Best watch your step."

She chewed slowly, savoringly. I wished to savor our surroundings instead, so I replaced one of my *tortillas* in its wrapper and finished my meal with a double handful of the cool water from the pool. Felipa finished before me and scrambled back up the valley. She strode across the rocks as nimbly as the goats, and with her badly cut bristling black bangs and thin, sinewy form, resembled her charges in other ways. Her animation was a welcome change, for during the morning she had been grave and quiet as she seldom was with Claytie to inspire her. I trudged after her, gawking at whatever presented itself to gawk at, until she beckoned to me and pointed proudly down to some cylindrical depressions in the rock in front of her. "My ancestors made those, when they lived here."

"Other Comanche?" I asked, regarding the built-in metates doubtfully.

"No, older than that. Before the People. But they were like us. They also made those pictures." She pointed to an overhang on the side of the canyon farthest from us.

The whole underside was covered with orangish drawings of horses and stick-figure men.

"You seem to know a lot about your people," I said.

"You mean for an Indian raised among whites?" She smiled with one side of her mouth, a smile too old for her age. "Yeah, I guess. I could have gone back with the People, you know. Five Horses is from another branch of the tribe but he is my mother's sister's son. He would have taken me long ago, if I wanted him to."

She was squatting beside the metate holes, her finger tracing the smooth and ancient edge, the red line that encircled it.

"You didn't want to?" I asked.

"No. I want my revenge."

"What? You mean for killing your parents? I—"

"See, when Drake's not there, I do all the translation. My people tell me things and ask me things, and me, I tell them things too. When I spoke to Five Horses this time he said I should come with him, that this land has been cursed, that the men who brought the curse upon us by taking you have been cast out. But he invited me. I said no. Drake killed my parents, who would feed me, clothe me, teach me. Now *he* feeds me, clothes me, and teaches me or sees that I get taught. First his wife did it, and made him do it. Now he does it out of habit. And because of Claytie. With what I'm learning, I've got a better chance of fighting him and hurting him than Five Horses does. As long as I keep out of his way and don't let myself be caught alone with him, I'm all right."

I wasn't shocked exactly. I knew what she meant. Those years of hauling my father out of places filled with inebriated frontiersmen had left their imprint on my innocence. While I struggled to think what to say, she grinned at me again.

"Hey, *señorita*, don't worry. With Five Horses' band I'd be married by now. Maybe I will be soon anyway. I just don't want to leave Claytie when there's such big trouble. And also, I think Five Horses is right. I think this land is cursed. I think I don't want to miss seein' the *patrón* get what's comin' to him. Come on, I'll bet you I can climb that ledge before you can."

She could and did. I added several scrapes and bruises to my already vast collection of injuries scaling the cliff face by means of a path more suitable for goats than people. Felipa added to my discomfort by kicking rocks back at me. We finally both found uncomfortably lumpy stone seats on a precarious eyrie from which rocks deserted at regular intervals to tumble into the pool below. As the rocks splashed, Felipa laughed, enjoying the activity as much as any child. She groped for other rocks to throw in after the ones that dived voluntarily.

"Hey, what's this?" she asked, holding the dark green object aloft for inspection. "It looks like one of the feathers Five Horses had on his lance."

It did indeed. *And* like the feathers Drake had found near his slaughtered animals.

"Let's take it down and show Mrs. Ledbetter, shall we?" I said a little briskly. I was suddenly very anxious to finish this task and be out in the open again. Felipa tucked the plume behind her ear. It hung crazily over her shoulder, tickling her spine, making her twitch as she climbed down after me.

Mrs. Ledbetter dismissed the feather. "Might be some new kinda cactus, I reckon, but pshaw, honey, even if that critter Benito made up did drop it, he probably dropped it as he was passin' through. Drake and the boys found all them cows miles from here. If I was that crazy about eatin' cows, I'd stay where I stowed 'em, wouldn't you?"

I wasn't sure, never previously having enjoyed the opportunity of eating my way through one beefsteak, much less half a herd of cattle, aside from my recent dreams. I contemplated Hulda's commonsense reply while I dipped water into the first barrel with the speed and accuracy of a tipsy bucket-brigader saving his favorite saloon.

Mrs. Ledbetter deserted her own bailing operations to assist me, and together we hauled the full barrel to the goat cart. I immediately tripped over my cavalry sword and had to unbuckle it before we tackled the chore again. The barrel was far too heavy to carry, and the ground was highly uncooperative in its formation. We rolled the cask on its bottom, first one side and then the other, scooting it gradually. We were both wet by the time we hefted the full barrel onto the cart. Felipa finished filling the barrel Mrs. Ledbetter had started, and as we hauled that one, began filling the third. By this process we soon had three barrels filled and the goat cart loaded and ready to be pulled back down to where Paquita and Dolores waited with another barrel and travois.

Since Felipa got along with the goats better than anyone else and since Mrs. Ledbetter possessed the most effective weapon among us and the knowledge to utilize it effectively, the two of them set off to deliver the goat cart to its first station and pick up the next empty barrel. Meanwhile, I stayed in the canyon and filled the fourth cask, the one Mrs. Ledbetter and I had pulled behind us. It was not supposed to hold as much as the others, since it would be pulled by travois rather than being loaded on the cart when it returned from its round trip to the fort and back, escorted every two miles by the team left at that station.

The plan was rather complex and dangerous, and it offered no protection to each isolated pair. But then, seven women, a young girl, and an old man did not exactly constitute a formidable deterrent force.

As soon as the goat reached the first checkpoint and the barrel held at that point was delivered to Mrs. Ledbetter, Dolores and Paquita would lead the goat cart back to El Mellado and his volunteer nurse, pick up their cask, and return to the station. El Mellado and company would lead the goat back another two miles and pick up an empty cask to replace the one they had given Dolores and María, and so on, with the goat eventually ending up at the fort to be unloaded and led back team by team to the three of us in the canyon.

We who had done the heavy hauling would then lead the goat cart while Paquita and Dolores bore the travois to the second team, who relieved them until they in turn were relieved. In this fashion we would rejoin each other, gathering numbers and strength as we returned to the fort.

The only problem with this plan was that it left me alone in the canyon for a good three or four hours while I waited for Felipa and Mrs. Ledbetter to return. It took me only a quarter of one of those hours to fill the barrel to the required depth. Actually, I might as easily have accompanied Mrs. Ledbetter and Felipa, since a water-barrel guard was a ludicrous idea. The cavalry sword was reassuring to clutch while I sat watching the shadows lengthen, but it was too dull to cut anything. I would have surrendered the water quickly to any needy puma or coyote, not to mention (I hardly dared think it for fear of putting myself in an unhealthily nervous state) something larger. However, everyone seemed to take it for granted that I would wish to remain behind and rest and think my deep literary thoughts, and I was indeed too tired from my sleepless night to want to protest.

I made a cursory reconnaissance of the area and found myself a place to nap on a rocky shelf overhung by the cliff. My cavalry sword was useful for ascertaining that the ledge was currently snakeless. Reasonably cool and sheltered from the eyes of the swarming crowds who probably would be arriving any minute (not to mention the thunderstorms) it constituted my idea of a place to rest my eyes for a few minutes before taking up my notebook again. I admit I did not make a thorough inspection of the area. Uncharacteristically for a journalist of my stature, I had decided I was not going to look for trouble. I tried to pull my sombrero over my eyes Mexican style, but the overhang would not accommodate my face and my hat both, so I left the sombrero by the pool with the remains of my lunch and my cavalry sword.

The Drastic Dragon of Draco, Texas

The still moist air, the heavy heat of the afternoon beating up in waves from the sunlit rock while leaving the shadows deliciously cool, all served to lull me to slumber, despite my certainty that I would awaken to find myself draped with coiling rattlers.

I dreamed of them, and the dry rustling of their scales upon stone. I dreamed of their spadelike faces staring malevolently at me, their eyes unblinking and cold, their bodies writhing. But when the real sound of scales upon stone occurred, it was preceded by a small avalanche, so I had plenty of warning and was wide awake when the putrid poison-green mist rolled out from behind the pool, concealing in its cloud the belly and feet of the great serpent slithering around the overhang. The monster was as large as the sheepherder's jacal. It dipped a forked tongue the size of a pitchfork into the pool for a long drink, then let its glowing green eyes sweep the area. I cringed back into my hiding place, away from those eyes, but they did not look at me. Instead, the beast spotted my *jalapeños*, flicked them into its mouth with one deft snap of its tongue, and incinerated my sombrero and Drake's cavalry sword on the next exhalation.

9

The odor emanating from the beast was definitely not that of sanctity, but it was overpowering. Rolling from the cavernous nostrils and seeping around every scale, it saturated the valley with its carrion stench and me with a realization of my horrible puniness. The pure physical aspect of the monster was only a part of it. Artistic interpretation flattered it. Essentially it appeared to be a gila monster of somewhat larger dimensions than an elephant. But gila monsters, especially ones of that size, don't fly. And they don't bear green fronds that flutter out from their necks when they ignite swords and sombreros. And they don't carry themselves with the majesty of immense dignity and age that was as much a part of the dragon as its stink and its scales.

I cowered back on my ledge, unable to breathe for the smell or to tear my eyes away for fascination. If a dozen rattlers had twined about my limbs like bracelets then, I would not have moved or uttered a sound. Had it been within my power to still the uncooperatively loud thump of my heart, I would have done so. I knew beyond a doubt that this creature was the "we" of my dreams. It was too large to be "I." While the knowledge gave me a certain feeling of affinity, I felt no temptation to presume upon it. Seeing the dragon was like seeing the Queen of England. I did not think either of them would care to chat with me, though of the two I'd have preferred the queen. Though my family had never cared for her politics, she was at least a human being with no known tendencies toward pyromania.

I did not, therefore, feel in the least slighted when the dragon ignored my ledge. Heedless of me as if I was some peasant at a parade, it dragged its spined tail across the stone, surveying its surroundings.

It bore a veritable mane of green serrated spines which raised and lowered like a porcupine's quills. Without warning, they bristled, and a blinding stream of green fire shot from the monster's maw, exploding our water barrel into a collection of steam, liquefied iron, coals, and cinders. Though there was a perfectly clean water supply right beside it, the dragon chose to lap up the still-sizzling water from among the ashes, just to prove it could do so.

My breath was coming in short little gasps now and my head prickled as my hair tried to separate from my scalp and crawl away to some safer place. Nevertheless, the beast's demonstration of its powers reminded me that I simply could not lie here dragon-watching all day but at the first opportunity, provided there was one, must run away and prevent the others from returning to the valley. At least we no longer had to worry about carrying the extra barrel back to the fort.

Surely the creature would leave sometime soon. I had not heard it arrive. Had it been here all along as we innocently fetched water? Where had it been hiding so safely from our view and vice versa? Or perhaps it had flown straight through the mountain. Had we not seen its light as it bored its way through two nights ago? While I was wondering these things, the creature spread its wings, membranous and leathery appendages like a bat's, folding closely to its body when it walked, but unfurling as wide as Drake's corral. The wings were camouflaged perfectly in color and texture, except that their downward edges were trimmed with curled spines like those in the mane. The dragon hopped as much as flew up to the ledge Felipa and I had previously investigated. The ledge was less than a foot above its head when it stretched its neck upward. It settled down for its nap with its face toward the wall, its muscular tail wrapped around its stubby feet and reptilian countenance, and gave all evidence of immediate slumber.

I lay cramped for what seemed ages, fearing to move before it was deeply asleep. I watched the heat waves shimmer off the armored hide and an occasional blast of eerie halitosis escape around the dragon's fangs to join the rancid mist. I grew somewhat calmer as I watched it. After all, though the creature had eaten a lot of cattle, it had inadvertently saved me from a wide choice of unmentionable fates at the hands of the Indian raiding party. Perhaps it really was a protective entity, as the ancient tribesmen claimed. I wriggled slowly forward on my ledge until my knees and shoulders were overhanging the smooth stone below. The beast snored and snapped its tail across its mane, swatting down a passing redtail hawk as if it were a fly. The hawk's squawk covered the noise of my descent. The bird plopped to the ground and the monster flexed in its sleep, resettled its snout, and I inched farther away from it, back down the mouth of the canyon. I wished I were wearing moccasins instead of my buttoned boots, which slipped on the smooth but uneven stone. My saddle sores were irritated again, too, and made it difficult to walk in a coordinated fashion. Nevertheless, the dragon provided sufficient motivation and I moved more silently than a cat, tiptoeing across the few loose boulders strewn near the metates and pictographs, walking ever sideways, with one eye on the rhythm of the green haze blowing to and fro like a curtain in the wind.

Once around the corner, I picked up my heels and made all possible haste down the trail. Each time I stumbled, my heart all but choked me. The beast had scared me when I faced it, but not so much as it did when I imagined it flying up behind me, its hot breath singeing my scalp, my face, and my shoulders, broiling me as I ran, just as it broiled the cattle, the mules, and the horses. I broke into a run at the bottom of the ascent and pelted down the trail, barely feeling the sores on my legs break open and the blood trickling warm and sticky, soaking my breeches. My mouth parched even as visions of the emerald pool interspersed themselves with those of Felipa and Mrs. Ledbetter walking into the canyon to face the fully alert monster squatting triumphantly over my messily mutilated form. My eyes fried in their sockets, and stars and whiteness replaced the trail in my sight. Several times I bumped or fell into cactus. After each time, I looked back to make sure I wasn't followed, but I could see nothing but dancing heat and a sky of burning blue throbbing down at me as if ready to burst open, spewing forth the dragon. I stumbled forward all the more quickly and clumsily, until at last I bumped into something soft and insufferably warm.

"Lord have mercy, honey, why didn't you say you wanted to walk along?" Mrs. Ledbetter asked, her voice roaring in my ears like a cool mountain cataract cascading into a deep and suspiciously familiar emerald pool.

"You must go back!" I cried—a very subdued cry. "The dragon is in the canyon."

"Dragon? Whereabouts is your hat, miss? I believe you've gone and got yourself sunstroked. Felipa, honey, give Miz Valentine your hanky to put over her head."

"No, truly," I protested. "There is a dragon in there." I proceeded with an eloquent plea which she insists to this day made no sense whatsoever.

"Any dragon, bear, puma, coyote, wolf, bobcat, owl, or jackrabbit who gets between me and the water supply had better be prepared for trouble," Mrs. Ledbetter said, shouldering her rifle. "Suppose you just show me where this critter is."

"Up the path, turn right into the canyon, and look up," I said sarcastically. "You can't miss it."

From behind us Dolores' voice rang out, terrifyingly

loud under the circumstances. "What is it, *señora*? What has befallen Señorita Valentina?"

"Never you mind, honey. Just some nonsense about a dragon or somethin'."

"*Madre mía!*" Dolores cried. She and Paquita and the goats stopped in the middle of the trail.

Felipa's eyes widened and she grinned as if she could not believe her good luck. Without a word to either of us, she ran back up the trail. Mrs. Ledbetter hooted at her, then trotted behind her at a distance-swallowing pace. I tagged painfully behind. The path had developed the annoying habit of undulating before my eyes.

When we turned into the canyon I all but crashed into Mrs. Ledbetter again, for she stood stock-still, staring up at the still-slumbering beast.

"My Lord in heaven, there it sits like a big old broody hen," she breathed.

"*Madre de Dios!*" Dolores said softly behind us.

Mrs. Ledbetter set her jaw and lifted her rifle. Dolores lunged and tried to wrestle the gun away from her. Mrs. Ledbetter snatched it back. About that time, Felipa emerged silently from behind the overhang. Her eyes were almost as large as the dragon's. The struggle over the firearm was forgotten as all three of us prayed silently while the fool girl picked her way toward us. The beast's tree-trunk-size tail switched an avalanche of loose dirt and small rocks down the incline. Felipa expertly dodged them.

Dolores was on her knees now, staring up at the beast. Mrs. Ledbetter hugged Felipa, then gave her a swat on the seat to send her back down the canyon. Then she raised her rifle again.

Dolores tore it from her grasp, this time carrying it back to the ground with her, where she hugged it to her while she crossed herself.

"Dolores, have you gone *loco*?" Mrs. Ledbetter hissed. "Give that back this minute. This is the thing that has been eatin' our stock."

Dolores' mouth moved silently for a moment; then

she sighed and seemed to collect herself. "Ah, *señora*, I know," she whispered. "I know. It is much more terrible than I planned. I thought the god would send only a drought, you know? Or a disease of the cattle. But he has come instead. The feathered serpent himself has come to punish Don Francisco. Your gun will be of no assistance."

Mrs. Ledbetter gazed at the monster for a moment, then down at Dolores, who also gazed both rapt and appalled at the thing she had summoned. With a grip that allowed no room for argument, the housekeeper reached down, took Dolores by the arm, pulled her to her feet, and walked her out of the canyon.

"Aren't you going to shoot him, *señora?*" asked Felipa, trying to dance around us to see back into the canyon.

"No, I am not," Mrs. Ledbetter replied. "It's no smarter to shoot a critter like that with a deer gun than it is to hit a lion with a broom and tell it to scat. Far sight dumber, in fact. As for you, young lady, what did you mean by slippin' off like that and sashayin' right past that thing? I thought he'd made a meal of you already."

"I didn't see him, *señora*. You said he was only the sunstroke of the *señorita*, so I went looking around to see if I could see what she saw. But I did not happen to look there. I looked behind the pool, though. *Señora*, you should see. There is now a big hole burned in the mountain in back of the pool. A very great cave, very deep. It was not there before."

"Felipa—" Mrs. Ledbetter said warningly.

"I swear it, *señora!* The stone was melted."

"Hmph. I must say then that I'm glad I didn't rile that thing by takin' a potshot at it. Question is, what will we do about it?"

"There is only one thing to do," Dolores said, her voice still hushed and her tilted dark eyes dazed, her face deceptively calm. "It was I who appealed to the god to help me. You must understand. I prayed to Our Lady, I prayed to her Holy Son. I lit candles. But the hearts of my enemies were not softened. They did not return my children. And the man who said he was my protector would not lift a finger or ask the simple question that would restore them. He is rich, powerful. He has not known sorrow like mine. So I think to myself that since pleas for mercy from my father's God avail me nothing, I will ask one of my mother's gods for aid. I remember a prayer she taught me in the old tongue, an herb to burn, and I think: 'Now the plumed serpent will send a drought, will kill the cattle, will blast the land, and Drake will be made poor. He will lose what he most loves, and will know what I suffer.' "

As she spoke, her voice rose a little and got much faster, her calm deteriorating, her breath catching.

Mrs. Ledbetter frowned at her. "Honey, I'm the first to admit that the boss is an out-and-out stinker and hasn't treated you very good, but that thing back there you say you called in is a *dragon*. A full-length, flyin', fire-breathin' *dragon*. Now, don't you think that's just a little bit drastic?"

Dolores gulped and nodded, her eyes swinging wildly from Mrs. Ledbetter to me as she struggled to free herself from the housekeeper's grip. "Yes. Yes, it is too drastic. Too much. Even for the sake of my children. I was wrong. I committed a sin against God, so that he has forsaken me, abandoned me to my sin, and allowed the plumed serpent to come again among us. I, in bringing him among us, have brought disaster upon us all. Nothing will appease the feathered serpent now but a sacrifice. I must go."

She rose, but Hulda Ledbetter jerked her back again. "Don't act any dumber than you have already, girl. You gettin' yourself killed isn't goin' to fill up the Rio or bring dead cows back to life."

"I must atone—"

"Hogwash. Only atonin' you've got to do is to me by stoppin' all this foolishness and helpin' haul this water back to the fort before it dries up. Like as not, soon as Mr. Drake and the boys get home they'll make feather dusters out of your feathered lizard in three shakes of a lamb's tail.

We could all get mighty thirsty before that happens, though, so come on, now, *ándale*."

I can only approximate some of these conversations now, though I have tried to hook them together more or less in the order they must have occurred. My memory is inaccurate at this point, because the other ladies were uncooperative. They kept popping in and out of time and space in an erratic fashion, their voices first murmuring, fading, then growing so loud I feared the dragon would hear.

My skin felt as if needles had been driven in it, and everywhere I burned, though my scalp, my legs, and my feet burned the worst. I accompanied my companions as far as the goat cart where Paquita waited sleeping in the shade of the barrels while the goats tried to eat the bush to which they were tethered. All of the details registered with diamond clarity—the shadow of Paquita's hat extending far beyond that of the barrels, the goats watching us, singling out Felipa in their stares, as we approached.

And then, as if by magic, I was lying on the trail with someone's sash wet and tied around my head like a fakir's turban. Soon I, instead of the fourth barrel, had been loaded onto one of the travois and was being dragged across the desert. All the while I felt weighted down with a sense of disappointment, frustration, and loneliness that I could not give vent to. Vaguely I was aware that it did not belong to me.

I recall rousing only twice before we reached the fort. Once was to try to ascertain the reason for Mrs. Ledbetter's angry berating of the next team down the line: "Josefita! Is that how you take care of him? Benito! Shame on you! A man of your age! Put your pants on and let's vamoose."

The other time was when my bearers hit a particularly nasty ditch and my litter was jostled so that my eyes flew open. Behind us I saw a cloud of dust and squeaked as loudly as possible, though I immediately broke into a cough. The dragging of my travois bestirred a mighty dust cloud of its own.

We could not outrun the newcomers even had we wanted to. The dust was raised by horses and they overtook us rapidly. Horses and a wagon, to be more accurate. And one other creature, as fantastic in its own way as the dragon was in his.

"Whoa!" A deep bass voice rang out so loudly I cringed for fear it would wake the dragon sleeping miles away. "What have we here?"

"Why, Chief Rain-in-the-Face, can't you see?" another voice cried in well-bred tones of shock and sympathy. "It is a party of ladies in distress. Dr. Alonso Purdy, purveyor of scientific miracles, and Chief Rain-in-the-Face of the Ojibanoxie tribe, owners of the secret of life-giving moisture, at your service, ladies. I need not tax you with further conversation to see how we may assist you. Chief, if you please, climb down off the wagon and help these ladies into the shade of our canopy. Gently with the injured one, poor dove. Now then, tell me, ladies, what catastrophe drives you into the desert?"

"*Madre de Dios!*" Josefita cried. "What is that he rides upon?"

The gentleman patted his extremely ugly, extremely tall hunchbacked, dust-colored mount on the neck. "This, madam, is Colonel Beauregard Sam Houston Burlingame, a ship of the desert. Or a camel, as they're less poetically called. The good chief and I found him wandering about bereft of gainful employment while we were traveling north of here a few months ago. Fortunately, I learned the art of camel navigation during my time in the French Foreign Legion. But that's another story."

I checked with others before writing down this speech, though I remembered the essence of it simply because it struck me as outrageously colorful, worthy of Buntline himself. I closed my eyes gratefully within the shade of the canopy, and though the tossing of the wagon did little to decrease the tossing of my innards, I made no notes, mental or otherwise, of the wagon, which should show the reader, by now used to my constant awareness of such matters, how far gone I was.

We were just within sight of the fort when a hideous scream pealed through the desert air, bounced off the mountains, and reverberated for several moments. I endured long minutes of agony while the horses bounded forward, whipped on by their driver.

My companions pounded on the gates for what seemed like centuries, until at last someone admitted us. I was alert enough by that time not to wish to be left alone in the corral while the others investigated, so I half-jumped, half-fell out of the wagon. I rushed across the courtyard several feet behind the last swish of skirt hem. Our flight ended in the main dining room, where Mariquilla, clutching her arm, her eyes flashing and bosom heaving, crouched by the fire on the hearth. By her side was a cast-iron skillet. I didn't notice the grease until Felipa, racing across the room, slipped in it and slid past me.

The heavy tramp of male feet preceded the sight of a large black man wearing a crown of eagle feathers pushing a half-clad Indian before him. Another man, slender and nearly as dark as a Mexican, covered the two of them with a rifle. The Indian did not seem to need much controlling, for his hands covered his face and he was moaning piteously. The large black Indian said something quite abusive to his prisoner as the lot of them presented themselves to Mrs. Ledbetter.

"The other aborigines remembered urgent prior engagements, madam," the slim dark fellow said, "but this gentleman would not hear of leaving without explaining himself. I fear, however, he was somewhat damaged upon arrival."

Mariquilla grinned ferociously. She rattled in Spanish until Mrs. Jenkins arrived on the scene and spoke sharply to her. "Mrs. Ramírez, how many times do I have to tell you that it is unrefined and very rude to talk that foreign flapdoodle in the presence of folks who understand plain English?"

Mariquilla nodded with mocking formality. "I beg your pardon, *señora*. I told my *compañeros* here that this Comanche bastard tried to grab me and I fried his filthy hide with hot grease." She fanned the air above the reddened and blistering flesh of her arm. "Alas, I have also fried myself a little."

With so much happening at once, none of us had any wish to be separated from the others, and once the Indian was bound, the gentlemen brought their assorted steeds onto the patio to be fed and groomed. As the only horses on the premises, not to mention the only camel, the animals were too valuable to be left in the open corral. Mariquilla and the maids departed briefly, the maids returning with the water barrels and buckets of extremely muddy water from the Rio for the horses and camel. They also carried some large droopy-looking leaves. When Mariquilla returned, her arm glistened with clear shining ointment. She was carrying three stoneware jars. Her good arm bore a load of goatskins and a potted plant.

"Oh, that'll look nice over here, Mrs. Ramírez," Mrs. Jenkins said. "But don't you think blankets would add a tad more color than goatskins?"

I don't think anyone even heard the remark but me. Mariquilla was busy pouring seeds from one jar and seeds from another into the metate by the fireplace and mashing them up. Meanwhile Dolores, at her behest, carefully broke open a long daggerlike frond from the aloe plant and rubbed the moist juicy end against the savage's wounded face.

Mariquilla spread her seed mash onto the leaves the girls brought from the river and placed them on my forehead and temples. Dolores continued rubbing aloe juice into the Indian's burns. He would not have allowed it, except that the black man spoke roughly to him and the slim one absentmindedly threatened him with his gun barrel in between pleasantries addressed to Dolores.

Mariquilla nodded like a symphony conductor to Josefita, Paquita, and Merenciana, and the three of them stood with their backs to me, spreading their skirts. With a goatskin over my lap, I removed my breeches. The blood had crusted them to my leg and I had to soak the trousers loose before removing them. Felipa found a skirt and the jar of salve in my room, and after donning the one, I applied the other.

"I was nearly healed," I said mournfully, touching my reopened sores with the utmost delicacy.

"Soon you will be almost healed again," Mariquilla promised. "This is made from the thick blades of yucca and yucca elata," María said, sounding as enthusiastic and normal as a wife sharing a recipe, "mashed with the fat of goat kidneys. It works very fast."

"Oh," I said. "Must be the goat kidneys." When I finished treating my sores, the girls scattered and Mariquilla applied a second round of coated leaves to my face. The burning and prickling I had suffered for so many hours immediately diminished to an astonishing degree.

I breathed a sigh of relief and lay back. Mariquilla asked me if I had any pains in my heart and I assured her I did not. We did find it prudent to keep an empty pail near my head throughout the rest of the night, as my stomach continued to rebel.

I slept through Mrs. Ledbetter's description of the dragon and most of Felipa's dramatization of her discovery of the cave. I opened an eye once and spied Claytie. She was so envious she was almost as green as the dragon.

When the various versions of the story were finished, the darker of our rescuers whistled appreciatively. "You got some kinda wildlife in these parts, ma'am," he said.

"We'd be much obliged if you gentlemen would be kind enough to carry us back there tomorrow so we can get some more water. I believe there's some dynamite in the storeroom—"

"If there was, it would be my brother's property to dispose of as he sees fit," Mrs. Jenkins said sanctimoniously. "However, when I took inventory, I did not see any explosives."

"Foot!" the housekeeper swore. "Pardon my language, but the good Lord only knows how long it'll be before the men stop chasin' Indians and hightail for home. If the redskins took the dynamite, catchin' 'em might not be an especially good idea." She sat down on one of the supper benches, her back propped against the wall near me. I glimpsed her through half-closed eyes and for the first time saw some reflection of my own feelings. Though flushed with too much sun, her face looked drawn and weary, her hair wet clear through the braids piled on her head, the stray strands darkened with sweat and lying like welts against her skin. She clasped her hands, unaccustomedly idle, tightly in her lap. "In that case, gentlemen," she said in a voice prim with effort at control, "perhaps you'd oblige me by takin' one of us up to the army fort to tell them what's goin' on down here."

"Due to certain diplomatic difficulties, that won't be possible, I'm afraid," Dr. Purdy said smoothly, but looking more jumpy about mention of the army fort than Mrs. Jenkins did about the dragon. "But the chief and I could solve your problems without outside help, I'm sure. Our specialty is rainmaking. Once we generate sufficient precipitation, your need to utilize the pool under the beast's control will be alleviated and you may wait at your leisure for your employer to dispose of the varmint."

"I wasn't born yesterday, Mr. Purdy," Mrs. Ledbetter said.

"Hulda! Your manners!" Mrs. Jenkins said. "Hear the good doctor out."

The doctor's companion gave him a look of the purest disgust.

"Furthermore, madam, if we do not produce sufficient rain in time to solve your problem, the chief and I will use our patented dragon-slaying techniques to rid you of your menace."

"What do you mean, 'the chief and I,' Al?" his companion snorted.

"Chief, you wound me. Didn't I ever tell you about that time along the Nile when . . ."

In the midst of this, I acquired a third application of leaves. While Mariquilla patted them in place, I noticed Felipa kneeling beside the captive Indian, speaking softly to him. He glared sullenly over her shoulder during the time that I observed them, but later on I saw her looking anxiously out the window in the master bedroom, the one connecting with the dining room.

Felipa returned to the dining room and sat beside me. "It is not fair," she said. "This man and his brothers were cast out for taking you, and you're not the cause of the dragon at all. Dolores is."

I peered more closely at the disgruntled brave. I was grateful to be able to peer at anything without my head pounding. "Yes, well, I'm sorry, Felipa, but I am unable to generate much sympathy for his plight."

She ignored my remark. "He and his brothers are now exiles because of you, and they came seeking vengeance."

"And got a faceful of hot grease," Mariquilla said, pausing at her metate to take a long pull at her cigar and blow a triumphant smoke ring.

"I hope they don't choose to avenge themselves on me for that," I said nervously.

"They ain't gonna avenge shi . . . anything, lady," Chief Rain-in-the-Face said. "In fact, I don't know why I don't just blow this one's brains out."

"Because, my dear Chief, we are compassionate and also curious men," Dr. Purdy told him. "This gentleman may yet be of use to us in deterring his friends from further rash action."

"Them are Comanche friends you're talkin' about, Al. This fella is a dead man as far as they're concerned. They'll just make sure we all join him in the happy hunting ground."

"Tsk-tsk, Chief, you are such a pessimist."

"I'm a *live* pess-whatever-you-call-it. I mean to stay that way."

Purdy shrugged off his associate's misgivings and proceeded to try to butter us up with flirtations and long stories about his travels and the miracles of moisture he and the chief had wrought.

The rest of the ladies, to my surprise, seemed to take his tall tales for the gospel. Even Mrs. Ledbetter's eyebrows unknit and her mouth quirked up in an indulgent half-smile. Dolores, having conjured up the dragon, now gazed at Purdy as if he had ridden in on a white charger instead of a camel. Mrs. Jenkins simpered and Claytie practiced flirting. Felipa asked the chief suspicious questions about his tribe.

I participated in none of it, and not just because I was still ailing, either. I knew a hustler when *I* saw one and was surprised that these shrewd, practical people appeared to lack my insight. Of course, they had not the educational benefit of growing up as my father's daughter, but they did live in the shadow of Drake's deception. But then, while Drake's lies got him what he wanted, they were pretty specific and not very entertaining. These fellows, like my father, lied magnificently, and about everything in general. Good fun, especially for hardworking people in an isolated place, as long as someone kept an eye on the pea while the verbal shell was being shuffled.

When I drifted off, two candles burned on the table and a fire glowed in the hearth. Felipa, Claytie, and the other children bedded down nearest the fireplace. I moved away, for despite the improvement in my condition, I still felt intermittently feverish. Dolores and Dr. Purdy engaged in silent communication which consisted of staring deeply into each other's eyes. The chief guarded the captive, who decided he was not to be boiled alive just yet and sank into snoring slumber.

I awoke in the middle of my sleep, suffocating with rage. Stolen water. Running water. Someone stealing water. I still heard the tinkle and swirl even as the dream cleared. The sound came from the patio, along with the stamp of horses and the jingle of harness. I tiptoed over prone bodies and stalked to the door. One of our self-styled benefactors was dipping a portion of our precious water from its barrel into a large waterskin. The other already had the wagon rehitched.

They finished their respective jobs, slung the water into the wagon, and led the horses into the open. I grabbed E.F. Ledbetter's deer rifle and raised it, stepping out from under the spiked moon-shadows of the *ramada*.

"Hold it right there," I said from between appropriately clenched teeth. "One more step, you moth-eaten misbegotten coyotes, and I drill ya."

"Like hell, lady," the chief said, raising his own far more powerful weapon. "No offense, but you women are not exactly dealin' from a full deck, you know what I mean? Dragons! Huh. This country's got wild Indians, it's got rattlesnakes, it's got sun hot enough to fry eggs on rocks. It don't need no dragons to be bad. And no crazy ladies either. At least, no crazy ladies keepin' company with Shadrach Lafayette and Slim Purdy. Ain't that right, Slim?"

Dr. Purdy bowed his head slightly and favored me with an ironic smile. "The chief has ancient Indian magic that reveals this sort of thing to him. I never argue."

"Sheee . . . Get that ugly humpbacked cayuse of yours and let's get out of here, Purdy, before I make a nasty mess on this nice lady's front porch. Come on, you." The last command was to the horses, which he led toward the gate.

Purdy felt constrained to explain a little further, mostly, I thought, because he liked to hear himself talk. "We took only what water we will need to get us to San Antonio."

"You stole what we risked our very lives for, sir," I told him. "And we defenseless women can hardly brave the dragon again to—"

"Now, there you go again, darlin'. I swear, some

people just shouldn't go out in the heat of the day. You go on back in there and get you some sleep like a good girl. Take you ol' Uncle Slim's word for it that there ain't no such thing as—" His mouth fell open abruptly as his face turned skyward. "Oh, my God, what the hell is that?"

Above the eastern edge of the roof, spiked wings spread as the dragon rose like the dead on judgment day and circled briefly above us, its wings barely twitching as it glided in circles, using its tail for a rudder. It smelled even worse than it had in the valley, its hot vapor nastier than the case of gangrene I encountered while covering the story of a miner who lost his foot in a cave-in. The green drifted down upon us, covering us in a nauseating fog, while above us the great beast's eyes blinked slowly as its head swung from side to side, searching. I knew immediately that the beast was the source of my dream feelings, which gave me the uncomfortable awareness that while it might be out for a midnight snack of horseflesh, it had something else on its mind too, and that something did not bode well for us.

Chief Rain-in-the-Face's rifle cracked, its report ripping through the night and bouncing off the walls. Screams erupted from inside the dining room, redoubling as one after the other, the ladies saw what was occurring. Both screams and rifle reports were puny as a kitten's first mews compared to the dragon's shriek, the same hellish howl I had heard the night of my abduction.

Purdy threw me aside and himself fell across the dining table as the chief, the horses, and the wagon clattered into the dining room ahead of the giant predator. Bodies which had been sleeping but a moment before barely rolled out from under terrified hooves. Feminine screams joined the dragon's as it ignited the *ramada*, the dining-room door, the shingles, and the bars at the window.

Mrs. Ledbetter dashed past me, grabbing E.F.'s rifle from my hands as she ran. The chief was flat on his belly inside the flaming door, his rifle aimed upward through the shower of sparks and flying embers. Both guns spat at once and the dragon screeched again, belching blinding green fire once more. Purdy grabbed another rifle from the wagon but the dragon cleared the roof on the opposite side and vanished.

Mrs. Jenkins' voice shrilled over the screams and the crackle of flame. "Let's not lose our heads, girls! Grab the bucket, Dolores. Paquita, the skillet. Josefita, help me with this thing!" And before each quite managed to figure out where the other was aiming, she and Josefita ineffectually dumped out the flaming window most of the barrel Purdy had partially drained into his water bags. Mariquilla dragged bowls from the cupboard and handed them to Mrs. Jenkins, who looked as if she wanted to put the nicer dishes aside but nevertheless passed them on to the next in line in the bucket brigade. Felipa swarmed up the untouched ladder to the roof, took the pot of water Claytie handed her from below, and splashed it across the flames.

We had a bad moment as the fire started eating through the woodwork into the shingled ceiling, but another potful and half of another solved that. The horses were saved, most of the fort was saved, including the *ramada*, but all but a quarter of one barrel of water and the skinful that Purdy threw into the wagon was lost.

While the chief was mopping his brow and checking to make sure all of his parts were present and unroasted, Mrs. Ledbetter relieved him of his rifle.

"Now, then, boys," she said, when the confusion had died down somewhat. "You helped bring this upon us by rilin' that critter. Suppose you just help us go ask it nice tomorrow if we can have a little more water, please. It's not likely we'll be able to make it to the cavalry post to get help with that thing loose. But we've got to have that water. Otherwise we're gonna all of us die of thirst right here before the menfolk return from chasin' Indians who had sense enough to clear out while the gettin' was good."

"If I may be so bold as to make a suggestion, ma'am," Purdy said, this time sounding genuinely somewhat modest about putting in his two cents' worth.

107

"I didn't see what I thought stoppin' you before," Mrs. Ledbetter replied.

"I think the chief and I could sidestep this whole problem, bein' as how none of the other solutions seem to hold much hope for happiness or longevity for the participants concerned, by practicin' our specialty. Why don't you just let us make a little rain for you?"

"Make away, mister. But it had better be a frog-strangler and a gully-washer to do us any good now. And a dragon-drownder too, if you can manage it."

10

The rainmaking took place as soon as the sun came up. Our guests grew as anxious as the rest of us for moisture. This new solicitousness on their parts for the improvement of our climate was no doubt enhanced by the fact that Mrs. Ledbetter held their weapons, one of which, the chief's powerful rifle, she kept trained on them throughout the remainder of the night.

"Sure do hope I don't doze off, boys," she told them. "My arthritis has a tendency to tighten up when I sleep, and might just accidentally tighten on the trigger."

"Ma'am, you have misunderstood our intentions," Dr. Purdy averred in an injured tone.

"Sir, I'll trouble you to keep your voice low. There are folks tryin' to sleep here."

"You seem to think we meant you ladies some harm. We were merely standin' guard against that beast you told us about, and as you can see, it was a very good thing we did."

"You had purloined that waterbag to throw into its mouth and douse its flame, I presume?" I asked, just in case the housekeeper was inclined to believe him. "And hitched up your horses to give chase just in case it didn't care for a drink of water?"

"No, darlin', we naturally were not plannin' any such fool thing as that," the doctor said deprecatingly. "We needed that water to prime the sky to send down more. It's part of the rainmakin' process. The chief here needs to take it out upon the desert and meditate over the life-givin' elixir before he performs the magical part of our proceedin's."

The chief's portion of the ceremony, when it came, consisted of skipping around in a circle, grunting, and making dreadful faces. The rest of us stood in a semicircle around him, watching, including the captive warrior. Sober, he was a great deal quieter than he had been drunk, and before the chief began dancing, wore a rather hang-dog expression.

The captive was not the only one to look less than pleased. Felipa sat close to him, talking low and unintelligibly. She occasionally glanced at Dolores with disbelief and at me as if I had betrayed her, which was hardly fair. I had never claimed any control over the dragon, to her, her tribesmen, or anybody else. If anyone had bothered to consult me on the matter in any language I understood, I'd have promptly set matters straight.

Claytie listened in on the Comanche conversation, but looked daggers at the warrior who was usurping Felipa's attention.

Dolores was a study in desperation overlaid with a quick whitewash of adoration. She looked at Purdy as if what he was about to do would save her life. And maybe it would. But there was a strained quality to her voice, her eyes, and the purposeless way she wrung her hands in the fabric of her skirt that had nothing to do with rain. Purdy, for his part, looked plenty grand and spoke confidently, but his Adam's apple traveled up and down the length of his throat faster than cannonballs being loaded in a barrel in the heat of battle.

Watching Dolores gaze so raptly at Purdy, it struck me as totally unjust that she, who had summoned the dragon, dreamed of the spurious doctor, while I, an innocent bystander, had been nocturnally plagued with the ruminations of *her* reptilian protector since my arrival. Well, at least I could be fairly certain my dreams were not lying, which was more than Dolores could claim.

The chief tried to enter into the spirit of his dance and muttered phrases in what sounded to me like a mixture of bastard French and pure linguistic invention but if his dark complexion had allowed him to blush, I think he would have done so. He kept having to brush back the feathers of his warbonnet, which flopped into his face while he hopped. Mrs. Jenkins buried her face behind her fan. She was a seriously disillusioned woman after the events of last night and was in no mood to be reillusioned quickly. Mariquilla used the occasion as a good opportunity to smoke up the open desert, though she did not appear to think there was much else special going to happen. Only Mrs. Ledbetter looked mildly hopeful, and as soon as the chief began his foolishness, her lower jaw snapped to meet her upper one, and her knuckles tightened around the rifle.

The beginning of the chief's Ojibanoxie rain stomp had a brightening effect on someone, though, and that was the captive, who first seemed to look right past the cavorting charlatan, then watched him with pained disbelief, mumbled a question to Felipa, who mumbled back. At that the Indian let out a whoop. For a moment it seemed as if he might have declared war on us, but then, despite the ropes that bound him, he fell to the ground laughing.

The chief stopped in mid-stomp and stuck his lower jaw out belligerently at his critic.

The Comanche drew himself up off the ground, quelled his all-too-scrutable laughter to a snicker, and roundly reprimanded the chief, tossing his head around to make up for the gestures he was unable to make with his hands to express his vehemence.

"Heyyy," the chief protested. "It ain't that bad!" Then he said something back to the Indian in the same tongue, though I suppose his accent was not particularly good. The

Indian replied with a sharpness spoiled by a suppressed giggle. Rain-in-the-Face narrowed an eye at him consideringly, scratched his chin, said "Oh, yeah?" and gestured to his partner.

They carried on a whispered conversation of great intensity, ending with Purdy shrugging, saying, "It can't hurt."

The chief turned to Mrs. Ledbetter. "Y'all stand back, ma'am. I'm gonna untie this fella. He promised to show me some new Comanche wrinkles in my patented authentic Ojibanoxie rain dance."

"Fudge!" she said. "You boys have somethin' up your sleeve. You're not from these parts. I bet you couldn't understand a word that redskin said."

"You'd lose that bet, ma'am," Purdy said smoothly. "The chief, before goin' into private enterprise, was famed among his fellow buffalo soldiers as a scout. He knows the lingo of all the Indian folk hereabouts, besides speakin' his own native tongue."

So the captive was untied, whereupon he proceeded to gesture. Felipa monitored the conversation closely, her head swiveling from chief to captive during the lesson. But when she tried to mimic the gestures the two of them demonstrated to each other, Rain-in-the-Face waved her back to her seat.

"This ain't gonna work if you do it too, baby," the chief told her. "This here is a man's dance. Women's just s'posed to sit on the sideline and wait to get wet."

"If you ask me, you got a head start on us all in that department," Hulda Ledbetter said.

"I don't see why if a person from a whole nother tribe can try it, a Comanche girl can't," Felipa argued.

"Aw, let 'er, Chief," Purdy said. "She's bound to do it more graceful than you."

The Comanche captive suddenly grunted something and sat back down again, looking out across the desert instead of at any of us.

"Now see what you've done," Felipa said. "He won't

show us any more. Says white men are all alike, even if they're women or have black skin."

"I know some fellas I surely do wish agreed with him," the chief muttered.

"Well, I think that's probably enough real heap big medicine for one rainmakin' anyway," Purdy said. "Sit down, now, Chief, and let me get on with the scientific end of it. I don't much like bein' out here in the open after last night."

The chief subsided, puffing a little, onto the ground beside Felipa, who imitated the captive and stared off into the desert. At least until Purdy went into his act.

The so-called good so-called doctor unbuttoned his top shirt button, removed his brown gabardine suit jacket (he must have been sweltering—I was, even in the shade of the wagon where I had been seated out of consideration for my condition), removed his cuffs, pushed his shirt sleeves up his arms like a stage magician, and said, "Sorry to appear before you in such disarray, ladies, but rainmakin' is heavy work."

The sky waited patiently, a serene and unrelenting blue studded with the blazing sun, confident that it was in undisputed charge of the situation.

Purdy rummaged in the wagon and with a flourish drew forth two items. These were sufficiently exotic that he no doubt could convince the other ladies that they were rainmaking equipment. To me, however, they were familiar. They were sky rockets. Wy Mi set them off every year for the Chinese New Year.

"Dr. Purdy, sir, you are a fraud and a charlatan," I told him straight out. "Those objects are nothing but Chinese fireworks. The Chinese in San Francisco use them all the time."

"What an honor it is to be able to demonstrate sophisticated equipment for someone so widely traveled and knowledgeable as yourself, ma'am," Purdy said, using one rocket like a hat to sweep in front of himself as he bowed. "Indeed, it is from China, an ancient civilization possessed

113

of much advanced scientific knowledge, that I learned of this apparatus. It is true that similar items to these you see before you are indeed used as decorations in Chinese pageants. However, ma'am, you mentioned the location of the demonstration you observed as being in San Francisco. Rains quite a bit there, don't it?"

"I . . . It—"

"See there?" he said to the other ladies before I had a chance to reply properly that sometimes it did and sometimes it didn't and that an outsider might mistake our distinctive fog for actual precipitation. I decided to let him continue uncontested. No doubt he would make a fool of himself without my help.

Besides, though I very much wished to see to it that these specious precipitation producers got away with nothing, I felt foolish. Purdy grinned broadly at me even as he addressed me so politely. I couldn't blame him. I must have been a sight. My hair was piled high and gummed to my head with a green lather of wild sunflower plant, leaves, stems, petals, seed mash, and all, which Mariquilla had that morning applied like a shampoo, swabbing it on the edges of my face and the back of my neck before massaging it into my hair and scalp. Thin and slimy and yellow green, it looked stranger than one of Mrs. Jenkins' fancy hats. It smelled sunflowery though, and when, during the initial application, some of it had dribbled into my mouth, its taste was not unpleasant. I hoped against hope for at least enough rain to rinse it truly clean.

Purdy planted his rockets in the ground, bamboo tails sticking into the sand. The rockets were bright red, capped with gold foil paper. The doctor harrumphed and flapped his arms and pranced around them until he was sure all eyes were on him. Outside the ring of tensed bodies and watching faces, dust devils swirled up as if they watched too, and tumbleweeds bounced past. Was wind a sign of rain out here? The sky remained placid and implacable.

All but wearing himself out with excessive dramatic gesticulation, Purdy lit the rockets and they did what rockets do—flew high into the air and exploded with a brief flash that would have been far more spectacular at night. The ladies oohed and aahed appropriately, though Mrs. Ledbetter, who did not appreciate the way she had been taken in before, sniffed and said that she had seen better on a reasonably festive Saturday night in Alpine.

"Just when may we expect the rain, Dr. Purdy?" Mrs. Jenkins inquired, her tone as starchy as it ever was but her eyes wide enough to swallow him whole, an appearance not too far from the truth unless I missed my guess. I had good reason to know what really occurred under the bonnets of some prissy widows.

"Soon as we're paid, ma'am. The effects are guaranteed then. Ordinarily we ask for donations, but in view of the current situation, we will accept water in lieu of a portion of the payment."

"That's fair enough. We've plenty of water right up yonder at the spring," Mrs. Ledbetter said. "We'd be obliged if while you're fetchin' yours, you'd fetch back some for us." She pointed toward the canyon, and though she was not looking where she pointed, the rest of us followed her finger.

Mariquilla saw it first, and breathed an awestruck "*Ayyyy.*" A very large and jagged hole in the landscape grew larger as we watched, the green haze around it intensifying.

Dolores dropped the lapful of *jalapeños* she had gathered from her patch for lunch. Mrs. Jenkins tried to swoon into Purdy's arms, but he sidestepped her and she drooped hard against the wagon wheel instead. Chief Rain-in-the-Face threw down his warbonnet and grabbed the reins of the wagon.

"Musta come back to finish what it started," Mrs. Ledbetter said, shouldering the chief's rifle.

"The rockets must have attracted it," Purdy surmised wonderingly.

"That's just jim dandy!" the chief practically whined. "Thanks to your stupid rockets, Purdy, that damn thing thinks we're a giant flyin' lizard of the opposite gender and I don't even want to think about what'll happen when it finds out we ain't no such thing!"

We were no more than a few yards from the open gate and most of us fairly flew across the distance. I am ashamed to say that I was one of the front runners, finding that sunstroke is no impediment to rapid movement in an emergency. I held the door open and encouraged the others. Claytie aided the mothers with their children, who kept wanting to go back and see Purdy and Rain-in-the-Face do another trick. Not for long. Our two self-proclaimed heroes nearly ran everyone else down galloping at full tilt through the doors. Mariquilla disgustedly supported Mrs. Jenkins, who it seemed was genuinely affected with fright. Purdy had snatched Dolores up into the wagon with him and I saw her stricken face blur past as the chief drove the wagon into the dining room. Mrs. Ledbetter and I were pulling the gates shut when we paused for less than half a heartbeat to exchange dismayed glances.

"Where is Felipa?" I asked. "Where is the prisoner?"

"Didn't they come past you?"

"No."

"Too late now," she said. "Take cover. Don't know what we're leanin' on this fool door for when the dragon can fly right over it."

I have noted already that sound carries well in the desert. I think I shall never forget the sound we heard as we all huddled within that one suddenly small room. Purdy and the chief held the mouths of two of the animals shut with their hands. The camel apparently had more sense than to make noise with a dragon in the vicinity. The middle Morales child started to scream but barely emitted a peep before he, his siblings, and the other children were each gathered into an empty lap, their mouths muffled against the bosom of a mother or surrogate thereof. The women's tenseness must have communicated itself to the children then, for none of them that I saw so much as wiggled a toe after that. Our respirations bellowed in my ears; our hearts were louder than tom-toms. But the measured, almost leisurely slap of wings was deafening.

Louder it grew, and louder, nearer, until I could imagine the spiked head clearing Drake's office. Another beat and it had crossed the patio, another like a thunderclap directly overhead, two more took it far enough away that the sound was distinctly fainter. The next beat after that boomed again. The monster returned, having failed to find the rockets. The beats pounded a circle around the patio and I craned my head just slightly to see out the window. The dragon landed, its back to me. It had grown. The tail alone was now the size of the creature I had seen before, a creature which could not possibly sit upon the ledge overlooking the pool.

I wondered with that odd sort of objectivity one sometimes experiences in an emergency how many victims of the fabled dragons died of flames, how many of smoke inhalation, and how many of the heart failure I felt would cause us all to expire if the beast did not soon depart.

The creature's great head swayed to one side and the other, and I noted a slight movement of the jaws. The green haze drifted back and through the window, so sickening I feared someone—and I feared it would be me—might start retching. No wonder the dragon could not smell us. It must have been completely overwhelmed by its own foul breath. I began to fear that it would be unable to leave, but at last it simply raised up on its hind feet and planted its front ones on the roof above Drake's office, elevating itself until it could spread its wings, and flapped off, the reverberations shaking the solid building so that the whitewashed mud plaster fell from the walls, exposing the adobe bricks.

There was no more mistaking the beast's absence than its presence, and when it was well and truly gone we revived those who had swooned (among them Dr. Purdy), had medicinal snorts of Drake's brandy to calm the trembles, mopped tears with admonitions from Mrs. Ledbetter that it was plain foolishness to waste water that way, and unfittin' as well, since the dragon was in no way a sad thing but a fearsome one.

Mrs. Jenkins swabbed her eyes with an inadequate lace square and complained in a voice even more nasal than usual, "Hulda Ledbetter, if you had any feminine sensitivity at all you would know enough to cry yourself. Not sad indeed! Just think how poor Bubba's gonna feel when he comes home and finds us all roasted alive inside our home."

"With all due respect for your feeblemindedness, Lovanche, I refuse to give that any thought whatsoever," Mrs. Ledbetter responded evenly. "What I am tryin' to think of is how to keep it from happenin', and even more to the immediate point, how to keep us from dryin' up like a bunch of tumbleweeds and just blowin' away without that critter havin' to so much as lift a claw."

"It's getting the thing to lift a claw that's the problem," I reminded her. "If it continues to sit up there between us and the pool except when it chooses to attack us or Dr. Purdy's rockets, we'll never—"

"Did she just say what I think she said?" Chief Rain-in-the-Face, who was still quite gray and whose eyes continued to show an uncommon amount of white, asked Dr. Purdy, who was finally recovering, under Dolores' solicitous care.

"Shhhh," Purdy hushed him.

Mrs. Ledbetter emitted a whoop of relief and inspiration. "Miss Valentine, honey, we might make a Texan out of you yet. You're right as rain, and Lord knows nothin' could be righter than that."

"I am? In what way?"

"In what way? she asks," Purdy groaned, and then decided, as Father sometimes did, to turn the enemy's strength into his own. "What a dear modest darlin' girl you are. You sure you didn't train with General Lee, ma'am? Because you sure did hit on a strategy, is what you did. What we have to do is draw that dragon's fire, you see. We can take you ladies and your barrels up to the canyon and drop you off at a hidin' place, then hightail it over toward the mountains and fire our guns and shoot off more rockets to attract the critter's attention. When it comes, we'll take dead aim and let loose with the buffalo gun where it'll do the most good."

The only real hitch to the plan was that Claytie refused to be left behind. "I'm not stayin' here with the brats again," she said. "Let their mothers do it. With the wagon, you won't need so many people to do the haulin'. I want to see the rockets, and where the dragon killed the cows. They're my cows, after all. Not just Daddy's. This land was Mama's before he married her and it's mine when he dies. I want to see."

She looked very much like her father then, her gray eyes stony, the baby fat on her jaw firming with resolution and the threat of an imminent temper tantrum.

The chief protested, "That's no place for a little baby girl."

"I will go," Dolores said. I wasn't surprised. She and Purdy were tight as Siamese twins. "She can ride beside me. I will let—"

Mariquilla did not look up from her metate as she interrupted smoothly, "Stay with me, *niña*. I need help making the medicines. We must gather sotol for the animals and for ourselves, and cut other cactus for water. With the wagon, you will only be in the way. Here, you are needed." I think I must have been the only one who saw the *curandera*'s eyes flick sideways to Dolores, who gazed beseechingly up at Purdy for support.

"I don't see why it would hurt to take her as far as the canyon," he said. "The chief could bring her back."

"Let her do what she wants," Mrs. Ledbetter replied, settling the question. "If there's a safe place in all this land, I wish you'd show it to me. Besides, she's right. This is her land more than anybody's. Just see to it she don't

119

get hurt. Miss Valentine, honey, I hate to ask you to ride but I want you to take this peashooter here and mind these two gentlemen so's they don't run off. Paquita, Benito, fetch some pillahs for the *señorita* to sit on while she's ridin'. Benito, they need to go up by where you live—"

He shook his head and backed away. "*No, señora, por favor, no—*"

"I know the way, *señora*," Dolores said. "There is no need for *el viejo* to go." I did not like the idea of depending on Dolores as a guide any more than I liked depending on Purdy and Rain-in-the-Face for protection and/or deliverance from evil. I feared she would indulge in some well-meaning gesture such as flinging herself into the dragon's mouth, which would endanger us all and ultimately do no good whatsoever. I said as much privately to Mrs. Ledbetter, who shrugged. "We all have our crosses to bear. If she tries it, see if you can get a shot into that thing's open mouth and drill a hole in its brain."

I nodded gravely, not wishing to diminish the housekeeper's confidence in me. I refrained from telling her that I was unfamiliar with firearms save the little derringer my father had showed me how to shoot to protect myself when on dangerous assignments—rescuing him from prolonged interviews with fellow connoisseurs of strong spirits in time to publish a newspaper, for instance.

I held the chief's rifle under my arm as the wagon bounced slowly across the desert. We had to travel at a leisurely pace to save the strength of the horses, who could not be watered until they arrived at the spring. Claytie and I rode with Rain-in-the-Face, she on the wagon seat, I precariously half-kneeling on the pillows piled just behind it. Purdy and Dolores rode astride Colonel Beauregard Sam Houston Burlingame. I refreshed my mind by observing the camel's slender pacing legs, its knobby knees, and its supremely ugly face, rather like Mrs. Higgenbotham's. Purdy crooned to it. Dolores tentatively scratched its neck. There is no accounting for tastes.

"I wanted to ride the camel," Claytie complained. "Dolores said I could ride with her."

"There is no room, *niña*," Dolores told her.

"You could get down and let me ride," Claytie said. "You've had a long turn. If I were up there I could see farther. Maybe I'd spot Flip," she added, using her nickname for Felipa.

"Felipa has run away with the others of her savage kind, little one," Dolores said.

Claytie shook her head stubbornly. "She has not. She wouldn't go and just leave me like that. We're blood sisters."

Dolores momentarily developed enough backbone to spit. "She is Comanche. An animal. She does not care for you."

Purdy wisely goaded Colonel to a faster gait, giving Dolores the last word.

"She should talk about animals!" Claytie said when her sputtering rage had died down to mere spite. "She's the animal!"

"What do you mean?" I asked, hoping Felipa had not confided Dolores' part in summoning the dragon. Mrs. Ledbetter wanted to keep that secret, for fear harm would come to the Mexican girl. I agreed with her, but for different reasons. Whereas Mrs. Ledbetter thought Dolores deranged but innocent, I believed more with every passing hour that she *had* summoned the dragon. But I could think of about a half-dozen reasons why Drake shouldn't share my opinion.

"Flip and I overheard Mariquilla tell Paquita that El Mula, the long-eared muleskinner from the train at the fandango last week, is from Dolores' village. He told her he knew Dolores' granny on her mother's side. He said she was a *bruja*, an old witch, who used to turn herself into a jaguar and eat people before someone finally killed her."

"That's the silliest thing I ever heard," I said convincingly, I hoped. "Why would anyone believe such a story?

121

I mean, we've seen the dragon, but people who can change into jaguars . . . ?"

"That just shows how much you know. Witches in Mexico do that kind of stuff all the time. Ask Daddy. He told me about it a long time ago. Said it's because the *brujas* are from an old, old bunch of Indians who were like werewolves, only they were were-jaguars. He says back when the Mexicans were doing all them human sacrifices the jaguar people were priests and kings. So Dolores hasn't got any business callin' Flip an animal." She grinned. "I wonder if she was really in trouble if she'd change into a jaguar too?"

"She was really in trouble," I said, "and the Indians sold her and took her children. That should tell you something." To change the subject I asked Rain-in-the-Face, "Does having been a buffalo soldier mean you turned into a buffalo anytime *you* were in trouble, Chief?"

He patted his mat of wiry black hair. "Indians think my scalp looks like a buffalo's hairdo. See, I only been a practicin' Ojibinoxie since I met Slim. Before that, I was colored. My dear ol' massa down on de plantation didn't believe in happy darkies, no ma'am. He believed in de whip and de hounds and de sell yore a— sell yoreself, little girl, for dogmeat if you didn't do what he say. Soon as my legs could run real good I ran off up north and joined the army. Got sent up to Fort Stockton with General Hatch, Company C, Ninth Cavalry, in sixty-seven. All of us colored. Indians called us buffalo soldiers and tried to shoot us like the genuine article till they found out we shot back."

Three hours put us in the mountains, beyond sight of the fort and within smell of the dragon's cache of dead animals.

The camel stopped where the road took a sharp dip down into a dry riverbed. The chief reined in the horses far behind the camel and indicated with a disgusted grunt and a vigorous spit that he had gone as far as he intended.

Purdy wrinkled his nose at the rotten odor and rode the camel back to us.

"Reckon by the perfume, ladies, that this is where you dismount. We walk from now on. Not much further, though, or we're like to die of pure putrinhalation."

"Pure what?" Claytie and I asked in unison.

"Putrinhalation. That's a scientific term for a malady caused from breathin' in putrid smells."

We unloaded the rockets from the wagon and the chief drove back to the fort. He had offered to take Claytie back with him but Dolores objected that the beast was drawn to livestock so Claytie would be safer with us.

"Thanks, *chiquita*. That makes me feel real good about ridin' unarmed across the desert all by my lonesome," the chief said.

"We are all taking our chances," I reminded him. "If you drive straight back as we are trusting you to do, you will soon have Mrs. Ledbetter and the other women with you, and they will be armed. After a fashion."

"When it comes to arms, I don't give a hoot for fashion, ma'am. What I want is holes in whatever I'm shootin' at. Big ones, that get there *fast*."

"I understand perfectly," I said. "All the more reason for you to be on your way promptly." For good measure, I pointed his gun at him. I must have looked convincing because the others stood well clear of me. He hastily turned the wagon toward the fort.

The rest of us began hunting for a hiding place large enough for ourselves and the camel. I made sure that Purdy dismounted and remained within sight of my gun. Claytie reinforced my authority by stalking grimly beside me. Dolores walked as sedately beside Purdy as if they were fellow pallbearers, which was reasonably cheerful for her.

Only after we had braved the smell several hundred yards further up the riverbed toward the canyon or "shut-up" (so called because the canyon was shut up at one end) did we find adequate cover. The river, now dry,

123

had undercut the bank, forming a ledge shading half the valley. Like the canyon where the spring-fed pool was located, the rocky walls here smoothly melted into a seamless basin. The stone was pinkish, with small spirals and scallops embedded within it. In several places the walls were pitted with caves.

"This one here looks big enough for us," Purdy said, after a cursory investigation. "It's tall enough for Colonel and we can hide behind that little bend back there."

"Suppose the dragon figures the same thing," I postulated. "The dragon melted the cave by the pool through the mountainside. I don't think a cave is much protection."

"You got any better ideas?" Purdy asked. "If that thing melts holes in the side of mountains, I don't give much for our chances anyway. But if we plant the rockets a ways down the canyon, no reason the critter would be lookin' for us. Like the chief said, it's lookin' for another dragon. It can't possibly catch our scent in here." He sounded a little nasal as he said this, because he was wrinkling his nose and restraining himself for the sake of appearances from clamping his fingers to his nostrils. "If it can't see or hear us, we'll probably be all right. And before you say that probably isn't good enough, let me assure you that I agree with you wholeheartedly. However, ma'am, you are the one holding that big ol' buffalo gun."

"I meant to speak to you about that, Mr. Purdy," I said as firmly and authoritatively as possible, just so he wouldn't get the idea that lack of expertise in one area was any reason to lose respect for my leadership in others. "I am quite sure that should *you* try to escape, I could discover how this firearm operates, but in the event that it becomes necessary to defend us against the dragon, I doubt I will have time for much reflection on the matter before I must act. Therefore, it would save considerable time and trouble if you would be so kind as to show me . . ."

Purdy's eyebrow raised ever so slightly and his dark

eyes crinkled around the edges, though he wisely forbore to smile or laugh at me. I could have always hit him with the weapon, even if I couldn't fire it at him. "Why, ma'am, I'd be gratified to show you how to use that thing in case you need to use it in a hurry should I decide to be more of a scoundrel than anybody ever had the guts to claim I was. I do think you and I pretty much understand each other, but I can tell you, I got no intention of goin' anywhere till we do what we came here for. The chief and I aren't likely to make a whole lot of progress with no water and a dragon droolin' over our transportation. Furthermore, whether you believe it or not, it's not in me to leave three helpless ladies alone out here to face a critter like that. Especially if I have the Sharps so I can do somethin' about it besides fry along with you."

"I confess that I am as doubtful about your chivalry as about your rainmaking ability, sir, but I seem to have no choice." I handed him the rifle.

He bowed over it ceremoniously and checked it over. "I don't suppose you remembered to bring cartridges?" he asked politely.

"I happen to have a few in my pocket," I replied. I was once more clad in Papa's britches in order to facilitate movement.

He loaded the heavy rifle in what seemed a single deft motion and smiled at me as if he had done something very clever. "You will see that I am a man of my word when I actually go so far as to give it," he said. "You are wrong about the rainmakin' too. It will come. It may take a month or two but it always comes. Sometimes local law enforcement lacks patience and seeks to discredit us. Often by the time the rains do come, people fail to render us proper credit. But we always produce rain. Eventually."

"Indeed?" I asked. "Is it you who do so? I was always under the impression rain was the province of the Almighty."

Our eyes locked. Finally he smiled and said, "I'd be glad to take care of the rain if the Lord would tend to the dragon."

I drew a shallow breath and called a truce. "Personally I'd be happy if he just made a nice little wind blow the other way and carry that stench with it."

"I admit that would be handy," he agreed amiably, and handed the gun back to me. "But I'll leave that up to him. Meanwhile, how about if you hold this for me while I set up my rockets?"

Feeling like a prize fool, I complied, standing guard while, with more than ample assistance and advice from Claytie and Dolores, he planted the rockets. When they were done, he led the camel into the cave, made it kneel, and then lay down with his head resting on its side.

"What part of the plan is that, Dr. Purdy?" Claytie asked.

"This is the part where the dragon-slayer sleeps before the battle, little lady. It'll be another good eight hours, from what sweet thing here tells me, before the chief can drive back to the fort, pick up the ladies and the barrels, and reach the water hole. I don't know about you, but I missed a bunch of sleep last night. I aim to catch up. Fightin' dragons is tricky business. Got to be alert."

We were all as tired as he was, and once hidden in the concealment of the cave, everyone seemed to settle down. Claytie kept saying, "Pee-yew. I don't see how a person is supposed to sleep when it smells so bad." Purdy invited her to snuggle up next to the camel, who smelled bad enough at close range to keep her mind off the other stench. She said she would rather die than cuddle up to a hot old camel. It was indeed far too hot to sleep next to anyone. Even Dolores and Purdy kept some distance between them. We spread out as far as possible over the cool cave floor, which wasn't very far.

I closed my eyes for a few minutes, but it suddenly occurred to me that if I knew what the dragon was doing when I dreamed, perhaps it would also be able to monitor my activity through my sleep. Perhaps it seems strange that I was only beginning to be concerned about my connection with the dragon, but until I saw the beast in full daylight I had not been absolutely certain it was real. And only gradually did it occur to me that my dreams were not true dreams at all, but the dragon's thoughts that I somehow was able to read. Again I wondered: why me instead of Dolores? She had called the dragon, not I. She was one of its chosen people. True, I did have a bit of the second sight, which I chiefly used as another sense, my nose for news. But then, Dolores apparently did too. I hadn't realized how deep in a doze I was while pondering these matters until I heard the susurration of Dolores' skirts as she rose and left the cave. I waited in a sleepy stupor, and when she did not return after the maximum period I reckoned a sanitary chore might take, I rose and tiptoed to the cave's entrance. Far up the canyon I saw a flash of white blouse. How she could continue walking into the stench without dying of asphyxiation was beyond me. Something very urgent must be drawing her on. My curiosity was no less urgent, so I followed her, keeping as much in the shadows as possible in deference to my sunstroke.

I wore another borrowed sombrero over the rapidly hardening green slather on my head, and tied a shawl over it to shelter my neck and shoulders from the sun. I lost sight of Dolores almost as soon as I set forth, but as I rounded a curve in the cliff that followed a corresponding bend in the riverbed, the sight of her white blouse and flouncing black skirt rewarded me.

My exertions certainly merited a reward, for though my pace was little more than what westerners might term moseying, the atmosphere in which I perambulated stifled me. The odor of putrescence, to which I might have become accustomed in time had it remained at the same level, grew steadily stronger as I advanced. Something else grew stronger too. When first I felt it I took it to be my own pulse beating in my ears, and indeed, that may have been what it was at the start. Gradually, however, the thumping grew louder and stronger, a beat to each step I took. I unconsciously kept cadence with it, as did

Dolores ahead of me, her black skirt swaying like a pendulum to that deep reverberation.

Beyond us now was a wall, grown up with moss, its stones worn smooth and rounded on the upper edges. I rested against the cool cliff wall for a moment, my hands to my eyes. My sunstroke seemed to have returned. The wall blurred ahead of me, its green extending beyond its solid perimeters, the color hanging in the air around it, shimmering with each thump of my heart—and that other. The very stones that comprised the barrier looked as if they expanded and contracted with each thump. Dolores marched gracefully to the lowest edge and climbed over it, rose, walked several more paces, and turned to face me.

She still did not see me, however, and for a moment her face hung there in the haze, staring slightly down at the wall, which covered her as high as her shoulders. She looked fascinated as a farmer-turned-miner watching his first kootch dancer.

I advanced two more steps before realizing that for the last several seconds I had been stupidly staring at her stupidly staring at the dragon. I had not seen it before simply because I was not expecting to see the dragon blocking this canyon—when last seen it was flying toward the pool. Furthermore, it had its back to us. Which presented the additional difficulty that it would not be able to see our rockets, which were actually unnecessary anyway since the beast was already here. Our only task would be to keep it here until the water had been safely collected and the wagon carrying it had returned to the fort. I hoped the dragon would have the kindness to sleep the day away. In case it did not, I hoped Dolores would have the wisdom to move before it awakened. I did all this hoping with the speed of greased lightning. The intelligent thing to do in this sort of circumstance is to think about screaming a deep and terrified scream, genteelly stifle said scream, and run very quickly and very, very quietly back from whence one came. By taking such a course, one might hope to preserve one's hide and live to tell the tale. However, my professional curiosity would not permit me to retreat without learning why the girl stood there as if entranced. Nor would my humanity allow her to remain.

I mention these ruminations so that the reader will realize that I do *know* better than to go clambering over the tails of mythical enormous reptiles in the depths of deserted canyons, but that I nonetheless had my reasons for doing so.

The dragon's heart—for that was, of course, the loud drumbeat accompanying my own pulse—had to keep time by itself for the next few moments. My heart, if it did not stop entirely, pounded a hummingbird's staccato counterpart. It is no easy affair to climb over a dragon's tail and hold one's breath at the same time. When I reached across the tail for something other than the scaly tip to use to pull myself over, my hand gooshed into slime and came away covered with dark old blood and other substances too sickening to mention. I slid backward, then gathered myself to vault over the spiny tail, touching it with a mere pat as I sailed across it to sink ankle-deep in slick putrescence.

Beyond the beast, as far as I could see, similar foulness covered the ground, while scattered throughout the canyon were the carcasses of Drake's slain herd. There were not as many of them as I expected, and that stood to reason. The dragon was at least three times larger than when I had seen it on the ledge above the pool. What would it eat when the livestock was gone?

Dolores stared into the face and did not seem to see my benastied hand when I extended it in a silent plea to her to be sensible and creep back up the canyon with me. I would have to bodily pull her away. If we lived through it, it would be a devil of a story to tell. If we died, it would be fast, if not painless.

Committing myself to my maker, I stepped around more dead meat and walked slowly toward the enthralled girl. When I was close enough to touch her arm, which hung limply at her side, my eyes locked upon her face, around which her raven hair writhed, stirred by the dragon's green breath. Her face was impassive, her eyes wide. Her gaze compelled mine to follow.

I stuffed my knuckles in my mouth to cut off the shriek clawing its way out of my throat. The dragon's eyes were open. Or so I thought. Sagging against Dolores, praying wordlessly as I watched in horrified fascination, I slowly realized that the light and movement coming from within the beast's brow did not emanate from its pupils, but from images playing across the closed milky membranes that covered the eyes.

The images were not clear, merely hazy patterns of light and darkness intermingling and altering so quickly that they held me by their very unpredictability. I gazed deeper, my heart gradually slowing to match the dragon's as my eyes shifted and my mind swam with images. The minglings assumed shape, and that shape was imprinted not upon the eyes but within me, a code I understood as clearly as if the light shapes were actual photographs of events, or printed words. And deeper yet those meanings penetrated until they were not something outside of me but part of me. Before, I had caught the dragon in my dreams. Now, while watching its mesmerizing eyes, I was caught in the dragon's dreams.

All is in perfect order and harmony. Below us our world glows richly, variously green, brilliantly bejeweled from the daily rains. Opulent blossoms, vermilion, lavender, fuchsia, searing sun yellow, orange, and lapis blue, clusters of tiny flowers and great cushiony blooms burst through the jungle carpet bowing beneath our wings.

We repose upon our landing platform, high above the plazas our people constructed at our bidding. In the plaza below, fountains dance on the colored tiles we taught our people to fashion. Long lines of grateful subjects parade up the steps of our landing platform. They bear as sym-

bols of their gratitude cages of exotic birds and butterflies, garlands of fresh flowers, succulent fruits, jewels and gold crafted, as we instructed, into intricate shapes. They come humbly, adoringly, offering thanks, requesting favors, seeking instruction for some new project if they are particularly bright and ambitious. No project proceeds without our approval, naturally, but we try to encourage initiative whenever possible. Our landing platform was widely copied throughout our lands, the grandeur of the structures reminding our people of ourself even when we were not in residence and thereby consoling their simple hearts for our absence. They particularly liked the steps which gave them access to our visage and enabled them to commune with us. These steps, we feel, are an improvement on the landing platforms designed by our fellow refugees in the lands of Asia, Europe, and Africa.

The steps also bring us pleasure, for we like nothing so well as to converse with and instruct the oldest, most intelligent, fearless, and fearsome race among our pupils, the jaguar people. Unlike the other indigenous peoples, these folk are unafraid of us. We speculate at times if they are perhaps cosmic travelers such as ourselves, but they cross-breed readily with the less nobly endowed species, avoiding genetic defects.

We pitied our three counterparts that they had no intercourse with these superior humans. When we came to this planet, our needs were simple: we wished only to subjugate and civilize it, starting with the populations of a few major landmasses and progressing until we spread enlightenment and culture throughout the world. Four perfect beings who each know all that is needful to know must have room so that our presences would not seem a plague, the teachings of each of us would be perceived as properly awe-inspiring, and be duly appreciated, and our hunting territories would not overlap. We did not meet, or wish to. The other engineer founded an empire upon a great river, the inventor/scholar in a populous land of

*varying climates, and the navigator in a cold realm with a
vast and varied continent and many islands to roam.*

*We do not miss them. We are content with the society
of our supplicants, particularly our jaguar people, who
understand our less complex thoughts.*

*A maiden of their kind climbs toward us now, in her
hands a net frothing with gem-toned butterflies.*

*"An offering, Wind-bringer," she greets us with her
mind-tongue. The language of our kind, with certain variations, has become the language of our pupils, though we
use no words to communicate. The girl lifts the net and
the fluttering profusion bursts forth, their wings so fragile
and colorful compared to the massiveness and linear nature of the home world. As usual, we sigh with wonder
and incinerate them, pleasing the girl, who considers her
offering acceptable. We dislike destroying such a beautiful
gift, but this is how we accept offerings. We flick in the
ashes of the butterflies.*

*"Delicious," we say, the ritual response for comesti-
bles. "Thank you, but you really should not trouble yourself so. You know we are here only for your sake."*

"Yes," she says, and we are content.

*We fly north to inspect our irrigation project. We
teach our coastal people navigation, time calculation and
management, and star knowledge. They have brought a
stranger in our midst. An ugly, hairy fellow who sailed to
our shores in a boat shaped like ourselves. His fellows
have drowned, but this in no way diminishes his overween-
ing confidence.*

*One day, while we supervise the installation of an
irrigation system involving the broad smooth lake in the
center of our realm, this outlander contradicts us. The sky
blackens, thunder rolls, light flashes, and as the smoke
rolls away, the outlander previously known to us is nowhere to be seen. Then, when the water below our landing
platform ceases boiling and the steam recedes, we see that
this man had another guise, one similar to ourselves but
more horrible. So horrible, in fact, that we flee from this,*

*our first sight of he whom my terrified people come to call
Smoking Mirror.*

Unfortunately, after so many years of peace, plenty,
and contentment, our people are excited, stimulated by
the violence of the transformation. They mistake Smoking
Mirror's appearance and believe we have begun taking
outlanders to ourselves as food. A trend has begun, soon
to spread throughout the land. We fly farther north,
confused, unwilling to share our domain with Smoking
Mirror by acknowledging his existence, fearing to appear
fallible before our people by informing them that if we did
indeed incinerate the outlander, it was by mistake. We are
never mistaken.

It is time to begin the dormant period which enables
us to renew ourselves. This is our first dormant period
since arriving on this world. Though our work is not
complete, we lie upon the topmost slab of our landing
platform in our northernmost land. We are too weak to fly
farther, too slumberous to do more than nod as the procession begins. This time there are no butterflies, no gems,
no birds. Only people leading other people, with no gifts
to offer but themselves. We are too sluggish to ingest the
offered ones, as we must to reassure our frightened subjects that we protect them still. That is when a jaguar
priest, considerate as a mother prechewing the food of her
hatchlings, cuts out the choicest bits for our delectation.

Suddenly the plaza is invaded with the kin of those
whose hearts we ingest. These people are making war on
those who honor us, and their battle cry is for Smoking
Mirror. We attempt to stir our wings, to correct their
error with a demonstration of our might.

We leap from the platform and soar low and wide,
past them, into the gray-green foam of the sea, where we
pass into oneness with the water for a time. When we
touch land again, it is centuries later. Though not yet
through with dormancy, we briefly arouse to hop-fly back
to the city where we find our landing platform half-buried.
A jaguar-man passing by looks with wonderment into our

eyes. Unable to instruct him, we merely draw from his dreams and those of his descendants a few fleeting visions of war, devastation, invasion, blood, and gold. More outlanders come clad in shells similar to ours, and above us they slay our people, trample our resting place with their horses, plunder, waste the land, and build ugly palaces. . . .

The dream had wound down from high tragedy to longing thoughts of *jalapeño* peppers and the cool green pool, when a sharp blow struck my thigh and I jumped. My head snapped sideways, my eyes breaking the hypnotic contact. The next moment I almost breathed fire without the help of the dragon. Claytie, one of her braids flying loose from its moorings, her face red with exertion, pounded anywhere on the scaly body she could reach.

"Let them go, you cattle-rustlin' monster!" she grunted, swinging the club. My thigh still throbbed from the blow that had connected while I was still linked to the dragon. Dolores jerked with each blow. I grabbed her hand and pulled her over the beast's tail before it could wake enough to exhale all over both of us. Claytie was so busy with her stick that she didn't stop until we were over the monster's tail. Dolores, her eyes blazing, clawed the club from the child's hand. I grabbed the stick from her before she got the notion to use it against Claytie, a definite temptation if ever there was one.

Purdy loped up the valley, the buffalo gun in his hand. I flung myself back over the dragon's tail and into the man's wake, frantic to stop him. Though I knew I could not trust the dragon to light my stove instead of me if the occasion arose, I felt I knew the creature better than my own father. Even if at best it was a little stuffy—all right, a pompous bag of hot air—I was not about to let anyone molest it, in case such a thing was possible. Dolores and I were in agreement on the matter. Her belly skimmed over the rocks as she took a flying leap toward Purdy and pounced on him.

"I'm real pleased you're so glad to see me, darlin',

but you are disembowelin' my ribs with this rifle. Your schoolmarm friend forgot to load it and took the blamed cartridges with her."

By the time I grabbed Claytie and intercepted Purdy and Dolores before they woke up everyone in Denver and Mexico City, as well as the dragon, Dolores was dragging her admirer back toward the cave. The dragon didn't stir. It was a wonderfully sound sleeper. Or was pretending to be.

Once in the shelter of the cave, Purdy renewed his demand that I give him the cartridges, but I was adamant. "No. Don't even think about it. You'll only make the dragon angry."

"You haven't observed the capacity of this shootin' iron for doom and destruction, ma'am."

"No, but I have observed that dragon at close range, and it is not a creature to trifle with."

Purdy licked his lower lip nervously. His eyes, dark as an Indian's, flicked back and forth from Dolores and me to the entrance of the cave. He reminded me of a wild beast looking for an escape route.

"If you knew that thing was the dragon, what were you all doin' just standin' there?" he demanded, his tone pettish with bewilderment.

I attempted to explain and he attempted to understand, but the truth fell somewhere between us.

When I finished he looked at Dolores for confirmation and received further clutching and a moody stare. Shrugging her off, he glared stubbornly at me. "Give me the rest of those cartridges," he said.

"Haven't you heard a word I've been saying?" I asked. "That thing isn't even from this world, and on top of that, it's so ancient that you might as well just call it immortal— Chinese dragons are, and from what I understand from our friend up there, they're close relatives. There's no way you're going to kill it with that little old rifle."

"Lady, I understand that you are tryin' to be helpful instead of a pain in the . . . neck, but I think that if indeed this creature has spoken to you, as you say, it's a damned liar. You talk like it's a sort of know-it-all traveler from Lord-knows-where. Why, I wouldn't trust somethin' like that any further than I could throw it. Furthermore, I don't see how a big lizard could talk to you anyway. More likely you're in-e-bree-ated or crazier'n a peach-orchard boar. Now, if you'll just hand me the cartridges, we won't debate the point any further. I'll put that critter down like a good horse gone lame. I'll be gentle, I promise. And this part of the country will be a lot safer for us all."

Men are such bullies. I had no choice but to let him have the cartridges. He was stronger than I was. Besides which, once separated from the power of the dragon's eyes, I was beginning to distrust what had seemed so convincing a moment or two before.

But that did not mean I was any more convinced that Purdy was right. Physical resistance having failed, I tried logic—in my experience a far less potent tool in dealing with the supposedly rational sex. "If you attempt to kill the beast now and fail," I said, "even supposing you survive the experience, which you surely will not, the dragon is apt to fly back to its other roost and be there to greet your friend when he brings Mrs. Ledbetter's water-gathering party. Why not let sleeping dragons lie for the time being? Perhaps the creature will doze until enough time has elapsed for the others to collect the water and return to the fort. At that point, you can blast away as long as you're able without endangering anyone except yourself and perhaps Miss Drake, Dolores, and myself."

"I could shoot him in the eye right now and have it over with. Or in the ear."

"The dragon has no ears that I could see, sir, and its eyes are, as I mentioned, covered with heavy membranes from which issue the hypnotic messages you so scornfully dismiss."

"Long range, then," Purdy muttered.

"No, mi amor," Dolores sighed. "Less than the full

force would do nothing. Nothing. The dragon is a god. I know. I called him."

"Then I wish to hell you'd send him on home, sugar," Purdy growled at her.

"Ah," Dolores sighed, "if only I could. I never thought the god would take my plea so personally."

Purdy's belligerence was fueled more by a taste for the dramatic than by a need to be martyred. He sighed, leaned the gun against the cave wall, and sat down with his back against the camel. Attempting to look casual and contemplative, he took out his pocketknife and began cleaning his nails. His hands were shaking so it was a wonder he didn't amputate a finger. "That's what you get for messin' with religion, sugar," he told Dolores, as if theology was the subject at hand. He looked down at his nails instead of at any of us. "I coulda told you that. Used to be a circuit preacher myself. Still do a marryin' or a buryin' now and then to keep my hand in, but mostly I gave it up for rainmakin'. It's more profitable. People expect you to pray to the Lord for free to bring rain, but if you make the rain yourself, they're more apt to see their way clear to rewardin' your enterprise."

Claytie sat down beside him, watching him and clearly waiting for him, as our protector, to make up his mind about whether we needed protecting or not.

But he was stalling in much the same way my father stalled when faced with the necessity of balancing the account books, by trying to overwhelm us with a barrage of words. "Now, I know there's some here as doubt me"—a hard look in my direction—"but like I said before, wherever we ply our trade, it always does rain. Sooner or later. As you may have noticed, clouds are up there pretty high in the outer cloudosphere. It takes even the most scientific modern devices a good long time to reach 'em—days and days sometimes. And of course, for the chief's dance to reach the Indian Rain Manitou, it takes ever' bit as long, not to mention takin' the message a while to soak in. But it does, and I know it will, because I got this power, you know. I know about rain like a water-witch knows about ground water, only in the opposite direction. Sometimes it just takes the clouds a while to catch up to me."

"In that case, Dr. Purdy, I must caution you against trying to eliminate the competition by raising violent hands against a colleague," I said, my need to have the last word getting the better of me, as it sometimes does. "In China, dragons are rain-bearers."

Purdy looked belligerent, frightened, and generally unhappy all over again. "Is that sooo— Damn, what's that?"

The earth trembled and rocks spattered like hailstones outside the cave entrance.

"That, Dr. Purdy, is opportunity knocking a second time," I informed him, rising.

"What?"

"The dragon, man."

Claytie beat both of us to the cave mouth, and pointed upward. "Look! It's goin' to fly away."

Purdy had the gun by then and was balancing it in the crook of one elbow while using both hands to try to light a cigar. The cigar lit, he hunkered close to Claytie and followed her finger.

I was right behind him. "Up there, see it circlin'?" he said unnecessarily. A dragon the size of a house is rather conspicuous. It flew above the portion of the canyon where the carcasses lay.

"We must act quickly," I said. "After it feeds, it will want a drink."

Purdy was not listening. "I'm goin' to slide in as close as I can while it's thinkin' about its dinner. You hear me shoot, you set off the rockets and draw it off me." With that cryptic command, he handed me the lit cigar and tiptoed toward the dragon, keeping to the shadows and displaying stealth both admirable and astonishing in such a noisy fellow.

The cigar died before I could touch it to the first fuse.

"Here, let me," Claytie said, and grabbed it from me, puffing expertly until the end glowed.

As we fumbled I strained my ears for screams indicating that Purdy had kindled more readily than the cigar. Dolores fluttered about in the open, in plain sight, getting in my way by circling the rockets and wringing her hands.

I spotted Purdy again when he climbed atop a rock and took aim. The Sharps buffalo rifle is a weighty weapon and its report must have roared, but the dragon's roar absorbed it, careening off the canyon walls, filling the riverbed, and gonging from the cliffs. Somewhere deep within all that sound must have been Purdy's scream. His mouth opened wide with agony and fear at almost the same moment the dragon's mouth also opened to spew a gout of green fire toward him. Purdy didn't wait for it to reach him but dropped the useless weapon and ran.

I dabbed the lighted cigar to fuse after fuse. Fire sizzled up the wick to ignite the gunpowder in the first as I lit the tip of the last. I dived for the cave, tripping over Dolores and Claytie. We sprawled in a heap as the rockets whooshed skyward, one singing after another into oblivion.

The dragon screamed again, its dark and windy shadow cooling the ground beneath us, its scream tumbling dirt and rock from the mouth of the cave. The camel brayed and tried to rise. Claytie threw her arms around its muzzle and held on. I peered out through the falling rock and prayed.

The dragon shot upward in pursuit of the rockets, its shadow shrinking, its frustrated scream diminishing in volume.

I prayed in Spanish for the first time that day. Fast Spanish too, my lips mimicking the prayer Dolores muttered until Purdy crabbed around the bend in the canyon, scrabbling toward us. His hair was more crimped and blackened than the chief's, his eyelashes and brows missing, his darkly tanned face red as with sunburn, and his hands already blistering. The burned hair almost smelled worse than the rest of the canyon combined.

"Melted the damn gun, bullet and all," he breathed. "Never . . . saw anything like it. Shot straight into its mouth and it melted the . . ." His eyes rolled back in his head and he crumpled, mercifully swooning before he could waste more energy in redundancy.

We dragged him inside as the last of the rockets died and the enraged dragon swooped down the canyon in search of its assailants.

We did achieve our primary objective, nonetheless. The dragon stayed away from the water hole. It kept us penned inside the cave for hours while it swooped up and down the canyon, its wings thundering, its frustrated scream threatening to bring the cave roof down on top of us. By the time it found our hiding place and poked its head inside the cave, we had found the tunnel.

11

I *should* say the camel found the tunnel. Despite Claytie's desperate grasp on its face, the panic-stricken animal lunged and jerked its legs spasmodically, trying to rise. One of its back feet caught in a small hole, and the frenzied kicks quickly enlarged it. Claytie lost her grip, but Purdy grabbed the bridle. The girl scrambled back as the camel flailed upward, and found herself sitting inside a new hiding place.

"Get out of there, you little nitwit," I said. "You'll be kicked to death."

"No, I won't. It's deep in here. Look." The enlarged hole telescoped from its small opening to a place fully deep enough for the four of us.

When the strip of sunlight from the cave mouth was suddenly blotted out and the cave filled with asphyxiating vapor, Dolores and Purdy needed no further persuasion to dive into the shallow tunnel alongside Claytie and me.

The dragon's head followed its putrescent breath, the latter somewhat filtered through the fragrance of frantic camel. The ship of the desert tried to crowd its bulk inside the tunnel with us as a giant snout and fangs materialized from the green mist. The snout bobbed experimentally from the wall shielding our hiding place to the other side of the cave. The great scaled craw opened ever so slightly and a thin pencil-lead of green fire disintegrated the wall to the left of the tunnel. No sooner had the flame shot forth than the snout jerked back, waiting patiently until the rock in front of it had melted. Then, once more the snout appeared, turning a little so that the next fire melted another section of rock, only an inch or two leeward of the camel's rump.

The solid stone bubbled and ran like hot fudge thrown against a wall. A droplet of liquid stone hissed against the camel's hide. The poor beast screamed a hoarse and hideous scream that died into a piteous burble.

"Ah, the poor beast, to suffer so . . ." Dolores murmured, for a remarkable change pitying someone other than herself. Claytie's hand, visible to the bony wrist in the faint green phosphorescent mist, reached out and stroked the twitching and trembling hide. "Poor Colonel. Don't be afraid. It won't get you here."

The green glow intensified as the snout reappeared. Suddenly Claytie's hand and wrist were joined by her forearm, elbow, shoulders, head, torso, and the rest of her as she toppled head over bloomers up *over* and across the camel's back and directly into the dragon's path.

"Heyyy," she hollered before her face, lit with an eerie green glow, screwed into a screaming knot as a talon the size of a wheelbarrow snaked in front of the dragon's snout, seized her by the back of her dress, and hauled her outside.

"Ohh, Lord!" Purdy wailed, and shoved past me. He was too big to fit between the tunnel's upper lip and the camel's back and lost precious seconds shoving and cursing his mount.

He broke through so suddenly that I ricocheted off the wall before following him through the cave mouth.

The dragon hunkered patiently in the middle of the riverbed, its other-worldly eyes glowing, its claw dangling the child in front of its face. It tried to turn her and the cloth of her garment ripped from its claws.

"Run, Claytie!" someone cried. Not me. Not Purdy. Not Dolores, who lingered in the cave mouth, watching the whole scene as if it were a play and she a not very amused theater patron.

The cry came from above us, momentarily distracting the dragon. On the ridge above the cave stood Felipa, the burn-scarred warrior, and his two accomplices. The three warriors, stripped of modern weaponry by their retreating tribesmen, pitted their skill as archers against the dragon, all three firing arrows down at the beast's inquiring face. The dragon opened its mouth as if to eat the arrows and they disappeared within the green light. The great lizard raised its bristling head to regard its assailants more closely. The three resorted to spears. While the dragon watched Felipa and the scarred brave, the other two leapt from the canyon rim into the riverbed, rolling lithely to their feet upon landing. The first to recover from his jump charged the dragon's rear with his spear, trying to duck low to reach the belly. The dragon rounded on him. Meanwhile the remaining brave jumped and Felipa half-jumped, half-slid after him. Claytie ran to catch her friend while the first two warriors charged the dragon with their spears. The dragon, covered on three sides, didn't seem to know whom to barbecue first.

It caught the spear jabbing for its left eye, its talons clutching as neatly as if they were hands, and thrust the missile back at its owner. The Indian was fortunately not firmly planted on the ground. Though the butt end of the spear barely tapped him, he sailed backward across the canyon to sprawl in the cadaver of a scrub brush clinging to the cliff wall.

The dragon peered at its fallen foe without interest and started to flap its wings, when another of the braves, loudly singing what I later learned was his death song, repeated his comrade's assault, this time trying to catch the monster in its mouth. The dragon seemed to have used up its patience on its first assailant. Or maybe it thought the Indian was trying to feed it something. At any rate, it spewed forth a gush of flame that turned the spear into ashes in midair. The barest tip of the green flame set the brave on fire.

The dragon seemed frustrated and besieged, despite the helplessness of those who pitted themselves against it. With a mighty beat of its powerful wings, generating enough force to totally extinguish the flames engulfing the hapless warrior, the monster took to the sky. The last Indian threw his spear quickly, unenthusiastically, and most inaccurately for a person accustomed to using missiles for hunting. His heart clearly was not in it. Fortunately for him, the dragon was well out of range by then and soaring off in the direction of the water hole.

Claytie, Felipa, and I rushed toward the charred warrior. His fellow braves tried to cow me by rattling their spears at me, but I would have none of that. I glared at them and used my handkerchief and a few precious droplets from my canteen to dab at the poor man's skin, which was by now really and truly red where it was not black.

Purdy sauntered over, trailed furtively by Dolores, who had snapped out of her dreamy daze enough to eye the Indians with dread. "Might as well shoot him," the good doctor opined on viewing the aborigine's wounds. "I got a horse pistol in Colonel's saddlebag."

"You'll do no such thing," I said.

"Why not?"

"For one thing, it is not a Christian thing to do, even to a heathen."

"I sorta gave that stuff up, like I told you, ma'am."

"Very well. It is not even a humanitarian thing to do, and if you have given that up, you may stay out here and consort with the monster for all I care, but the wounded man will be carried back to have his burns treated by Mariquilla."

"He's likely to be about as grateful as a cow pulled out of a mudhole for that kind attention," Purdy scoffed.

"Perhaps. But there is another consideration. Those spears his friends are aiming at us may not be effective against dragons but I venture to say they would not improve the health of any of us who are less well armored. I trust we may count on Felipa to explain to her kinsmen that we intend to see that the man is properly tended."

"Never let it be said that Alonso Purdy shirked his Christian humanitarian duty to the bloodthirsty savages entrusted to his care," he said piously.

Felipa argued with the braves briefly before they lowered their spears and unceremoniously hoisted their comrade and carried him to the cave entrance. Trying to get the wounded man on the back of the terrified camel provided the only levity of the day.

The Indians, quick to recover from the crisis, reacted to Purdy's trusty steed with awe. Once they were assured that the good Colonel was not another demon, they laughed and poked at it while they slung their companion more or less tenderly across the soft woolen camel blanket. Purdy had regained his horse pistol while coaxing the camel from the cave, thus restoring the balance of power to his favor.

His face was redder now and his speech became less precise. His eyes appeared feverish as he passed his hand over his browless, lashless, and quite naked-looking eyes. "How about if I was to hold this gent on?" he asked. His usually limber tongue seemed to have trouble twisting around the words. "Here you go, lady. You want to be in charge, you carry the horse pistol home."

He mounted behind the wounded man, collapsing only a little less thoroughly. He did manage to encourage the beast to rise and convey its human cargo forward. Dolores held onto his leg and steadied him while the braves walked on the opposite side, guarding their own wounded. Felipa and Claytie fell in beside me. Claytie stayed far to the outside and hung behind.

I did not need Purdy's horse pistol to maintain order. The Indians seemed more baffled than hostile. Felipa did her taciturn Comanche impersonation. Claytie whispered nervous and rather whiny questions to her occasionally, but was otherwise quiet.

Even Dolores refrained from demented behavior and made a quite sensible suggestion that the sun wasn't doing the burn victims much good. At her urging we took shelter in El Mellado's abandoned hut.

"Excellent idea," I said. "Perhaps if we travel after dark the beast will be less likely to find us when it has that nicely lighted hacienda to attack."

I was not being so callous as I sounded, for, truth to tell, I finally realized that the scene I had just witnessed lent credence to what the dragon had intimated in its dreams, that being a reassuring but shockingly unprofessional disinterest in devouring humans. It could have eaten a minimum of four people when the Indians so valiantly but futilely faced it. It had almost gone out of its way to avoid damaging its attackers any more than necessary. Perhaps its nap and its snack of decaying cattle had put it in a mellow frame of mind. For whatever reason, I felt better about braving the desert than I had at any time since I was abducted from the mule train.

Very little could be done to make the injured more comfortable inside the jacal with its mud floor and bare adobe walls. I poked around with the horse pistol, daring snakes to slither out of holes, but none took me up on it. As soon as the camel was safely installed under the *ramada*, Purdy managed to crawl off into a cool corner of the abandoned building while the braves carried their friend inside and placed him on the mat of tanglehead grass old Benito used for a bed. Claytie huddled close to Felipa, half-mumbling, half-whining at her while the older girl nodded and patted her shoulder.

Dolores searched Purdy's clothing, which he affected not to notice, and produced a small knife. "I will go now and find some things that will treat these burns and help the pain. I need carriers." She smiled winningly at the girls.

"I'll go," Felipa said. "*Momentito*." She huddled with the two braves briefly. One of them rose to accompany her and Dolores, while the other remained behind, staring at Claytie, who scooted closer to me.

Purdy cleared his throat and rolled over. In the dimness of the shady jacal, his eye glittered like water.

I did not even have to rise to reach his side. I crawled two paces and was kneeling beside him. "Shh, Mr. Purdy. Do you need a drink? There is little left, but if you think you would—"

He shook his head with more energy than I thought he possessed. "No, darlin'," he rasped. "Just wanted to tell you—don't let Dolores get within reach of the little towhead. Next time that dragon of hers might be quicker."

"Are you trying to tell me that Dolores pushed the child into the dragon's path?" I demanded in an urgent whisper.

"Well, ma'am, I sure as the devil didn't, did you?"

I shook my head and pondered.

Purdy coughed and raised himself on one elbow. "I could use a little sip, but save the water. There's a flask in one of the saddlebags."

I dug until I found it, and fetched it to him. He took two gulps, replaced the cap, and seemed much improved. The Indian groaned, and I had to give him some too. "Don't hold it against her none, ma'am. Poor girl's had a bad time. Hates Drake for keepin' her from her babies, so I guess she thought she'd give that critter one of his. Seems fair enough from her viewpoint."

I lost patience with him. Had a plainer woman committed such a foul deed he'd have been ready to hang her. "If Dolores called the beast, I don't understand why the little fool doesn't just have it fly off, get her children, return them to her, and let Drake and his family alone."

"I can think of a lot of reasons," Purdy said, "such as: maybe she don't want her progeny returned to her cooked. And maybe the dragon don't know one kid from another. And maybe—probably—she might have called the damned thing but it don't listen to her so good now. Anyway, the kid is safe. Just keep her away from Dolores, and Dolores in range of that horse pistol, and you'll do all right. Now, if you'll excuse me, I believe I'll sleep a spell."

The culprit and her party returned shortly. I was torn about what to do with her. She had proved herself useful. From the store her gathering provided, we ate and drank cactus for dinner, though I made certain Claytie partook of nothing previously unsampled by Purdy or myself. After due consideration, I decided Purdy's advice was sound. To accuse her now would only cause further trouble. The girl was not in her right mind, if one charitably chose to believe that ordinarily she did not murder young girls, and she was dangerous. Better to pretend nothing untoward had happened, guard Claytie, and speak to Mrs. Ledbetter about the matter upon return to the fort. If we ever reached it.

Meanwhile, we munched cacti and soothed fevered brows, Dolores favoring Purdy's hairless brow while Felipa personally attended to the wounds of the badly burned Indian and to the older burns of Mariquilla's victim, Growling Porcupine. Like Five Horses Running, Growling Porcupine was one of Felipa's uncles.

"Growling Porcupine says I can be his son. He says he'll give me my own pony as soon as your papa buys new ones he can steal," I overheard her telling Claytie. Then, pointing with a downward thrust of her chin toward her current patient, she said, "This one, who fought that monster off you, is my cousin Rabbit in Hawk's Shadow. *He* promised to pay three ponies if I marry him." Claytie's eyes grew wide with alarm but Felipa grinned at her. "Don't worry, I told him I'm too young. Besides, I'd rather have one pony of my own than have to marry Rabbit while the ponies go to someone else."

Claytie seemed to agree that that was sensible and they had a bite of cactus together before falling asleep between Growling Porcupine and me.

By moonrise, as rested as any party of eight people and one camel can be after napping in a hot mud room the size of a pantry, and as refreshed as the cactus cuisine could make us, we set forth once more, across the night, heading for the single low saddle of mountains to the left of the hacienda.

I will not go into the fears and trepidations I experienced that night. I had to be very careful not to start when an owl called or a coyote yipped and bawled. The Indians watched me closely and smirked at each other if I betrayed the slightest distress, or so I fancied. All of us got a bit of a turn when, coming within distant view of the fort and of the little range of hills concealing the water hole, we saw that the top of the ridge was lit with individual fires. I knew by now what caused them. Felipa translated my reassurance to her cotribesmen that the fires were not supernatural in origin—or not very—but were merely more examples of the dragon's idea of target practice, trying its flame on greasewood bushes. The Indians nodded and seemed a shade more respectful after that, so I tried mightily to refrain from cringing at every large cactus with limbs like a man's arms.

We walked for hours, keeping pace more or less with the camel, until at last we reached the fort. The place was silent, the gate open. Inside the corral a mound of ashes and twisted metal blocked our way. The smell of burning flesh and hair clogged the night air.

"It got the horses," the chief told us when, much to our relief, we learned that the dragon hadn't eaten anyone else. "I'da come after you like we said except for that. Dammit anyway, couldn't you have stalled that horse-eatin' son of a bitch a little longer. We got—"

Purdy gave a put-upon sigh from his pallet and let Dolores administer Mariquilla's burn medicine while he sipped an internal remedy of his own. He seemed to need it. Though he tried to pretend to enjoy her ministrations, he watched every move she made with great interest.

"At least we got the water back here and unloaded first." Mrs. Ledbetter sighed, looking thoroughly done in.

"When we saw that critter comin', we thought you were goners for sure and we were about to be."

"It didn't hurt any of you, though, did it?" I asked thoughtfully. "In fact, through several rather violent attacks, it has failed or perhaps declined to hurt any of us, except for Rabbit in Hawk's Shadow there. And that was almost accidental. Tonight the creature was even kind enough to light signal fires to guide us home."

"You on good terms with it, are you, lady?" the chief demanded gruffly. "I wish to God you'd get it to buy us some more horses and a wagon, then. We are hereby wiped out." He fell silent for a moment, then grunted, "Those were damn good horses, too."

The poor man was down to his most distinctive piece of clothing, a colorful and very smelly pair of trousers fashioned from a jaguar hide so well-used the fur was wearing off and the spots were almost obscured. His red long-handled underwear covered his top portion but his sombrero and even the feathered headdress were lost with the wagon. He buried his angry face in his arms and brooded himself to sleep.

The rest of us sat in the darkness of the dining room, backs to the walls, facing the patio as if by common consent. The children slept, some of them whimpering and kicking in their nightmares. The chief slipped down the wall and curled in the corner, his robust exhalations punctuating the halting conversation. Our voices were hushed because our throats were full of dust. The light of the crescent moon, called the horned moon by the natives, glowed feebly through the now barless window and the gaping portal where the wooden doors once hung.

Everyone who had remained behind looked faded, with the possible exception of Mariquilla, whose eyes still sparkled with anticipatory wakefulness while she smoked like a chimney and ground seeds, roots, and leaves into a burn cure. Felipa sleepily applied a second application of the poultice to the injured brave. His brother warriors had made themselves scarce before we entered the compound.

150

This proved to be a wise move, since before I could apprise Mrs. Ledbetter of my suspicions regarding Dolores' murderous intentions toward Claytie, the clatter and rumble of horses and wagons and a loud pounding at the gate announced my host's return.

Old Benito awakened at the noise and gamboled like a spring lamb to greet the master who had imprisoned him. Though the aged shepherd had finally stopped trembling constantly, he remained far from blasé about having a dragon in the vicinity.

"Good thing that critter overlooked the chickens when it took everything else," Mrs. Ledbetter told Mariquilla. The strain of recent events had taken its toll on the sturdy housekeeper. When she rose from the bench, she put both palms on her ample thighs and thrust herself ponderously to her feet. "Cook 'em up quick as you can. I s'pect Mr. Drake and the boys'll be hungry enough to eat the dragon, but they're gonna have to settle for chicken."

Everyone roused and staggered out to the corral to greet what we felt with a rather fleeting sense of security to be our deliverers. I confess I almost enjoyed the sound of Drake's voice issuing orders, thinking it would be very nice from now on to let someone else worry about whatever disasters the dragon would wreak.

Hulda hugged E.F. down off his horse and held on. His dust-coated skin and clothing matched his gray hair. The seams in his leathery face were deeper, and his bushy brows drew together in a baffled frown as Hulda gripped him with a white-knuckled embrace. He held her and patted her shoulder and his face wore a look that boded ill for any dragon unwise enough to pester his wife further.

Kruger's face was both less reassuring and far less welcome. The blackguard was more full of orders than Drake. Many of Drake's *vaqueros* who had ridden out with the party were now missing. Instead, a quite different group jumped to obey Kruger's orders. The missing *vaqueros* had seemed to me a hard enough lot, no less chiseled from stone than these men, no less inured to hardship, and no less scarred. But they were mostly Mexican, experienced cattle workers. Kruger's henchmen were the trashiest of white border trash, as they would have to be to make their living taking not only Indian but also Mexican scalps. Though their behavior varied from wild to calculatingly calm according to the nature of each individual, a certain deadness underlay the expression of even the rowdiest.

Drake caught my appraisal of the group. "The savages took my dynamite," he said. "Ambushed us. Fortunately, John's old *compadres* were right near and helped us fight 'em off. But we lost a lot of men."

"So did they," Kruger added, grinning with death's-head gaiety. With a teasing wink at me, he opened his stained satin vest to reveal a belt fringed with bloodied black scalps.

Drake's lips folded inward to a narrow line as he surveyed the ruined corral. "Looks like we lost a few other things too," he remarked dryly.

"You did at that," Hulda replied. "And the way things have been goin', bringin' indoors the animals you got left might not be a bad idea. I wouldn't recommend the dinin' room. Since the rainmakin' fellas got here, the whole place smells like humpy-back camel."

Drake lifted an eyebrow but questioned her no further until the stock was safely lodged in the dungeon, a distinct comedown for the animals, since it smelled worse than any stable.

Hulda stood close to E.F. as he supervised the new stabling.

"You rode late tonight," she said. "Thank the Lord the boss didn't have you camp somewhere till dawn."

"Didn't feel right out there," he said. "Soon as we hit the southwest corner of Drake's land, the air smelled wrong. You want to know somethin' funny? There ain't no drought in New Mexico. The Rio's full just about fifty miles west of here and then it sort of disappears into the ground. Spooked us all, even Kruger. We saw a cloud of black smoke late this afternoon and a lot of little fires lightin' up the mountains back of here from a long ways off. We figured we'd better make tracks."

A shriek issued from the dining room and Mariquilla, brandishing the mano from her metate, chased a dripping scalphunter from the patio. Laughing and spitting, the man played tag with her, hiding behind the last of the horses.

"Old woman, have you lost your mind?" Drake asked. "Mr. Kruger and his men are our honored guests."

Even with Drake's personal intervention it took all of us to restrain Mariquilla from braining the culprit and five minutes of Spanish invective flowing from her mouth more rapidly than the recalcitrant Rio had ever flowed to learn the reason behind her displeasure. "Your pardon, *patrón*, but your honored guest just dumped over his fine and glorious body, which is soon to be his corpse, one of the five barrels of water for which we have all of us this day risked death."

Drake glared at her and stalked toward the dining room. He was too late to prevent several of the other men from lavishing another precious barrelful of water on their toilets. With a few well-chosen curses Drake forestalled further depredations and sent Mariquilla back to her dinner preparations.

By the time the Ledbetters returned from the stables, Mariquilla and Dolores were passing out chicken-filled *tortillas* to the new arrivals.

Drake polished his off and leaned back from the head of the table, lit one of his cornshuck cigars, and told Hulda, "I would be gratified if someone would tell me what's been goin' on and where these extra people came from. Like the nigger and the fella that looks like a plucked chicken. And who cooked the Indian, and why didn't they finish him off?" Claytie had moved from her sleeping position next to Felipa and half-dozed with her head on

153

the arm of her father's woven leather chair. Her thumb was in her mouth.

Lovanche Jenkins hovered in the background until her brother's attention was not divided, then made a perfect ninny of herself, flinging her ripped ecru lace bustle onto the bench beside Drake's chair and lifting a similarly lacy wrist to the spot just above her eye where ladies having the vapors for some reason usually place their wrists. "Oh, Bubba, it was a *night*mare," she said. "A perfect *night*mare. Why, I was nearly killed a dozen times. Then Dr. Purdy and his slave came to our rescue and tried to make rain but that awful monster attacked. I can assure you it was quite without my approval that Claytie Jane accompanied Miss Lovelace and the doctor up to the shut-up. As you can see, the poor child is in shock and her dress is simply *ruined*." Were I punctuating her sentences as she spoke them, I would place a question mark at the end of each, where her voice rose as if asking for agreement.

Drake stared her to a stammering halt and, rather to my surprise, Kruger slipped onto the bench alongside her and patted her shoulder with one hand, her lace-clad fingers with the other.

That night I had some idea of why Drake had succeeded in that country as well as he had. He must have simply worn down the competition. We were all exhausted, but he and his men had ridden nonstop since before dawn. The *vaqueros*, the scalphunters not standing sentry duty, the horses, the lower-echelon maids, and the children were all allowed to go to bed—in their own rooms for a change. But Drake stayed up, showing no sign of slackening his questioning until he was satisfied that he had a full report of occurrences in his absence.

Mrs. Ledbetter provided him with a rough sketch, not sparing the accounts of the trouble and anxiety we had experienced, nor the pains to which we had gone—twice—to procure enough water for the needs of the hacienda. Dolores flickered at the doorway while helping Mariquilla finish the cooking chores. She glanced at Purdy, who was struggling to stay awake on his pallet by the window, and, with an unmistakable pang of shame, at Claytie. Then she looked directly at me and put her finger to her lips before returning to her work. I had no intention of concealing what she had very nearly done to the child, but I thought I might at least wait, now that she appeared more or less lucid again, until she had a chance to explain herself before turning her back to Drake's tender mercies. As it turned out, she was safe enough for the time being, since Mrs. Ledbetter included in her synopsis of events what we had told her of our adventures in the canyon, and I was not asked to tell anything. Drake ordered the rest of us to bed while he and Kruger repaired to his office.

The following day bristled with domestic activity. Drake directed most of his employees into the desert, to cut new ocotillo stalks for fencing and for rebuilding the *ramada*, to harvest sotol for the animals and also for human consumption, to cut barrel cactus for the slaking of human thirst, and to singe prickly pear for further animal fodder and thirst-quenching.

Drake interrogated various staff members all morning. After each conference, he and Kruger closeted themselves in his office. My turn came last. Kruger left as I entered, to my great relief. The man gave me a knowing grin quite out of keeping with the depth of our acquaintance.

Drake tilted his desk chair against the wall, his boots, the spurs fastidiously removed, propped up on his desk. He did not rise to greet me but continued to stare out the front window toward the dry riverbed. "Guess you're gettin' quite a story here, eh, Miss Lovelace?" he commented. His lower jaw worked back and forth as if his teeth hurt.

"Certainly not the one I expected to write, sir," I replied cautiously, standing like a schoolgirl in front of the teacher's desk, waiting for permission to sit.

He faced me and stared at me thoughtfully for a long moment, then ran his hand over his eyes and waved me into the leather-slung chair. "Pardon my manners, ma'am, but I confess I'm distracted near to death with practically losin' my place overnight. I'd be obliged if you could tell me more about this monster. Especially about what happened in the canyon."

I told him frankly what I had seen. I did not tell him what Dolores had confessed or what Purdy and I had guessed at that she had not yet confessed. I started to tell him about the dragon's dream, but before I could get beyond the images of pyramids and lines of worshipers bringing sacrifices, Drake interrupted.

Thumping his chair solidly on the floor, he jumped up, pacing. "You know what that could mean, don't you? You read the manuscripts. Kukulkan. The feathered serpent itself come back to earth. Whooee. If the blasted thing weren't so fond of my livestock, I'd feel plumb honored." He halted, his pale green eyes piercing, his hands flapping together like broken bird wings behind his back. "Kruger thinks you women have been eatin' peyote buttons, and I declare if it wasn't that the herd is gone and the Indians fought us like wildcats just to get away from us, I'd be inclined to agree with him. As it is, I got to believe you because I can't kill somethin' I don't believe in. How do you reckon I should go about it?"

"I'm not strictly certain it's necessary to kill the creature, Mr. Drake. It seems reluctant to kill human beings, even when attacked, and I gather from the dream that the only time it has done so is in ceremonial situations, when presented with sacrifices, and even then—"

"Miss Valentine, you are too softhearted for words. Of course it has to be killed, much as I hate to see it. We can't just keep lettin' it gobble every livin' thing on the place. Much as I would like to chat with it and see things its way, it is a big ol' critter and it is runnin' me off my own land. And it ain't like there's anywhere else for it to go. Lord knows, if I could think of some way to break it, I'd show the rest of the country a thing or two, but we

156

can't afford bargainin' time. Just tell me how to get rid of it."

"I'm afraid I'm at a loss there, Mr. Drake. As Dr. Purdy will tell you, a heavy buffalo rifle has already been used against it to no avail."

Dr. Purdy had not told him anything because Dr. Purdy, along with the chief, the camel Colonel, and the injured Indian, had been incarcerated in the dungeon with the livestock.

I suggested to Drake that he had acted hastily, since Purdy and the chief, along with Felipa and the Indian, had saved his daughter's life.

"Yeah, so I hear. Just the same, I think they'll keep pretty good in there until I make some sense out of things. I was kinda hopin' you'd help me out on that, Miss Valentine. Kruger and a couple of the boys and I are goin' to ride up tomorrow and take a look at the canyon and around the water hole, see if we can find a place to maybe mount an explosive charge. I'd like you to come along and show us just how it all happened."

"What if the dragon is in when we visit its lair?" I asked.

"Don't you worry your pretty little head, ma'am, Kruger and me will take care of you. You just show us what you saw and we'll handle the rest."

On that dubiously comforting note I was dismissed.

By bedtime the work of the day had drawn some of the scalphunters and *vaqueros* into cozy relationships with those among the unwed servant women who had no desire to await the arrival of a monster without a man to hide behind. On the previous night most of us had been too spent to care for anything but the elusive luxury of sleep. Besides, the dragon had already fed on the chief's team the day before. By now it would be rested and hungry again. Claytie begged to stay with her father, but he was not about to be saddled with a child. To the consternation of both Mrs. Jenkins and Mr. Kruger, he insisted that

Claytie and Felipa stay with Auntie Lovanche instead, with a guard outside their door.

The light of candelilla candles glowed in his office window all night, as I could clearly see since the dragon's fire had consumed the upper half of my door. I hung a serape there at first, but then felt I would rather see what was happening than not and pulled it down again. I lay fully clothed upon my rope-strung mattress and tried not to open my eyes every few moments to watch for a telltale glow in the sky.

I hoped Dolores would be able to smuggle in Mariquilla's treatments to Purdy and the Indian. At least Drake simply kept the men imprisoned instead of following Kruger's suggestion and summarily executing them.

I had just closed my eyes when I heard Drake's door creak shut. Spurred boots rang across the patio. I tensed. The light in the room shifted abruptly. Shadow flooded my doorway.

"How you doin' there, missy?" Kruger asked me softly, a finger lightly stroking the scar running from above his ear to his chin.

I blinked at him, making no move to rise or welcome him. "Trying to get some rest, Mr. Kruger, as I suggest you do."

"Oh, I intend to. But I needed to unwind, and thought I to myself: I'll just go visit that little gal and take her the present I brought her."

Even *my* father warned me not to take gifts from strangers. I doubt he could have conceived such a loathsome inducement as the bloody necklace Kruger dangled before me, a strand of woven glass beads, bone, and claw.

"See here, Mr. Kruger, I hardly think—"

"Nothin' to think about, darlin'." He knocked open what remained of my door and dropped the beads on my stomach, towering over me. "You're the first new white woman I've seen out here in a long time. Young too, if a mite over the hill for marryin'."

If he fancied I would consider myself wooed by such observations, he was mistaken.

I attempted to sit up but he pushed me back down again with the point of one finger in the hollow of my throat. When he withdrew the finger an inch or so I said, "Mr. Kruger, this is not seemly. We are both guests here and—"

"Wrong, missy. You are workin' off a bond and I am about to become part-owner of this place."

"That is *not* my arrangement with Mr. Drake," I said, knowing very well from the aroma of his breath that it was no good to argue with him.

"Things have changed," he said. "Like havin' half the fort burned down, all the stock run off, all the customers turned on Mr. High-and-Mighty Drake, and his women all crazy with chewin' locoweed. If there is some big ol' bogeyman out there, we'll get it all right, but Drake's needin' a little ass-istance. I need a place to bed down regular in my old age. I choose right h—"

He crumpled on top of me and Dolores dropped the mano stone with which she had clobbered him and hauled him aside with more distaste than if he had been a pile of horse manure.

"I must talk to you," Dolores said, wringing her hands as she stepped over the body on the floor.

"So I gathered. You have a way of making your presence known. I suggest we find somewhere else to talk. We'll let Mr. Kruger believe he awoke with a particularly bad hangover in a particularly unfortunate location. After which, I will seek lodging with Mariquilla—"

Dolores made a small face to indicate that that would not be such a good idea and left it to me to imagine why.

"Very well, then. The Ledbetters. Now, come, tell me what you have to say on the way."

"I know you think that I am *loca*—no, that I am worse, that I gave Kukulkan the child from malice. *Señorita*, I swear to you as I have sworn to Alonso, I did not."

"Like Dr. Purdy, I am aware only of my own innocence in the matter," I said, the intended sternness of my demeanor relaxing into puzzlement when I recalled that the girl had just spared me a most unpleasant ordeal. "You . . . er . . . you mean to say that perhaps she jumped over the camel? That you did not push her."

"Oh, no, *señorita*. Most certainly she did not jump and most certainly I pushed her. But I did not do it to *harm* her. I did it because the god told me to and I could not help but obey."

"The god told you to?" I stopped in the jagged striped shadow of the partially rebuilt *ramada*. Looking full into her face, I searched for signs of the dreamy derangement she sometimes exhibited but saw only frank appeal and anxiety that she be believed in her tilted black eyes. "When was that? I didn't hear anything."

"Ah." She sounded disappointed. "Alonso told me you brought me away when I faced Kukulkan. I assumed the god spoke to you as well."

"Not *to* me exactly," I said.

"But then, I suppose since you are not one of the god's special people, that is why he wanted to see you. And Claytie and Alonso. I only obeyed his command by pushing her forth."

"Your god was trying to burn us," I reminded her. I was still unconvinced of her innocence, but our conversation got no further because we were at the Ledbetters' door and I paused to hear what E.F. was saying about being damned if he was going to keep workin' at Fort Draco with Kruger on the place. After what he'd seen, he ought to talk to Drake, he reckoned, but he couldn't be sure Drake wasn't in on it, and Kruger would probably do for him the same way he had some of the other boys— them that didn't run away when they had a chance—nobody was going to convince *him* that was Indians who set up the ambush in New Mexico. He'd spotted Kruger flashing that mirror at his *avisos* in the hills a couple of hours before. Made him a little extra cautious ridin' between them cliffs and he was lucky to be alive and he meant to stay that way. But he had to come back for Hulda. Soon's he could figure how to get away unnoticed, they'd both leave.

Dolores bit her lower lip as if she still wanted to say something, but I knocked quickly, unwilling to have E.F. compromise himself and Hulda any further within her hearing. The girl gave me a mournful glance, pressed something into my hand, and fled. I barged in on the Ledbetters and explained that I did not feel safe where I was. I intimated that Kruger seemed more interested than I liked, but I did not tell Mr. Ledbetter how the villain forced his attentions on me for fear E.F. might take it upon himself, however reluctantly, to confront Kruger on my behalf, a measure which would serve no one. I need not have worried. We had enough to confront that night without picking fights with one another.

The dragon visited us again. Though it had finished off every large head of livestock on the place it probably figured that Drake had an endless store that reproduced itself as it was consumed. Or maybe not. Maybe Kukulkan just happened to be in the neighborhood as it hunted the coyotes which still flourished in abundance and happened to sense the new horseflesh as it made its rounds. Or maybe the ancient creature was lonely again and decided to have another try at convincing its prospective converts to see, literally, the light.

Around three in the morning the coyotes began singing lustily, keening what the Indians would have called a death song. The rising wind carried the ghostly hoots of owls within the undulating dust veiling the mountains and the moon. I rose from my pallet beside the Ledbetters as I felt more than saw a lightninglike flash outside the barred window. Cracking the door, I stood concealed in the *ramada*'s shadow, a borrowed shawl wrapped around me, swaddling my nose and mouth. Red lightning, heat lightning, flashed far beyond the northern wall of the fort. I hoped that was what was agitating the chorus of coyotes that seemed to surround the fort. All at once they all fell silent. Holding their breath, saving it, cowering.

A startling *ki-yi-ing* yelp rent the night. The sacrifice had been chosen.

Above me footsteps pattered and jangled as the guards on the roof ran to the edge, trying to see beyond the walls. Sand crunched under their boots and huaraches. Hammers clicked as guns were cocked, and shells thunked into chambers. Then silence again, except for the wind and the spatter of the blowing sand. The duststorm had risen after I joined the Ledbetters. Red lightning flickered again, piercing the gloom and throwing the mountains into spectral relief.

The guards stood listening, holding their fire, saving ammunition. The Indian raid had wiped out most of Drake's stockpile. Stepping out from under the *ramada*, into the open expanse of working courtyard, I saw Kruger's men standing easily on the roof, their postures reflecting relaxed watchfulness. Such men did not frighten easily. They were unaccustomed to encountering anything more frightening than themselves.

When they did fire, they fired almost in a single volley, and even then their shots were futile. I ran across the courtyard to get a better look.

As I ran, the dying yips of the coyotes were joined by frightened whinnying from the dungeon—the horses reared and pawed at the fence, screaming a warning. E.F. rushed from his room to calm them, Hulda in his wake. I huddled into my shawl, watching them run for the dungeon, where the horses shrieked their fear. The dragon was near, but I did not know how near until suddenly the cottonwood pole supporting the *ramada* in front of me slumped sideways, dumping its stalks into the courtyard. At the same time an explosion of splintering wood shook the ground as several tons of scaly beast rent the broken doors of the storeroom further asunder. I heard the guards screaming about it to each other. The dragon either flew in to attack under cover of the storm or got lost in it, ramming into the storeroom door with stunning force and suddenness.

The men on the roof stumbled backward from the crumbling edge of the roof, where the storeroom's entrance disintegrated underneath them. One *vaquero* lost his hat and groped blindly for it as he half-fell, half-crawled out of danger. One of his comrades trampled both the fallen man and the hat and clubbed at him with the butt of a rifle when the poor fellow reached up and grabbed at his leg for support.

The remaining sentries vaulted over the edge of the roof and onto the patio without waiting for the ladder. Kruger's enforced sleep had not incapacitated him enough to prevent him gaining the roof even as his henchmen deserted it.

He chuckled gleefully and smacked his hands together as he gazed down over the ruined west side of the storeroom. "Hah! Got it now! It's trapped." Only someone as crazy as Kruger would have greeted that particular development with optimism.

From the patio Drake bellowed up at Kruger an excretory expletive I will not repeat.

I had to see what was happening directly, to actually observe the dragon firsthand. I raised the bolt and ran through the west gate just as a spike of coiled tail flashed by the gaping aperture further up the wall where once the huge doors had safeguarded Drake's treasurehouse.

Drake arrived at the same spot from the opposite direction at almost the same time, having run around the building through the patio entrance. "It'll burn us out," Drake screamed up to Kruger, his voice anguished and his eyes transfixed by the squirming mound of muscle undulating across the break in the wall. "It'll set the whole damned place on fire."

"I think not," I told him, my voice muffled by shawl, shortness of breath, and a liberal inhalation of gritty dust. "When we were trapped in the cave it refrained from using its fire—I think it feared to use its flame where the heat would recoil on it."

The three-foot-thick adobe wall buckled on the left

side of the hole, the side nearest the river, and that portion of roof caved in.

"It's wedged inside between the pillars," Kruger cackled. "Lord God Almighty, Frank, did you see that thing? Hey! You! Norwood! Partain! Get that cannon over here pronto. We got us a dragon."

Kruger had obviously never heard the proverb of the fellow riding the tiger. I wondered how we would manage to "dismount" now that we had this dragon where we supposedly wanted it. Several of the hirelings apparently wondered the same thing, for they lifted the cannon from the roof above Drake's office and hauled it with the speed and strength of desperate men to the hole in the storeroom wall.

From the other side of the dungeon wall horses and men screeched in concert as the dragon bellowed its frustration and rage. Not to be outdone, Hulda Ledbetter hollered above everyone, "You there! You dagnabbed redskin, get that horse outta there and no blasted further, you hear me? Purdy, get that humpbacked horse of yours out of the way."

The louder the horses whinnied, the louder the dragon roared, its roar growing more and more strident as it strove to reach the horses it heard but could not see.

Something cracked with the force of an avalanche and Drake groaned, "It's snapped a pillar." The roof above the hole in the wall slid into the desert. I backed quickly away from it, right into a clump of Spanish dagger. Limping and hopping cautiously back and to one side, I found a safe place from which to watch as the *vaqueros* dragged the cannon into position.

"Anyone got a goddamn light?"

"Don't ask me. I swallowed my cigar."

"*Estúpido!* Where is the ammunition?"

Another crack and the spiked back of the beast humped above the crumbling roof.

A very large *vaquero* who looked as if his face had been hatcheted from granite by an inept sculptor, a man formidable enough to dissuade me from wanting to meet him in the dark or any other time, fainted as neatly as a fashionable matron.

Someone located the grapeshot for the cannon two shattered pillars later as the west corner of the roof was spun into the desert with hurricane force. Above the collapsed roof the spined ridges of the dragon's back loomed through the duststorm. Near the wall adjoining the dungeon a great gout of fire erupted through a jagged rip in the roofing.

Adobe bricks flew, men screamed, women screamed, horses screamed, the dragon screamed, I screamed, though I didn't know it until a raw throat and a mouthful of sand caused me to desist.

The dragon's head reared suddenly above the ruined roof, smoke and flame collaring the beast's massive neck. The cottonwood shingling and timbers of the ceiling were aflame. The dragon shrieked, unbearably high and shrill, its fire rebounding to bake it like a lobster in its shell.

It craned its neck toward the corral and shot another, weaker flame in that direction. At that moment Drake's men fired the first volley. The next bolt of flame, shot from about fifty yards above and beyond the attackers, did not quite reach them but melted the shot in midair and dissolved the mouth of the cannon.

As the men stood in various poses of disbelief, a horse galloped from the corral gate and toward the men. E.F. ran after it, swinging his rope. The dragon's flame cooked the horse before all four hooves touched the ground, and E.F. swore. I don't think he thought about what he did next. It was so illogical, he couldn't have. He did what any *vaquero* might do when something threatens his charges. He coiled his rope of spun and braided *lechuguilla* fibers and it spun from his hand, striking at the dragon's head.

I wish I could say that that heroic action solved our problem, but of course it did not. The dragon crisped the rope in midair and might have crisped E.F. too but I flung myself against the old wrangler, knocking him backward, out of range and into a patch of cactus.

The great tail sent another avalanche of bricks and mud toward us, but the debris fell foul of the whipping wind and short of us. The beast's flame was growing weaker now, and the wind deflected it as well. Its huge hypnotic eyes glowed above the flame. It screamed again, this time its pantherlike roar, that awesome half-hoarse grunting growl. I cringed into my shawl but I couldn't help peering into those eyes again and feeling something of their power, being drawn to it so that my mind stretched toward that crouched behind those passive wild orbs.

Trapped! Oh, the depravity of these barbaric people! Where is our priestess that she allows this? Ayyi! This structure disintegrates around us with a flick of the tail. Its flimsiness sends it crashing down upon our wings and would cost us scales, but the initial backlash of our torch dies into fuel-fed fire so we are no longer at risk. Is the increased diet we undertake for the sake of punishment and increased grandeur truly worth the strength necessary to transport it? As if having their shoddy building collapse upon us is not sufficient to try our patience, these mortals fling missiles at us—is this an assault by the disciples of Smoking Mirror or some new sacrificial rite? Really, we must have discourse with our priestess and instruct these folk upon proper ritual procedure. But our wings loosen of rubble—ahhh!

Adobe sprayed like water from a fountain as the great tail and torso churned its way through the wreckage. At last the wings flared above the flames, catching them with a golden edge for a moment as the heat sloughed away while the huge body rose into the air. It rose for only a heartbeat, then dived straight toward us. I stumbled backward again, painfully, my eyes still seeking the dragon's, but they were below me now, concealed by its upended body. Some of the men ran, some fell over flat on their backs and tried to crawl away like upended turtles. Ignoring them, the dragon's tongue, now as large as its tail once was, pulled the horse into its mouth. The beast ground its massive jaws twice, belched another fiery bolus, and launched itself skyward.

Its final lashings and the beat of its wings extinguished most of the most obvious flames, but the stunned men had to be rallied. Hulda and Mariquilla rushed forth with axes and wet serapes, chopping smoking timbers free and smothering them. The maids followed with more blankets; and E.F., Purdy, and the chief were right behind them. Even the children helped. Even Mrs. Jenkins. If this fire was not extinguished promptly, we would be homeless in the desert, with no shelter from the beast or the storm. We worked the rest of the night, muscles straining against the wind, sand in every pore, sustaining splinters, cuts, burns, and smoke poisoning. When most of the fire was finally under control and the worst of the damaged section of storehouse cut free from the rest of the building, E.F. and two other men set forth with their ropes to recover the escaped horses. Only a few had followed that poor fellow foolish enough to cross the dragon's path. Many of the others had run to the far corner of the corral, herded there by the chief and Felipa, to tremble themselves sick. Only the one, Mr. Drake's own spirited and beautiful black, had died.

The unconscious scalphunter revived, Claytie cried over the horse, Mariquilla chewed her cigar silently as she threaded through the smoldering rubble treating wounds, and another of the scalphunters, unwounded, sat curled into himself rocking back and forth, saying "Lordy, Lordy, Lordy, Lordy" over and over again. Though I knew of the dragon and what it was capable of, the extent of the destruction left me feeling empty, as if the end of the world was close at hand and the dragon its harbinger.

Drake paced through the ruins, issuing an occasional order and chain-smoking his cornshuck cigars. He did not appear to be in shock or even unduly upset. His expression was similar to the one Papa sometimes sported when he had gleaned new information which provided an important twist in a news story.

Kruger's reaction was the strangest of all. Once the battle was over, he inspected the cannon, capering around its melted barrel, scratching his whiskers, and laughing to himself. "That's some kinda critter," he said to no one in particular. "Yessir, that is *some* kinda critter. All hellfire and brimstone. I like that. Reminds me of me." Drake, far from being annoyed, glanced up from his reverie and smiled slightly at Kruger, as if actually amused at his antics. Kruger grinned fiercely in return.

"I understand now about them stories you told me, Frank," Kruger said, wetting a corner of his mouth with his tongue. "I allow as how if I had thought of it, I'da tried what you accused me of. But I never could have come up with a lalapaloozer like this Coocoocan critter of ours."

Drake nodded, staring down at the dust as he methodically crushed a cigar butt with the toe of his boot. Then he looked up at Kruger and nodded again. "You thinkin' what I'm thinkin'?" he asked.

"I reckon so. Powwow?"

Drake nodded again and the two retired to Drake's study and locked themselves in while the rest of us busied ourselves cleaning the site and taking stock of the damage.

During siesta one of the children found the second golden ornament.

Too nervous to sleep, I rested by sitting in the shade of a toppled pillar, where I recorded the new attack in my journal. Claytie and Felipa squatted in the dirt beside my pillar, sifting through the sand looking for salvageable merchandise. The wind had finally abated, carrying the vestiges of extra heat from the fire with it. Outside the perimeter of the ruins, Mariquilla moved purposefully, stooping low to gather this or that desert plant, searching for more that would heal the wounds of the previous night. She had removed the cactus spines from my flesh and treated them to prevent festering, remarking that if ever a stranger to this land had managed to inflict upon herself every minor ill it had to offer while luckily avoiding the hugest of disasters, I was surely such a one.

Dolores crept out of hiding as soon as the dragon disappeared. I ignored her probing glances, thoroughly fed up with her. Her cowardice angered me all the more because it was so silly. She had the power to call in a dragon, to converse with it and require it to eat a herd of helpless animals for her sake, but she was too spineless to do anything to halt the destruction because she feared to make her role known to Drake. Or perhaps she still wanted Kukulkan to pull the world down around us all. Never mind that many people besides Drake would go hungry, thirsty, and homeless, to end up at least injured and possibly eaten. And what of the rest of the country? I was inclined to agree with the dragon that its current priestess must be a far cry from her ancestors. If she was going to practice heathen witchery, she ought to be more decisive and responsible about it. Nor was I mollified by her apparent attempt the night before to bribe me into silence with the dirty little ornament—possibly a lapel pin—she must have picked up in the dirt somewhere. The frog design did not appeal to me in the least.

The discovery of the second jewel very quickly shed a new light on the first.

"Señorita, señorita, see what I have found!" A very young child tugged at my skirts, and I deliberately ignored her while I finished my paragraph. Felipa, whose patient had fled with his kinfolk as soon as Hulda opened the dungeon, once more decided I was not a bad sort and designated herself protectress of my adult prerogatives. Pulling the child away from me, she said, "Do not disturb the *señorita, muchacha*. She is creating a history."

"But I wish to give her this thing," the child declared.

"You may give it to me," said Claytie, whose pinched dusty face again resembled that of the spoiled little girl I knew before she was dangled by the dragon. "I am your *patrona*, after all."

Mariquilla and Dolores, their baskets loaded with

plant matter, returned to the house, Mariquilla rolling her eyes at our little drama as she passed.

"No!" The little girl clutched it to herself.

"I cannot work with you girls bickering," I said, not because I was any crosser with their noise than cactus stabs, burns, splinters, a sleepless night, heat, and a nagging uncertainty that I would live until the following day, or even the next hour, usually make me. I simply wanted to point out their bad manners. Since the older girls should have known better, I sided with the youngster. "I should very much like to see what you wished to give me, dear. I was simply preoccupied."

She placed the amulet, sticky from her hot little hand, in my own hand. It was blackened with ash and dirt but glittered yellow where a bit of adobe brick had nicked it. I wiped it on my skirt and it flashed in the sunlight. Worn absolutely smooth on one side, it bore the face of a feline on the other—a fierce, slant-eyed wildcat type of feline, not a gentle house kitty. Through the ears were holes, from which it presumably could be hung.

"Where did you get this?" I asked the child.

She pointed.

The sluggishness of the day vanished in a treasure hunt. Between the four of us, Felipa, Claytie, the child, and I found four more pieces of gold jewelry, including a diamond-set bracelet in the rubble. The pieces all looked far too valuable to pocket as lost trinkets. They were puzzling, too, in that some of them, such as the cat amulet, appeared ancient, while others, such as the bracelet, were of relatively contemporary design.

I showed the ornaments to Drake as soon as Kruger left him alone in his office. The *patrón* of Fort Draco turned the cat over and over in his fingers, looking as pleased as if he had not just lost his home and livelihood. The mission manuscript papers, parts of which bore new underlining, lay scattered across his desk. The similarity between some of the drawings and the ornaments was easy to see even upside down. He fingered the other pieces one by one before asking, "You found these over by the storeroom this mornin', you say? Never seen anythin' like 'em before?"

"No," I lied blithely. My gift from Dolores was none of his business. "Should I have?"

"No, I reckon not. They sure don't belong with my usual inventory. I can't see any bunch of miners or settlers carryin' gewgaws like these around, though that bracelet might be a Spanish heirloom, maybe. The dragon—" He stopped himself with a cough. "Danged duststorm," he said. I was glad I hadn't told him about Dolores' bauble. His sly tone was not reassuring.

As if sensing my disapproval, he fixed me with a confidential and sympathetic smile. "I don't suppose after all you've been through you'd be up to takin' that little ride we were talkin' about yesterday, would you?"

"Yes, but I thought that was so that you could determine the dragon's strength and size. I should think you've seen enough of it for one morning."

"I have. Still want to have a look around, though. Could be somethin'll come to me. You see Mr. Kruger out there, you ask him to come back on in for a minute, will you? I want him to take a look at these things."

Kruger was lurking near the door, abusing the scalphunter who had fainted earlier. I gave him the message, and once he stopped trying to intimidate me long enough to understand that I was saying "gold," he sped into the office without so much as another leer. I returned to what was left of my room, the back wall having half-buckled in and the bed full of adobe mortar. Pulling on Papa's britches, still filthy and bloody, I was filled with foreboding and decided that the source of it was that I knew Drake was probably right. In the course of our ride, somethin' probably would come to him. The somethin' would be the dragon, which would eat the horses right out from under us if it followed its customary pattern. Actually, having survived several encounters with the monstrous creature, in the course of which I had gleaned some

171

insight into its personality, I was less worried about it than about having to sit a saddle horse again and keep my peace around Drake and Kruger for the duration of our trip. But Drake's suggestion that I ride with him had been issued as more of an order than a request.

We rode into the canyon as far as the place where the beast had lain before. My sores bothered me less than I anticipated, though they gave new meaning to the term "tall in the saddle," a position which at least kept me alert and allowed me some advance warning of things to come. To my vast relief, no scaly form blocked the dry riverbed. I showed Drake and Kruger the cave where we had hidden and also where the dragon had lain. We rode up the canyon, now totally devoid of carcasses, though not of their stench. Even the bones were gone, charred and digested with the rest of the bodies, presumably.

"I cannot believe it," Drake said, twisting in his saddle to survey the utter desolation of the valley. "Horses, cattle, oxen, sheep, goats, wild burros, even coyotes—gone. That dragon is worse than the railroad for clearin' stock off a piece of land." His voice held no little admiration, and the smugness in it was so inappropriate under the circumstances that it sent a small chill across the back of my neck.

Kruger and the others rode cautiously ahead but I sat with my hands crossed on my saddle horn, watching awe and guile wash across Drake's face in successive waves.

We sat there, eyes locked, I with all that practice from staring down bill collectors, he with all that practice looking sincere for government officials, until Kruger shouted.

He had found something and it was not more of the jewelry the dragon seemed to be littering the landscape with while pursuing its path of destruction.

At the closed end of the canyon, where it was supposed to be "shut up," a network of cracks extended from a gaping hole, over which Kruger and the two henchmen accompanying him leaned. Our horses had to skirt the cracks, the smallest of which were large enough to swallow horse and rider. The dry edges crumbled and broke under our weight, so the footing was uncertain. I was not nearly as concerned about all this when I approached the hole as I was after looking down into it. And deeper down, and deeper. Like the pit in Poe's story, this hole appeared to have no bottom. Kruger did the adolescent thing one would expect of a man of such mentality and threw a rock down it. I smiled, thinking that if the hole went all the way to China, as it seemed to, and the rock hit someone on the head, I would willingly translate whatever insults the victim wished to convey to Kruger. However, the rock elicited no response, Chinese or otherwise. Kruger tried a larger rock, but it too, seemingly, failed to land.

"Remember that little earthquake a couple of weeks ago, Frank? There you have it. Ol' Coocoocan got hisself born right here, if I'm not mistaken."

"Maybe," Drake said. "But I'm more interested in its family jewels than its birthin' place. I have a feelin' some of that jewelry is fairly local. Did you see the crest on that bracelet? That's the Rodriguez family's. There's been stories around here for years about how they buried all their gold and jewelry in one of the old Indian mines before the Comanche got ahold of 'em."

"You think the dragon has found a buried treasure?" I asked, only a little incredulously. I should have thought of it myself. Dragons were supposed to have hoards. Even Mexican dragons.

"Yes, ma'am, I do. And I mean to have it in compensation for my ruined land and animals."

"We mean to have it," Kruger corrected.

The fools! For all their posturing, and in spite of the graphic illustration with which they had recently been provided, they still seemed to lack a realistic idea of the dragon's power. It was my turn to look smug. "I beg your pardon, gentlemen, but it seems to me that unless you have a better cannon than the one the dragon melted last night, you'll do very well to keep the creature from depriving you of your lives, much less trying to deprive it of anything."

"Right there, little lady, is where we've been makin' our mistake," Kruger said. "See, Frank here's been readin' up on this dragon. Seems the old-time Mexican Indians worshiped somethin' just like it and they had plenty to eat, lots of water, and more gold than you could shake a stick at. We been goin' about this all wrong, sort of tryin' to kill the goose that lays the golden egg. Right, Frank?"

"That's about it, John. We are hereby fixin', Miss Valentine, to cease and desist all attempts to kill this rare and fascinatin' specimen honorin' our premises with anything more deadly than lovin' kindness," Drake announced. "In other words, havin' discovered that we can't beat it, we fully intend to join it."

12

"I beg your pardon," I said. "I'm afraid my heat stroke must be making me hear things. I thought I understand you to say you were going to join the dragon."

"You heard right," Kruger said.

"I did? Ah, yes, well, um, perhaps you'd be so kind as to explain what that means?"

"Now, come on, Miss Valentine, darlin', you know that as well as we do," Drake chided me. "You're the one told me how this critter was just dreamin' of havin' people worship it again and bring it presents and such, just like it said in the manuscript. Mr. Kruger and I had us a long talk out on the trail about the raids, and got to studyin' on what I should do to turn the tables on whoever was tryin' to ruin me. That's before we knew it was a real dragon, of course. A real dragon with a real treasure."

"Don't matter that much in the long run, though," Kruger said. "The stakes are just a little different."

"I'm still not quite following," I said, but recalling what Drake had said before, I was following all too well.

"Well, you may remember me thinkin' out loud that if somebody was fixin' to ruin me by pretendin' to be a dragon, and I could catch 'em and make 'em tell how they did it, there was no reason I couldn't do the same thing to somebody else to recoup my losses?" He sounded as if it was a perfectly rational and socially acceptable, even brilliant, idea. I nodded. "In the course of explainin' to John here how I thought he might have faked all that dragon stuff, we hashed it over some more and decided it was a pretty good idea. My place was already about shot. But with a little grubstake, I knew I could turn this to my advantage. That's when John offered to come in as partner."

"I always did set a lot of store by Frank," Kruger said, and spat a stream of tobacco juice to cover his embarrassment at making what was for him an emotional statement.

"Umm, just a moment. Mr. Drake, may I speak with you privately for a moment?" I asked. Drake shrugged at Kruger, who wiggled his eyebrows lasciviously. We rode away from the other men a bit.

"Mr. Drake, I think you should know that Mr. Kruger set the ambush that killed so many of your hired hands," I told him, hoping that the realization of just how far Kruger would go might shake him.

"Now, how would you know about a thing like that?" he asked me, not shocked, but wary.

"I . . . uh . . . he got drunk and came to my room and bragged about it to me," I said, avoiding implicating Ledbetter.

"I see. Well, that's a real serious matter. I'll have to talk to John about that. Don't mind havin' his boys on the place, but I insist on doin' the hirin' and firin' mostly. John's no good at it. Got too trustin' a nature."

I stared at him in disbelief as he led me back to the main group. "You know, I got to hand it to you, darlin'," he said. "You were sure right about that bein' a bona fide dragon. I've got to thank you for openin' my mind to the possibility so it didn't take me as a total shock. And I also appreciate you kinda playin' hostess to it for me, so that I know it's the kind of critter that can be bargained with, not just some big old prehistoric dinosaur with a big belly and no brains."

"You prefer an ancient alien god?" I asked, as if it was a perfectly ordinary question.

"Sure. If it's thinkin', it wants somethin', and if it wants somethin', it can be bought. You say our friend Kukulkan misses people worshipin' him and sacrificin' to him. Well then, we'll give him worshipin' and sacrificin' and he'll give us the rest of the country and the pot of gold where he got the appetizers he left behind last night."

"I . . . see," I said. I could not believe we were having this conversation. "No doubt the dragon will be glad that you wish to be reasonable, but you're expecting quite a bit, and I'm not sure in your current impoverished state what you have to offer in return."

Actually, I had a good idea, but what they were intimating was so preposterously wicked I couldn't believe my imagination was not running away with me. Though I suppose human sacrifice was not all that radical an idea for a pair of scalphunters.

"Why, we'll do missionary work for it, natcherly," Drake said, "spreadin' enlightenment to anybody too dumb to listen, until we have ultimately converted all those souls sufferin' from excess wealth—"

"Yep," Kruger said. "We'll give 'em a choice. They can convert from rich to poor or from alive to dead."

"But of course, those are only our long-range plans. In the meantime, Miss Valentine, what we really wanted to talk to you about, since you've had more to do with this critter than anybody, was maybe gettin' an introduction. I wouldn't have thought a Texas dragon would have much in common with a San Francisco lady, but it seems to have taken a shine to you. We want to know what else would tickle its fancy—or else."

"Mr. Drake," I told him, "you, sir, have been out in the wilderness keeping company with crazy people entirely too long."

177

"We're in a crazy situation, missy," he told me philosophically. "We all got to do our part to make the best of things. For instance, you can either throw in with us or be our first offerin' to your scaly friend."

"That would hardly make you popular with him," I pointed out.

"Oh, he wouldn't recognize you. We'd just leave your heart. That's how they used to do it, from what I've read," Drake said.

"Your reading is spotty," I told him. "There was a great deal more to it than butchering people, if you studied the manuscripts thoroughly. Even the scanning that I did with *my* rusty Latin indicated that those old rites were performed by specially trained priests who knew all the right magic words to say and who were supported by thouands of believers. The closest you two will come is to be hanged by hundreds of cavalrymen or perhaps a dozen Texas Rangers. Murder is illegal."

"Don't think of it as murder, Miss Lovelace. Think of it as a religious contribution. Why, maybe we could get the Reverend Dr. Purdy, as I understand from Sister Lovanche he used to be called, to take up preachin' again. We'll have to work out all the details. But I figure we've got time. If we don't get it right with you, we'll just keep tryin' till we do. It says there in the manuscript that ol' Kukulcan will go for it. They used to feed their statue of him hundreds of human hearts, thousands sometimes, and he liked that."

"Not according to him," I said. "He said it was a mistake. He said—"

"Miss Valentine, I'm surprised at you stoopin' to fibbin'. And about a spiritual matter, too. Never mind. John here'll get to the heart of the matter. We're fortunate to have among us someone with his expertise in sortin' out body parts from one another."

Kruger tested the edge of his bowie knife, grinning through yellowed teeth, his eyes, madder than ever, impertinently fixed upon the front of my shirtwaist.

What could I do? I was surrounded by armed men on horseback. I am not particularly adept at hand-to-hand defense techniques—particularly without a parasol. My usual weapon is my pen. "Mr. Drake," I said sternly, "this sort of thing will *not* look well in your biography."

Never has my quick native wit stood me in better stead. First Drake, then Kruger, broke into idiotic braying laughter, beside themselves with amusement at my helpless bravado. The other men joined them, slapping their knees and laughing so hard they coughed and gasped for breath and almost fell from their saddles. Annoyed as I was at their infantile behavior in this grim situation, I took advantage of it.

Drake's rifle hung in its scabbard. No one had even had sufficient respect for me to have a weapon drawn while threatening my life. Drake bent double, clutching his middle, tears rolling down his face. Who would have guessed the man had such a sense of humor? All the better for me. I jerked the rifle free, turned my horse, and galloped madly down the canyon while the four ninnies cackled at each other. My steed was fortunately a surefooted animal and managed to find her way down the stony part of the canyon without breaking her legs or mine.

Behind me, Drake called, his voice still bubbling with laughter, "Wait up, now, darlin'. Dernitall, wait up."

I had no intention of doing any such thing, but fled for my life. Glancing over my shoulder, I saw one of Drake's men trying to coil a rope, but he was too far back and laughing too hard. Kruger recovered first and whistled sharply to my treacherous mare, who stopped in her tracks, turned, and trotted docilely back the way we had come. I dismounted in an undignified hurry, landing squarely on my posterior with the rifle tangled in my skirts. Pointing it with the proper end toward my enemies, I bounded to my feet and backed quickly for the cover of the cave. They followed, grinning like death's-heads.

"Oh, Lord, John, look at that. She's gonna shoot us for sure. I'm afraid we keep forgettin' that this pore little girl isn't from these parts—she's not used to our kind of funnin'."

No one drew a gun, though the one fellow still held his coiled rope.

"Yankee gals got no sense of humor, Frank."

"I'll admit that's how it looks," Drake said sadly. "C'mon now, darlin', you're gonna hurt yourself with that thing. You don't know one end of it from t'other."

"I don't imagine I'll hurt myself quite on the grand scale you were envisioning, Mr. Drake, and I have never been one to scorn experimenting when my neck is at stake."

"Darlin', you didn't take all that *serious*, did you?"

I glared at him and held the rifle more firmly.

"Don't be stubborn now or we'll take the horse and leave you out here," Kruger warned me.

"We can't do that, John," Drake said, pretending to be aghast. "That dragon's mighty hungry now. Soon as it sees she's all alone, it'll eat her up in a minute."

"I'll take my chances with the dragon," I said, and meant it. I preferred being killed by what amounted to a force of nature than by two of my fellow so-called human beings who would enjoy seeing me suffer. Compared to them, Kukulkan seemed downright moral.

"I could trick you into shootin', little lady, and you'd lose your advantage," Kruger said. "I'd bet even money you ain't much of a shot."

"I might get lucky," I told him. "It runs in the family. Irish, you know."

"Don't taunt the girl, John," Drake said. "We'll leave her out here tonight, since that's what she says she wants. By tomorrow she'll have either recovered her sense of humor or succumbed to the . . . er . . . elements or will have come on home by herself. Good day, ma'am."

With that, the vermin rode off, my horse in tow.

*   *   *

I was alone, and on foot, but I was not without resources. In the bag containing my notebook, pen, and ink I also carried a dainty pearl-handled pocketknife with a blade suitable for skinning rhinoceri. This was a gift to my father from Sasha Divine, who had received it from an admirer and had in turn given it to Papa, who gave it to me. He had his pride, after all. I also carried a hair comb, a handkerchief, and a flint. With these I was confident I would survive the wilderness far more easily than I could have survived Drake and Kruger.

The first part of my strategy was to try to remember all of Natty Bumppo's and Chingachgook's frontier tricks, which did me little good, since those worthy children of nature inhabited forested land and I occupied a desert. I also recalled some of the tips Ned Buntline passed along. Mariquilla's herb and cactus lore proved more useful than my reading. I had watched her and Dolores collect edible plants and knew I need not starve or die of thirst. I could build a fire and keep off wild beasts.

My chief problems were Drake, Kruger, and the dragon. Should I remain where I was or manage to be gone the next morning? Should I return secretly to Fort Draco or try instead for Fort Davis, finding my way by the stars, which I was not exactly sure I knew how to do?

One thing for sure. Sitting the rest of the day and brooding over my doom was probably the worst possible choice. I did what Natty Bumppo would have recommended in a similar situation. I headed for high ground. Natty Bumppo is not the only one who uses this tactic. As a small child hunting my native city for the precise tavern containing my revered parent, I often had to hike up the nearest hill and overlook the surrounding buildings until I spotted the correct one.

Shedding my skirt and using it for a shawl of sorts now that there were no men to see that I wore Papa's knicker-bockers underneath, I trooped up the riverbed. From higher in the hills I hoped to be able to see the cavalry fort.

I paused beside the dragon's pit, unable to help wondering what really lay below. Drake and Kruger had been so busy tormenting me they had not made a proper investigation. If only I had a very, very long rope I would do so. And perhaps some of those spiked things mountain climbers use. I was sure I could get the hang of them without much trouble. I circled the hole and found another jewel, caught in the narrow end of one of the radiating cracks. A gold ring with Kukulkan's portrait on it, though the beast had clearly gained weight and added legs since the ring was made. The ring was massive but not too large in diameter to fit my thumb. I slipped it on, thinking if I ever got back to San Francisco I would have to ask Sasha Divine's advice about a costume sufficiently redolent of splendid barbarity to complement my jewels.

If I ever got back.

I did my ruminating while I climbed, unable to afford the luxury of sedentary self-pity. The climb was long and hot but I kept my head covered first with just my bonnet and later by draping my skirt over it. Though the skirt nearly suffocated me, I kept it on, having learned my lesson about the sun. I also cut sotol and chewed it on the way, as Mariquilla had suggested. Nevertheless, by sunset, when I had gone as high as I could and found a rock to sit upon, I had to wait a moment while the rock pulled itself together from two wavery and transparent-around-the-edges rocks to a single solid, substantial stone.

I sat for some time recovering from the unaccustomed athletic activity, thinking dully to myself that had I stopped sooner, I could have not only seen civilization but climbed back down and headed for it instead of having to spend the night on this hill. I had purposely scaled some very steep and slippery places where men on horseback would be unable to follow, and I knew I could not retrace my steps now or find a new path down the promontory. That would have to wait for daylight.

The distant lights of Fort Draco looked deceptively warm and welcoming. That reminded me that I would need a fire of my own. I built one on the low side of my rock so the flame would be sheltered. Mesquite sticks and a stem or two of greasewood made a short-lived flame but one that drove off the sudden chill of sundown. I turned slowly, exposing as much of my person as possible to the fire. As I toasted, the lights of Fort Draco serially blinked out.

Beyond them, another light sped across the desert, playing tag with the hills.

I stared at it stupidly for a moment, then kicked at my fire to douse it. The feathered serpent swept ever closer. It had an excellent sense of direction. I hoped it might stop at Fort Draco for a little snack of horsemeat or preferably a bite of Kruger or Drake. On second thought, so far the dragon had done me no harm; why should I wish it such massive indigestion? On third thought, from the appearance of the approaching ball of green light, the harm it had not previously done me could be an oversight the monster was coming to correct.

13

I stomped on the fire to finish dousing it, but too late. The dragon swarmed toward me, its wind almost knocking me off the plateau. As I struggled for balance, the great creature humped itself into a small hill. Breathing on a clump of greasewood, it kindled a fire to replace the one I extinguished. The lamping green eyes turned on me full force.

Saying that I preferred the dragon to Drake was one thing. Actually facing it was another. What would I say? How would I address it? My mind was a complete blank, and I feared if I met those eyes my thoughts would become dragon thoughts. I fumbled for my journal, as I always do when at a loss. I flipped back to the dream and found the passage I sought.

"Ah, yes," I said. "Greetings, Wind-bringer and . . . er . . . Fire-giver. To what do I owe this honor?"

The dragon did not answer. I waited expectantly with my eyes lowered, maidenly modest, but quickly became very uncomfortable, and looked up to see the dragon staring at me with frustration just this side of wrath.

"How are we to converse with you if you refuse to look at us?" it demanded.

"Excuse me, Wind-bringer, I'm rather new at this

. . ." I said. I caught myself starting to stare at my note-book again and quickly fumbled it into my pocket.

"What is it?" the dragon demanded.

"Uh . . . nothing," I said, quickly producing it again so that the dragon wouldn't mistake it for a weapon. Drake's rifle was fortunately concealed by my cast-off skirt. "Just a writing tablet, see?" I held it up. It was a relief to have those big eyes staring at something besides my person.

A tear started in the dragon's eye and quickly turned to steam as it rolled down the scaly cheek. "Writing! All of our teachings have not been abandoned then."

"I should say not, your Wiseness!" I replied.

"Ayya," the dragon sighed, and I stepped quickly out of the way while the rock which once shielded my camp-fire melted. "Writing—very good. We wrought better than even we, in all our wisdom, realized when we spared you from your tormentors, for which we naturally accept your humble and everlasting gratitude. Have you sought us out to express it? Did the jaguar woman send you? You wear the disk of power, the ring of sacrifice."

"Sacrifice?" I said, quickly removing the ring and holding it out. "There's been a mistake, your Immensity . . ." I should have left well enough alone. Dolores had given me the disk sensing that I might need it and trying to protect me. It had thus far worked like a . . . eh . . . charm. Would adding the ring prove to be not only exces-sive but also fatal? "I found the ring near a hole. I didn't realize it belonged to you."

"All things belong to us. But the disk and ring are remnants of the priestly regalia which remain from our former reign. We recovered them from below and left them for the jaguar woman so that she might resume her duties. We assumed you were she. The herds are de-voured, the river swallowed. The ugly castle has been ruined sufficiently to convince even the most unreason-able king of the wisdom of heeding us. Where is his obeisance? Where are the multitudes seeking our wisdom and knowledge? This is not proceeding as we planned. We sense incompetence and we will not stand for it!"

The dragon was losing its temper and *I* certainly could not stand for that. "Wind-bringer, Wind-bringer, Wind-bringer," I said soothingly, "calm yourself. Why, don't you think the jaguar woman realizes that you aren't receiving the adulation and appreciation you deserve? Of course she does."

"She does?"

"Yes, indeed. In fact, she sent me to help correct the problem."

"Ah," the dragon said, as if it understood perfectly then. "As a sacrifice? For none but the jaguar people are priests—no substitutions accepted."

"No, great one, not a sacrifice, and not really a substitution. For, as you say, I am not one of your jaguar people. However, where my own people come from we have legends of beings like yourself—I was wondering if this might not be one of the other teachers who came with you. Perhaps the great affinity I have enjoyed with your illustrious self is because your colleague chose people from *my* line to be its priests. We're somewhat short on jaguar people where I come from. But we did have druids and fairies and that sort of thing."

"The Navigator never was especially particular," the dragon admitted. "In fact, we are quite certain it was one of his pupils who, by his impudence, brought Smoking Mirror among us. Smoking Mirror, who—"

"Yes, your Benevolence," I said quickly. "And that is exactly why I am here. You see, there aren't many multitudes around here anymore. Word has to be spread by writing to alert people to the honor you're bestowing on us all by reappearing. Your future worshipers will want to know all about you and, of course, this Smoking Mirror, so that they can adhere to your path and learn how to please you. That's why Dolores—the jaguar woman—thought it would be a good idea if I borrowed her regalia and came up here to interview you."

"Interview?"

"I ask you questions and write down your answers so that I can share what you tell me with others."

"Ahh, that is good. Such a device would enable us to spread our wisdom to the farthest reaches of this desolate land. Begin."

I extracted my pen and ink, and as I prepared to write, asked, "Wind-bringer, just for the record, you are, are you not, the famed Kukulkan, ancient god of the Aztecs?"

"That is one of our aspects, yes, though we never knew these Aztecs you speak of. They learned of us from our original peoples, the Toltecs and the Mayas. We learned of them in dreams."

"You communicate in dreams a lot, do you not?"

"We do. We make ourselves known to those with whom we have had primary contact through their dreams, and may, especially with jaguar people, visit theirs. At times we share one of our dreams of wisdom, as we did with the jaguar woman and yourself on one occasion. We have, while in our dormancy, periodically dreamed of events occurring on the surface. In this way we learned of the Spaniards. That fiasco was so disheartening we declined further dreaming until awakened by the jaguar woman."

"What do you dream of when not communicating?"

"The glories of civilization, sacrifices we have known and relished, and food."

"On the subject of sacrifices, Wind-bringer—that is the proper way to address you, isn't it? Or do you prefer to be called Kukulkan?"

"Either will suffice. Our true name is unnameable, naturally. But you wished to inquire about sacrifices?"

"In your dream, you intimated that the practice of sacrificing human beings to you was not your idea, but the result of an error"—the dragon's eye grew baleful and I quickly hurried on—"an error on the part of your worshipers, who mistook the arrival of your archnemesis Smoking Mirror for a desire on your part to devour humans. Is that essentially correct?"

"Essentially, it is—"

"Is it true then that you disapprove of human sacrifice? That you prefer flowers and birds and jewels and abhor the taking of human life?"

"We would not go so far as to say that," the dragon replied. "All contributions are, you comprehend, graciously accepted. We would particularly like a sacrificial beast now, or perhaps a harvest of maize or fruit—you do not happen to have such?—no, clearly you do not. Unfortunate. The land has suffered decline since last we dwelt here. Then we could have eaten daily as much as we have taken here altogether without depleting the supply. Though we have relished the sacrifice of the herds of the jaguar woman's enemy, we are still in need of food for daily sustenance." Its spade-sized tongue licked a cupful of dragon drool back in between the fearsome fangs.

"Perhaps I didn't make my question clear enough," I said, my own mouth dry and my pen shaking slightly. "What would your reaction be if someone, say Mr. Drake, the man you refer to as the king, and perhaps another person, presented you with the hearts of people you knew—even Dolores or myself—so that he could win your favor?"

"Our reaction? Ay yi, daughter of the Navigator, our reaction would be to pray you, if you have any influence with this King Drake, to see to it that he does not."

I allowed myself to swallow and my pen was somewhat steadier until the dragon continued.

"We are far too hungry for that practice. A human heart has much blood, but little mass—little capacity for energy for a creature of our magnitude. Fresh, there is no gas of decay for our flame. Decayed, the mass is even smaller. Altogether a most unsatisfactory repast. We were particularly dismayed during our dormancy to enter the dreams of these sacrifices and learn that their hearts, their thousands of hearts, were being thrown into the mouths of stone figures from which we could not possibly extract them, or burned in fires unconnected with our own except symbolically. You do comprehend, do you not, that symbolically is not the same as fillingly?"

"But didn't you care that those hearts belonged to people? According to the manuscripts, the best, brightest, bravest, and most beautiful of those you claim were students of yours were murdered by having their hearts torn out and fed to you. Even if it was only figuratively, didn't it concern you that they were slain in your name?" My voice rose in spite of myself and I gripped my pen hard enough to leave creases in my hand.

The dragon, however, replied mildly and without menace. "You exert yourself unnecessarily, child. Naturally we cared that our students were slain. We were not commenting on the quality of the bodies from whence came the hearts, merely on the nutritional value of the organs to ourselves. But it is true that the brightest, bravest, and so on were slain, and it is true, as you have pointed out, that this saddened us. But our people had already seen the face of Smoking Mirror, who would tear down all we build. That demon suggested to the jaguar people that they could rid themselves of enemies and rivals and provide themselves with the flesh of the victims as a source of otherwise forbidden food. This was most attractive to them when I had long lain dormant and the land grew fallow, the crops failed, and the animals died unculled by our hunting forays. Oh, Smoking Mirror wrought cunningly to time his appearance so near to the time of our dormancy. He reigned in our place, lying to and deceiving our poor students, leading them into degenerate practices so that their finest specimens died without issue to maintain the strength of the gene pool—no, you do not understand gene pool—their inborn heritage then. By the time Cortés came, he found a people still benefiting from the accomplishments of those who had heeded our immortal lessons. A final bitter delusion our enemy foisted upon our poor students was that Cortés was the reborn form of ourself. This was not true, naturally, though we did enter the dreams of the woman known as Doña Marina a time or two. Naturally, we did not intend that our pupils be exterminated, as they nearly were, but on the whole we think it less ignoble for them to die in battle than to die one by one as a reward for their accomplishments. Such a practice undoes all we taught. When those who excel are killed, a certain lack of incentive develops among the student population, you understand."

"Then you *would* refuse to accept that sort of offering in this life, I presume?" I asked, hoping I understood at last. The dragon, however, was a politician.

"Alas, child! We have not that luxury. The practices of Smoking Mirror have been written, even as you are writing, for many years. The people believe them to be correct. They believe them to be our decree. We cannot contradict a decree—even one merely attributed to us. Much as we deplore some ideas, some practices, if they are meant to honor us, we must accept them."

"But if they're only meant to bribe you . . ." I said, trying hard to keep my tone from seeming dangerously argumentative.

"That is the same thing. If someone wishes to pay us with a sacrifice to try to win the knowledge it is our primary function to provide, we must naturally provide that knowledge."

"But it's Drake. And a horrible man named Kruger. And all they want is the gold like that gold you shed the last night when you were trapped in the storeroom."

"Is that all? They want our hoard? But there are hoards all over this country. They could easily make their own instead of bothering with that that encrusts itself beneath our scales—we will gladly teach them the skill of finding and crafting the gold."

"But if they want to kill your other students, even your priestess, sacrifice them to you in order to get your gold?"

"That sort of thing is for you people to settle among yourselves. We do not destroy. We construct and civilize. If you destroy, if you kill each other, that is your concern. You have long been under the influence of our enemy and we understand this. Therefore your sacrifices may be less than entirely appropriate. Nevertheless, we accept any sacrifice to transfer our knowledge. While we are fond of gold and jewels and fine workmanship, it is of no real value to us. We sleep with it. We admire it and accept it as homage.

"But we have no qualms about dispensing such wealth in the interests of fulfilling our primary function. We would accept the sacrifices and allow the supplicant to obtain the knowledge of a treasure now and then, while trying to teach him sounder values."

"Surely you have had supplicants whose desires contradict each other," I suggested.

"Those matters they must resolve among themselves," the dragon replied. "If we concern ourself with what each granted desire means to all individuals concerned, we would have no time to fulfill our primary function. Generally speaking, our supplicants have been limited to those who apply to us under the supervision of our priests, those who wore the disk and ring. That seems to provide some sort of order."

"Since I'm wearing the disk and ring, could I ask you for something?" I asked hopefully.

"Of a certainty, child, provided you have a suitable sacrifice. Though we would not turn down a chest full of golden jewelry, we hope you have noted in our previous conversation that we would much prefer a large offering of comestibles."

"I haven't got any large chests of jewels or comestibles at the moment," I said miserably. "Don't you take humbler offerings?"

"They lack sincerity. Also, you are not truly of our priesthood, and your kind has already been proven to lack the proper reverence."

I trembled and my disarranged coiffure stood at attention from the roots out. My hopes of turning this encounter into some sort of triumph were crushed. I had counted heavily on the fact that the dragon did not routinely slay people (unlike Kruger), assuming it would save us from Drake's plot if it knew of it. But routinely was not the same as ritually, I now comprehended, to my sorrow. Though it wanted to control everything it could possibly receive credit or offerings for, the dragon was not interested in taking responsibility for the lives its interference destroyed—that burden it had neatly displaced to Smoking Mirror, the creature it had apparently concocted from its angry mirror image. Much as Drake left most of his dirty work to Kruger, the dragon left its imaginary enemy. An interesting device, but understanding it would be no help if one were the subject whose heart was removed and broiled. In that event it really didn't matter whether the deity responsible was Smoking Mirror or Kukulkan; one was just as dead. In the interests of avoiding instant death by immolation, I refrained from informing the dragon of my theories and strove instead to look as agreeable as possible.

It was the correct course of action. Unchallenged and apparently adored by a sufficiently inferior being, the dragon was beneficently inclined to continue the impromptu audience. "Lacking as you may be in that respect, however, you do write, recreating events as we, in our wisdom, created them. On our home world, the younglings serve the same function. We once produced such histories ourselves, though of course far superior to what you could hope to produce. Still, there is a kindredness of spirit between us and yourself. We find it comforting after all of these centuries alone. Therefore," the dragon continued, "let us dispense with sacrifices and interviews for the time being and keep each other company—we will impart to you some of our teachings for you to preserve on your paper, and you must tell us of yourself and your world, particularly the world beyond this realm."

It then proceeded to lecture me on ancient irrigation techniques, which could cause my cotton, I was assured, to grow already dyed in rainbow hues, navigation techniques, and mathematical and astrological formulas so complex I nearly fell asleep despite the alarming company.

I told it something of my journeys but it was not interested in the features which had fascinated me. People and their exploits were less within its sphere than crops, herds, rivers, lakes, ponds, and seas. It asked about the current location of the Gulf of Mexico and seemed edified to learn that that body of water had not moved far since the dragon had crawled ashore from it prior to dormancy. Noting its predilection for water holes, I thought it might go mad with rapture if I mentioned the Pacific Ocean, so I refrained. We passed the night thus in a sort of truce, until the sun began to rise again.

"Ah, if only we could find a snack after such an edifying conversation," the beast grumbled, "we could then sleep. Though we are able to teach more efficiently when pupils are available while we are this large, we also require far more sleep. It is tiring to fly our body around, and more tiring to find the food to fill it and to make fuel for the flames. Wait—what is that?"

Its predator's eyes spotted the horses and the lone horseman long before I did. If only I could have stalled before answering that I had none of the livestock the dragon craved, perhaps I could have delivered myself and the rest of those endangered by Drake's plot. However, I had no sooner made out the horses and that the rider wore the red flannel shirt E. F. Ledbetter favored than the dragon was aloft, swooping down upon the hapless horses, and paying no more attention to E.F.'s shotgun protests than it had to my attempts to enlist it on the side of the oppressed.

I descended the hill by the quickest route I could find, waving intermittently to try to catch E.F.'s attention before he galloped away from the dragon and/or got himself killed. The dragon's words—those pertaining to our situation, not those concerning mathematics and irrigation—ate at me all the way down, flashing into my mind when I should have been concentrating on my footing. Here we were about to be sacrificed to something ancient and alien that looked like a giant lizard and had the zealousness of a Jesuit missionary and the scruples of a railway company lawyer. That beast was not going to be happy when it learned that its so-called advanced knowledge was outdated by several thousand years. I could think of nothing such a creature was good for these days but raising the price of cattle and providing crazy people like Drake and Kruger with an excuse to murder, which they didn't need anyway. Though the dragon was not exactly a demon, it was not by any stretch of the imagination related to Jesus, Mary, or Joseph, and in the absence of any real demons was giving a pretty good imitation. While it was not bloodthirsty—for human blood anyway—it didn't discourage bloodthirsty practices: its attitude was aloof, as befitted its station, the god who couldn't be bothered with the petty problems of its worshipers.

Still, I had been safer with it than with Drake and Kruger, and that alone was enough to warm my heart toward it on a purely voluntary basis.

From a shelf about halfway down the ridge I stopped and watched E.F. shouting and waving his rifle up at the dragon, which paid him no more attention than it would an ant but enveloped him in its shadow while it mowed down the horses he had so carefully herded together. When the dragon did finally seem inclined to take notice of him, E.F. suddenly recalled he had both his own life and his horse's to save and galloped for the shelter of the cliff wall. The dragon nonchalantly tipped its wings and abandoned Ledbetter to gather its kill. It flew toward the water hole with the carcasses, now just so much dragon fodder.

The wrangler was cussing a blue streak as I scrambled down toward him. Having to swallow his words in the presence of a lady made his face momentarily red and puffy. His sharp gray eyes glittered from under their bushy gray brows. Even the hook in his long nose looked sharper. "I hope you had you a nice campin' trip, missy. When Drake and Kruger came back without you, nothin' would satisfy Huldie but I come out searchin' for you, and here I've lost four good horses."

His voice was rough with yelling in the dry, dusty air and his face grim with the loss of the horses, but I knew, despite his angry tone, that he was relieved he hadn't lost me as well.

"Thank you, Mr. Ledbetter," I said with heartfelt sincerity and humility.

He reached down, and I grabbed a strong bony wrist and swung myself up behind him. He did not ask me why I had been where I had been, what had occurred with the dragon, or what my status was at the fort. We didn't come within sight of Drake's hacienda until siesta time. When we were still several hundred yards from it, E.F. deposited me behind a mesquite bush.

"Huldie will fetch you by the west gate. Watch for her wave and come runnin'. I can't vouch for the lookouts lookin' elsewhere for long."

It was midafternoon, during siesta, and the compound was hushed. I heard E.F. shouting to the sentry that the dragon had killed the horses; at the same time, I saw Hulda. I ran quickly toward her. Thanks to the dragon, there was no longer any concealing vegetation for the last thirty yards between the gate and me.

Hulda wrapped me in a black rebozo and smuggled me into the kitchen. Despite the time, Mariquilla stood over her counter, dismembering peppers with such hard chops her whole body shook. When I entered she fixed me with a black-eyed glare that looked a lot like hatred.

She wiped her sweating forehead with the back of the

hand that held the chopper. I backed away from the anger in her face.

"So, worthless one, you return," she said with poisoned sweetness. "Please, enter, but do feel free to run away and make love anytime you wish. Do I care? No!"

"Who put the burr under your tail?" Hulda demanded, matching her glare for glare. "Miss Valentine needs hidin' and you're not bein' exactly dis-creet bellerin' like that."

"Miss . . . Señorita Valentina?" She stared under the black rebozo, which I slid back a little. "You are not dead after all?" And before I could respond, Mariquilla, knife and all, embraced me. "That Roberto, Kruger's man, he told me the dragon ate you."

"Rumors of my demise have been vastly exaggerated then, as you can see," I said a little feebly.

"I thought you were Dolores returning for something. That gringo—that Purdy. He came for her right after siesta began. He said he would take the camel and the two of them would sneak away to the cavalry fort for help. Ha! As though either one cares for what happens to the rest of us."

"Hmph," Hulda said noncommittally. "Well, maybe they do and maybe they don't. One thing's for sure, and that's that we need help from somebody. Anyways, I figure the safest place to hide Valentine is back in the pantry. Kruger ought to know enough to stay away from your kitchen now."

So I was stowed in the pantry with rows and rows of jars of pepper and sacks of other staples while Mariquilla returned to chopping peppers. Though no longer displaying her anger in the direction of my rebozo, she continued to sweep around her kitchen like a fury. When she turned to scatter the chopped peppers into the batter bowl, I had to dodge to escape being charred by the cigar clamped between her teeth at my eye level.

"For heaven's sake, calm yourself, woman," I said. "I just narrowly escaped being devoured by the dragon—I don't want to be branded by your cigar in the same morning."

"You *saw* the dragon?" Mariquilla asked.

"Yes, saw it and had a lengthy conversation with it, actually. It wasn't nearly as fierce as you . . ." I finished with an attempt at lightness undercut somewhat by the chattering of my teeth. Now that I was relatively safe, I began to feel the effects of my little adventure.

Mariquilla caught me as I dived headfirst for the floor, and eased me to a sitting position. While the room swam around me, she watched me for a long moment, tipping her cigar ash onto the floor with one rather elegantly long forefinger. "Forgive me, *muchacha*. Since Roberto told me what *el patrón* tried to do to you, I have been trying to think what to do to stop him and can come up with nothing. Dolores seeks help and Señora Hulda sends her man to search for you, but me, I am stuck here in this kitchen without an idea in my head. I thirst, I am inadequately aided in my work, I am surrounded by ruffians, and I have lost many old friends who did not return from New Mexico." She looked back up again, my last comment having finally soaked through her preoccupation. "You actually spoke with Kukulkan? What did he say? Why is he tormenting us?"

I tried to explain and got muddled, so I pulled out my journal and read aloud those scribbled passages from the interview that I could decipher.

"Ah, that Dolores," she said respectfully. "She knows how to curse. I give her that. But you know what distresses me most about this thing?"

"Other than the possibility of having your heart cut out and fed to a creature who'd rather have a nice fat steer or a string of chilis? No."

"Of a certainty, that concerns me very much, but around Francisco and Kruger, even without the dragon, dying suddenly has always been a better-than-average possibility. No. I am more concerned about the sacrilege. As I grow older I worry less about dying than about my soul.

You may think that funny, coming from me. I who have not been confessed since Padre Alfonso's visit last spring, nor taken Holy Communion. Frankly, I have not always been a very religious woman, and never have I had thoughts that Francisco worshiped anything but his own money and power, this more than his daughter or his poor wife, may she rest in heaven. But with this plan, he and Kruger will offend not only our Lord God but also desecrate the spirit in which Kukulkan was once worshiped as a benefactor by my most ancient ancestors. A very learned priest told me once that Quetzalcoatl, as he called it, was what made my ancestors better than savages, and perhaps even brought to them some of Christ's teachings before the Spanish came. I have always liked that idea, that God loved Mexico long before the *conquistadores* came. If this creature who rampages through our land and will eat our hearts if fed them is indeed Kukulkan, come back to rule the world as a demon at Francisco's command, such a connection is impossible."

Her voice was bleak. I understood. She felt somewhat worse than I would have had Saint Patrick reappeared on this earth as a werewolf. I was unable to be of much comfort. "Well, by its own account, Kukulkan isn't even from this world and it predates Our Lord's birth by hundreds of years. On the other hand, it wasn't until Cortés was mistaken for Quetzalcoatl that the Church was introduced to Mexico. So maybe there is some sort of a connection. How fortunate or unfortunate depends on your point of view, I suppose."

"Ah well, only children feel unhappy when they learn such stories are false, not old women."

"Don't worry. If Drake and Kruger continue, none of us will grow any older *or* unhappier. While we're feeling religious, though, I guess we can pray that the dragon will be satisfied with the horses it ate this morning until Dolores, Purdy, and the camel reach the cavalry post."

"*Sí. If* they return. I do not trust them, or the soldiers, and most certainly I do not trust Francisco and

Kruger to wait for them." She stubbed her cigar angrily into the counter. "*Ay*, I cannot help it. I like nothing about this situation. It is *malo. Muy malo.* If only I could think of a way to remedy it . . ."

I smiled. "A *curandera* would think in terms of remedy, I suppose."

The smile she returned was as tight and dry as an untanned antelope hide.

When Kruger gathered everyone in the compound onto the patio that evening, I began to understand why Drake had been so blasé about the ambush of his *vaqueros*. Kruger's scalphunters were much more likely to cooperate with certain schemes than honest cowhands. They were also much less likely to talk to the law.

The gates were closed and an armed scalphunter covered every door. Drake strolled casually out of his office once everyone was assembled. I watched him from the concealment of the rebozo. Mariquilla had pointed out that if I kept it pulled over my head, I could pass for Dolores, thereby delaying any suspicion caused by the girl's absence. Covering Purdy's disappearance was unnecessary, since Mariquilla was not responsible for Purdy. No one would come looking for him in the kitchen.

To all appearances, the only people missing from the assembly were myself, Purdy, and the chief. If Kruger believed the rainmakers to be within the compound, he evidently did not intend for them to be present.

Drake sent El Mellado back into the office and had him drag out the office chair, in which the *patrón* enthroned himself amid the chairless rest of us with the air of a father about to address his children. He tried to present a bland, benign countenance, but frankly, he had never looked so unconvincing. He wore several days' worth of stubble. His clothing was soiled and smelly, his hair dark with perspiration, and he plainly had been drinking. He looked harried, hunted, and haunted and I began to wonder if the methods that Kruger endorsed so casually really suited

Drake as well. The upward drafts of twisting shadow from the candle flames burning near his seat emphasized the hollowness of his cheeks and eyes. An owl hooted and I pulled my rebozo closer. The air was cooler now, time for rain—even snow, some years. But we had none. Just a few yellow-bellied clouds moving in to surround us at night, and the red tongues of heat lightning.

"I wanted to talk to you all about what's been goin' on lately," Drake began. He sucked on his cigar. The rest of us had to wait until he had blown it out again to hear what it was he thought *had* been going on. "We've had trouble before out here in the *despoblado*. Some of you folks been with me from the beginnin'. I always said I wanted to be the biggest and best, but I didn't exactly mean in the lizard department." He took another puff while an uneasy and rather forced snicker curled the lips of his audience. "Just the same, we have us a sort of special critter. Now, I admit, it's eaten all of our cattle and by now some of you may have heard that poor little Miss Lovelace disappeared while she was ridin' with Mr. Kruger and me up by its lair. We are truly sorry about that, but you all have seen us already try everythin' in creation to kill it, with no luck. Well, after we took a little trip up by the water hole yesterday afternoon, we began to think we've been a mite hasty. Mr. Kruger, shall we show the folks the saddlebags?"

Kruger hefted the bags, which seemed uncommonly heavy, and unlaced the leather thongs from around the buttons holding the flaps shut. Then he turned the bags upside down. Gold and precious stones sparkled in the candlelight as jewelry, loose gems, and coins showered into a drift at his feet. "The way I see it," Drake said quietly while the collective breath of his household sucked in with pure wonder, "this critter may have a powerful appetite for my stock, but unlike some settlers and Indians, it can pay its bills."

"The dragon *gave* you this treasure, *patrón?*" El Mellado asked incredulously.

"You might say that. Actually, it sort of let me find it.

There's a whole lot more up there, but we haven't negotiated terms just yet. Still, I think we can do that fine. Just have to let the critter know that we're reasonable folks. Now, what I want you all to do is give me a hand. We are, as you know, flat out of water except for the spring. Mr. Kruger and I didn't take anything bigger than canteens up there with us, so we couldn't bring any back. So what we figure is that all of us should go back up there. Not only are there more folks to carry water, but we can kinda make a welcomin' committee, lettin' that rich lizard know we mean it no harm—maybe take it another horse as a sort of goodwill gesture. Once we have the water, we can make the trek over to Mexico and pick up some more horses and cattle with this gold and we'll be back in business again. But we want to get enough water this time to last us awhile. I'm thinkin', now that we've figured out how to come through all this alive, it's a good time to throw one hell of a fiesta. We'll need enough water to see us through to Chihuahua to pick up stock, and we'll have to buy more than usual—our guest has a powerful appetite. I'll want you ladies to have enough to do some bakin', too. Day of the Dead is comin' up and I want you, Merenciana, to do us somethin' especially fancy this year. I know you've all been scared pretty bad, but everythin' is under control now. Once this little trip is over, we're gonna be back on our feet again, fatter an' sassier than ever. We may be out of the Indian-tradin' business and into swappin' with lizards, but I always did think there wasn't much difference between a Comanche and a reptile. Now then, everybody go get some sleep. Our guest ate four of the horses Ledbetter rounded up this mornin', so I don't reckon we'll have to do any unexpected negotiatin' tonight. I want everyone up at the crack of dawn with anything that'll carry water."

"Please, *patrón*, does not someone need to stay here to guard *el fortín*?" Old Benito still didn't care for that dragon, no matter how good a customer it was.

Drake laughed, not pleasantly. "*El dragón* ain't interested in *el fortín* as long as we're fresh out of stock for it to eat. And tomorrow we'll be takin' everything edible with us. No, El Mellado, Mr. Kruger and me and the boys would not feel right without you to help us guard the women and children—just till we get things straight with our guest. After that, we'll all be safe, mostly."

14

The skirmish ensued as soon as the procession reached the stand of mesquite where El Mellado had sheltered on our previous water-fetching jaunt. We would have been easy prey for a slightly larger or healthier band of Indians. All of us were afoot except for Drake, Kruger, and the four remaining men who were allotted horses. Everyone else walked, from E.F., who strode along in a pair of street shoes since he wasn't riding, to Mrs. Jenkins, who tripped protesting in the wake of her brother's horse, trying to maintain hat and parasol and fashionable riding-boot heels without stepping in something or tripping over her own skirts.

Claytie and Felipa tagged behind her, followed by Hulda. The poor chief was tethered to Kruger's saddle horn.

Mariquilla and I walked together, which was fortunate, since she kept me from falling over my own feet. My walking was exceptionally awkward. I had Drake's rifle strapped to my back under the rebozo, which was bound so completely over my face I had trouble seeing where I was going. I also found it hard to breathe in the heat, and like everyone else, I was intensely thirsty. Even cacti with a drop of moisture were becoming fewer and farther from the hacienda.

At least the rebozo kept out most of the dust. I choked on wool fibers instead. I had to turn my entire body from right to left to see anything but the back of Felipa's head.

When I saw the mesquite clump just a few yards head, I fastened my gaze upon it as if it were the Holy Grail, thinking only of its skeletally fragile and fleeting shade and of how I could avail myself of its maximum benefit for the maximum duration without drawing attention to myself. Therefore, I was the first to note that the bush wore a face—a crazed, disfigured face at that. I gasped and Mariquilla and Mrs. Jenkins both turned to see what occasioned the reaction.

The hapless Rabbit-in-Hawk's-Shadow leapt from the bushes at Kruger's horse. The move was suicidal, of course. The poor Indian was crazed with pain from his wounds, which had needed more extensive treatment than he had been able to receive before his escape. Why his fellow braves didn't prevent him from such a foolish action, I have no idea, but Kruger simply kicked him away and drew his pistol. The other two Indians caught up with their companion at that unfortunate moment. They were immediately surrounded. Kruger aimed his pistol at Rabbit's stomach, his aim slightly spoiled by the chief's attempts to keep from being trampled while the nervous horse stomped in place.

Though all of this transpired in less time than it takes to tell, Felipa grasped the situation and flung herself into the breach—between Kruger and his victim.

"Flip! Don't! Daddy, stop them!" Claytie screeched, flying toward her friend.

"Stop, John," Drake said calmly and quietly. So calmly and quietly that had I been Kruger, I might not have heard him, and had I heard him, I might have shot before his words registered. Kruger was a better listener than I.

He held his fire and his men did likewise while Drake clopped slowly back to investigate the ruckus.

The other two warriors already were, like Chief Rain-in-the-Face, being tethered to saddle horns. Felipa shielded Rabbit while trying to help him rise. Drake grabbed her elbow and jerked her back.

"This how you pay me back for takin' you in, squaw? Plantin' an ambush?"

"Daddy, she didn't!" Claytie cried.

"That's enough out of you, young lady. You set too much store by them that aren't your kind. I think you need a lesson."

From there on our procession was far more interesting, involving a lengthy trilingual discussion in English, Spanish, and Comanche. From what I could gather, Drake had trouble believing more Indians did not wait farther on. He accused Felipa of spying, which Claytie vehemently denied, while Felipa chose to play the stoic Indian-princess-in-captivity and refused to throw any light on the situation. Rain-in-the-Face, who was jerked around a great deal as Kruger rode back and forth between the captives and Drake, swore in all three languages, with a little Creole French thrown in.

The wonder of it was that the dragon didn't feel it was being invaded by a brass band. Whether or not it heard us, it did not greet us at the entrance to the smooth-rocked canyon, and our party reached the pool without difficulty. All but the prisoners were allowed to drink their fill before filling their vessels. Drake managed time-out from the argument by drinking and sharing his cup with his daughter and sister. He chased it with a drink from the flask I recognized as Purdy's before stepping cautiously behind the overhang.

He reemerged quickly. "Guess it's not home, John. Anyhow, have some of the boys bring that stone slab from the side of the hill down here."

"Good idea," Kruger said. "We can use that to dress 'em out."

The slab, about the size of a small table, was duly fetched and Drake looked at the chief, who had been watching and listening very carefully.

"Wait a minute," Rain-in-the-Face said. "What you talkin' 'bout? Dress who out? You gonna need somethin' lots bigger than that to do the drag—"

"I have no intention of trying to harm the dragon," Drake informed him.

"Well, there ain't many animals left," the chief said.

"Not four-footed ones, no," Drake agreed amiably.

Her timing impeccably bad, Claytie chose that moment to take some water in her father's cup to Felipa.

One of Kruger's men began to untie the chief's bonds, but Drake waved at him to stop. "Not him. Not now. I want to get rid of the traitors first. Our guest is used to Indians. Let's give it an Indian—one I gave every chance to be somethin' better. Guess you can't overcome inferior breedin'. Anyway, I heard them old Aztec gods were supposed to be real fond of young girls. We'll do her first."

Claytie dropped the water and whirled around. The armed horsemen had neatly boxed everyone else up against the lip of the pool. The stone slab sat beside the overhang, just outside the entrance to the cave. "Do what first?" she asked. "Daddy, what are you up to?" The horseman in charge of Felipa threw his end of the rope to another of Kruger's men, who jerked the girl to her feet. "What are you doin' to Flip?" Claytie demanded, her voice rising.

"Well, darlin', our rich guest is a mighty big, hungry fella and we just can't afford any more of the horses. I've treated this Indian gal like she was my daughter, just like you, all these years, and she betrays me, tries to ambush us all. You set too much store by her. You'd think she was kinfolk, the way you act. But you can't really trust this kind of trash, Claytie. I'll bet if the truth were known, she had a hand in bringin' that dragon here, not knowin' I'd find a way to dicker with it."

"That's not so," Claytie said. "If you want to know

about that dragon, ask your precious Dolores. She's the one who threw me out in front of it so Flip and Rabbit and Porcupine had to rescue me. Dolores is—"

Felipa threw her an angry look.

"Well, she is. Ask her!"

I was caught between the wall and the pool. All eyes were upon me. Under the circumstances, I thought I could at least dispense with the rebozo. As I unwound it with one hand, the other pulled Drake's rifle from its folds. I had the element of surprise on my side and was able to wrestle it loose before the men realized I had it.

"Well, how about that! It ain't Dolores after all. It's Miss Valentine, still pretendin' she knows one end of that shootin' iron from the other. Nice to see you all safe and sound."

"That's more than I can say for you, Mr. Kruger, unless you release the prisoners, have the men throw down their weapons, and allow all these people to go home before the dragon returns."

"You're a mighty particular woman, Miss Valentine," Drake said. "But in case you didn't notice, we have the drop on you this time. I suggest you set that thing down real carefully unless you want to lose both arms. By the time you figure how to fire that rifle, you could end up holey as a piece of cholla."

No fewer than ten firearms were trained on me. I followed Drake's suggestion.

"Now then, darlin', you just come on over here and see Mr. Kruger and we'll finish that job we left undone yesterday."

"Drake, what the hell are you talkin' about?" E.F. demanded, swinging himself in front of me. "What do you mean, pullin' guns on ladies? It's bad enough the way you've been treatin' this darky, who ain't done nothin' to you that I can tell, and pushin' around these Indians and F'lipa after Claytie Jane already tole you how they saved her life. But—"

"Old man, you don't understand the situation," Drake

said, his pistol now pointed directly at E.F. "Miss Valentine abused my hospitality by trying to steal a horse and runnin' off with my rifle, which you see as evidence before you. Normally, horse-thievin' is a lynchin' offense, but we had somethin' rather different in mind."

"Hold 'er for the marshal then," Hulda said. "The cavalry may not be any more convinced than we are that she wasn't plain murdered."

I didn't think I could joke my way out of this one. Kruger fingered his scalping knife. E.F. stood ready to take my bullet and both Hulda and Mariquilla looked eminently prepared to stop others. The only sensible thing to do was surrender. I couldn't help myself, though. I simply could not stand to let Drake have it all his own way. The pool looked cool and inviting, and I was hot and thirsty, so I jumped in feetfirst, splashing everyone.

In a proper story there would have been an underground tunnel leading to safety or somewhere I could hide with a reed to my mouth for breathing purposes while the villains pursued me in vain. Unfortunately, the underground spring fed through a hole no bigger than a skillet and all I got was a nice cold drenching.

I bounced up from the bottom of the pool expecting that Kruger and Drake would try to hold me under—a possibility far more attractive than allowing Kruger to cut my heart out—an immodest way to die, to say the least. But as I sliced up through the bubbly green veil I first heard the distant, muffled clarion of a trumpet and thought it was Gabriel calling me home until it was followed by a dulled crack of gunfire. I burst through to the surface, shaking water from my eyes.

The trumpet blared now and no one paid the slightest attention to me. All stood as if frozen, their backs to the pool. A strong wind rippled the water and a pall of darkness swept across it, chilling my exposed neck and shoulders. I craned my head upward in time to see the dragon's underbelly, broken into prisms by the water droplets still clinging to my lashes. Its wings spanned the width of the valley. I pulled myself out of the pool without hindrance or assistance from anyone and retrieved Drake's rifle. All eyes watched the dragon as it swooped down the canyon, a blue-coated squad of U.S. cavalry in hot pursuit.

I was not allowed time to dry off. As the cavalry galloped toward us, the denizens of Fort Draco crowded backward to allow the horses past themselves and the overhang. Along with Mariquilla, Mrs. Jenkins, E. F. Ledbetter, and two of Kruger's thugs, I plunged back into the pool, flailing to stay afloat as gunshots richocheted off the canyon walls, horses screamed, and hoofbeats thundered past. Purdy's camel, carrying the doctor and Dolores, trailed the cavalry mounts, but halted at the edge of the crowd.

"Dolores!" I hollered. "Purdy! Someone tell them to stop. Tell them they'll only anger it!"

And all at once the dragon let out its own terrible yodel. A long hiss of fire, a horrible stench of decay and the smell of fresh burning flesh coupled with the screams of man and horse. More people fell on top of us as the cavalry backed out from behind the overhang. Horses were never meant to reverse course with no room to turn.

"*Dismount!*" someone screamed. The trumpet let out a single blurt and died, E. F. pulled himself out of the pool and grabbed Mrs. Jenkins' hat. Her face, fat-cheeked as a chipmunk's, floated just beneath the surface, her skirts and hair spread around her. I grabbed a hank of hair and pulled, dumping one of Kruger's men from her shoulders, on which he had been standing to maintain his balance.

"*Dismount*, dammit! It's eating the horses! Oh, Lord, get off, boys, or it will fry you with 'em!"

The pool seethed like a river in flood while more men and horses retreated from the overhang, pressing Drake's people farther and farther back. I caught a piece of Mrs. Jenkins' dress, and it started to tear. When I tried to improve my grip to get her shoulder, I bent my fingernails backward and howled, but thrust my hand farther down and caught her before she disappeared. Her face, spitting

209

and blowing, came even with mine as another odoriferous sizzling hiss sounded from beyond the overhang. The earth trembled and rocks rained down on us. Then, abruptly, the sun was back, the wind was gone, the smell dissipated, and we were all hauled back to dry land while the cavalry counted their losses and demanded to know what Drake meant by smuggling in dangerous foreign animals who took unauthorized liberties with government livestock and resisted arrest, and what the devil did he intend to do about it anyway?

The lieutenant questioned Drake on the trek back and Drake responded in his characteristically smooth fashion.

Lieutenant Dougherty was the officer's name and I rode behind him. He had been one of my suitors when I was detained at the cavalry outpost. One of my married suitors, with an allegedly sick wife back in Boston. Some of the cavalrymen objected to their horses having to carry double, plus water bags, but when Dougherty explained that the alternative was to slow down enough to escort the pedestrians, the grumbling stopped. Even the wounded were so eager to reach the fort quickly that to a man they declined to be carried. Instead each rode with one of his comrades, since the wounded were those whose horses had been taken by the dragon. The dragon had also, to Drake's consternation, taken the precaution of sealing the treasure cave shut again. When Drake pointed out the still-sizzling stone to Dougherty, all parties concerned agreed to travel at once and talk later. Drake left the goats tethered in the canyon, just in case the cavalry mounts already devoured had not been sufficiently filling.

Once we were back at Fort Draco, the lieutenant showed his teeth. "Now then, ladies and gentlemen, I demand to know just what is going on here," he said, and despite our nervous protests, he kept us standing in the corral while his men unloaded the water and the wounded.

"Why, General, sir," Purdy said, "it's just like the

lovely lady here and I told you already. Mr. Drake is tryin' to illegally feed citizens of the Republic of Texas and members of the human race to that dragon whose ass you chased out of the valley, beggin' your pardon, ladies."

"Startin' with me," Rain-in-the-Face interjected.

"He tried to murder me yesterday," I said plaintively, clinging to the lieutenant's epaulets in a manner I'm sure Sasha Divine would have prescribed.

Drake held up his hand for silence. The group obeyed because they were used to doing so. "Lieutenant, sir, far be it from me to call a lady a liar, but Miss Valentine tried to steal one of my horses, and if you'll just take a look at that shootin' iron she's totin', you'll see my initials engraved in silver on the stock. Now, what say we rest after our narrow escape and discuss this matter over brandy and cigars like gentlemen?"

All seemed lost as soon as the lieutenant accepted, for he was not, as I well knew, a man of impeccable moral character. Not inherently dishonest, perhaps, but swayable. And Drake not only was a silver-tongued devil but also had all that gold in his saddlebags.

Back in the kitchen Mariquilla blasphemed rapidly and thoroughly, wondering how she was to feed so many more gringos on nothing but *tortillas*, beans and chilis— mostly chilis, the beans being almost as scant as water by now. Had she not kept a good portion of the food stores in the pantry rather than the main storeroom, we would have run out of food long before then. Still, she hated to set a scanty table. The soldiers had always praised her cooking and she knew they liked meat. She cursed Drake for leaving the goats in the canyon—*cabrito* would have been a dish fit for guests. She made a large drama out of a small problem, thus distracting herself and anyone who cared to listen from the larger and more frightening issues.

By the time dinner was served, the lieutenant, full of Drake's brandy and puffing one of his cigars, said that he had actually investigated Purdy's complaint simply to get his hands on Rain-in-the-Face as well as his accomplice—

the men were wanted for fraud in several states, and the U.S. marshal had asked the army to cooperate in apprehending them if possible. After several more snifters of brandy the young officer said that upon deliberation, it seemed to him that unauthorized Mexican dragons were more a matter for the immigration authorities than the cavalry. If Drake would kindly repay the army for its lost horses, the soldiers would take their prisoners and depart.

The other accusations were not repeated. Drake preferred to handle them himself. The only further action he wished to take was to have the three renegade Indians bound over to the cavalry with the rainmakers, and Felipa with them. "I can't handle her anymore, Lieutenant Dougherty," Drake admitted sadly. "These Indian kids are like wild animals, you know. Cute when they're cubs, but they'll turn on you as they get older."

I frothed at the mouth and would have said something except that Dougherty was no longer listening to me. I flounced away from the table, fuming, and stalked toward my own room. Dolores, her face bleak and pale in the frame of the black rebozo, grabbed my arm with taloned fingers and pulled me under the shadows of the *ramada*.

"*Señorita*, you heard?" she asked. "They intend to do nothing to help us and they will take away my Alonso. After we rode so far to bring them. Is there no justice?"

"Apparently not."

"But they should see that we speak the truth! All is well at Fort Davis. Their well is not dry. Their cattle have not been disturbed. Their horses roam free. Can they not tell that Drake has been singled out for punishment for a reason? Why will they not help us?"

"Well, they probably have other things to do," I said wearily. "You know, cleaning weapons, shining their boots, preparing for inspections. Uh . . . training. That sort of thing."

"They must be made to care. Kukulkan cannot be stopped alone, and me, I am not a strong woman. If Don

Francisco forces me, I will show him how to serve the god. And I will despise myself. Please. You must help me."

"Dolores," I said, "I have already done everything I can. When I spoke to the drag . . . to Kukulkan, it wanted sacrifices, and Drake is prepared to give it sacrifices—us. If the army is too thickheaded to see that, the only alternative I see is to abandon this place and strike out across the desert. Your large friend probably won't eat us, but we will surely die of thirst. If you don't like that answer, I'm sorry. I went in *your* place to talk to the dragon *you* called down on us, and tried to explain to it why you haven't been to see it. I went without sleep all that night and the next day and most of last night and all day today, and had precious little before that. Now it's your turn. *You* come up with a plan and *I'll* go to sleep. If I can be of any assistance, let me know no earlier than noon tomorrow. Good night."

I first congratulated myself on giving her a piece of my mind, then berated myself for not striving to be more helpful. She was discussing a problem that was most intensely mine as well as hers. But I could not continue to feel guilty—my mind was empty of anything useful and my feelings were all of a surly and disgruntled nature, if not downright disgusted and hostile. I fell onto my cot resolving to speak to her again after a good night's sleep. As my cheek touched my blanket, these thoughts flowed away. Sometime later I stirred long enough to hear Dolores murmuring and the distinctive drawl of one of the young soldiers answering, "Thank you, ma'am. That's mighty thoughtful of you. A man gets thirsty standin' guard all night." I smiled halfway into another dream, feeling proud that my upbraiding had gotten through to Dolores. She had finally quit feeling sorry for herself long enough to do something practical.

The dregs of a dream remained with me as shouting voices shocked me into wakefulness. This dream was different, for the dragon was addressing me in it. It curled around its crater, feeding. Someone was with it, but at first I couldn't tell who.

Generally speaking, we are pleased. For a daughter of the Navigator, you are an unusually worthy messenger. Somewhat tardy in producing results, perhaps, but considering your lineage, on the whole quite adequate. We take issue with only one detail of your service, and that is that the presenter of a sacrifice must always wear or at least carry the disk and the ring. If you are to assist the jaguar woman in the future, you must see to it that she is properly adorned. Such details seem trifling, perhaps, but in this case we cannot grant a further boon to the jaguar woman because her sacrifice is improperly presented. We must draw the line somewhere. Observance of good form is necessary to the orderly completion of lessons. Orderly completion of lessons leads to the orderly growth of society.

The dream and the shouting were explained by a single occurrence: Dolores, the chief, and Purdy had absconded in the middle of the night with all of the horses except one of the cavalry ponies. The soldiers blamed the Indians for the loss of their horses until they found that all of the Indians and Felipa were still locked in the tack room, the key in Kruger's possession. Purdy and the chief had been under military guard— the military guard I had overheard Dolores ministering to with a cooling drink the night before. She had made the rounds of the guards, spiking their water with generous doses of Mariquilla's sleeping potion.

Drake lost some of his customary aplomb, bellowing that he was surrounded by traitors and ingrates. He banished all of the women to the kitchen and the working courtyard. It was he I heard shouting at Mariquilla outside the kitchen door as I rubbed the sleep from my eyes.

"And just where were you while your helper was helping herself to the army's horses?" he demanded.

I peered around the corner. Mariquilla's face was drawn tight with exhaustion. She pulled her rebozo close to keep off the morning chill and the hint of—could it really be?—dampness in the still-darkened morning. She puffed her cigar in short little chugs, like a railway engine just getting under way. When she pulled it from her mouth after listening to him blame her for several minutes, she spat, barely missing his right sleeve.

"Me, I have all night been caring for the injured soldiers, treating their burns. Dolores helped me until she says she is too tired so I tell her go to bed. She asks me where are the herbs of sleeping for she fears she is too tired to sleep well. I direct her. How am I to know?"

Mrs. Jenkins wafted out of her room without the usual bustle either in her manner or in her costume. Drowning had had a subduing effect on her. "Oh, Bubba, she really was busy with those poor little old soldier boys. I heard 'em moanin' and screamin' all night, off and on. Can't you possibly quarter them somewhere other than the drawin' room? I barely slept a wink—"

"If you didn't sleep, how come you weren't awake to tell me when that bitch took the horses? You in on this too?"

"Why, no, I just assumed you men were doin somethin' with them. It never occurred to me to *pry*. But cheer up, darlin', do. Things aren't as bad as they could be. She did leave us one horse, so we can send a messenger to the army for more help."

Drake's eyes bored through her. "Stay with these other sluts till I decide what's to be done, Lovanche. All of you, keep away from the soldiers. They're rough men. No tellin' what might happen."

Hulda Ledbetter rounded the corner from the corral then, a sniffling Claytie in tow. She raised an eyebrow at Drake's departing back.

Lovanche looked as if she'd been socked in the stomach. She spread her fingers on her skirt, as if smoothing it, and said quietly to Hulda, "Mrs. Ledbetter, Mr. Drake seems to think the ladies need more supervision than they've been gettin' and has asked me to see to it. Naturally, I don't wish to subvert your authority. Where do you suggest I start?"

Her eyes were down and her voice shook. Hulda had heard part of the conversation. The rest she guessed. "Why don't you and Claytie go help Merenciana in the bakery? I think she had some idea of makin' those bread-dough skulls up to treat the soldier boys for Halloween. A mite frivolous, but fittin' somehow under the circumstances."

Mariquilla sighed and slumped to the floor of the kitchen, cigar dangling disconsolately from her lips as she balanced her elbows on her knees and stared off into the distance. "Instead of making replicas of the dead, we should be struggling to avoid joining them."

"Well, it may not be so bad after all," Mrs. Ledbetter said. "That Dolores is a flighty little thing but I think she's done us a good turn by takin' those horses. This way the major is goin' to have to come himself to see what's up, and he and Drake get along like cats and dogs. He's bound to do somethin'."

"Yes," I said, "but what? The dragon is invincible to most weapons. After it's eaten the cavalry horses, what's to stop it from eating the major's horse, every horse the army has, and every horse and cow in Texas or the whole country, for that matter? Dolores has only expanded the dragon's roster of possible victims. Much as I hate to say it, as long as the army is here to protect us from Drake, we really need to try to think what can be done about the dragon. Unless it is dealt with soon, the whole world may end up looking like ancient Mexico, with Kukulkan presiding while Drake and Kruger bully Dolores into serving up sacrifices and their suggestions for running the world."

Claytie ran up then, bearing the upside-down top half of a skull filled with slimy green brains.

"Aunt Lovanche wanted to know is this your disgustin' idea of a casserole," she said, handing the mess tc Mariquilla.

"No," she said. "It is the burn cure—the bowls are all still dirty from the night of the fire. Merenciana had this from her baking early this morning, so I dumped my medicine inside."

"It's bread, and you poured liquid in it?" I asked.

"The bread is hardened with glue so you can fill the center, if you like, with special treats to offer the dead on All Souls' Day, the Day of the Dead. It is the custom, Valentina."

"Well, I don't reckon the dead got much use for your burn cure, Mariquilla, and particularly not for the sleepin' potion—" Hulda scoffed. She sniffed the medicine and wrinkled her nose. "Seems right, keepin' it in a skull like that, 'cause it sure does look like poison when you don't know what it is. You know, too bad poison wouldn't work on that dragon. We could fill one of these things full of it and give it to the varmint. But I reckon it would just get burned up."

Mariquilla stuck the lit end of her cigar through the skull's eye socket. The orange glow winked out. "Poison would. I thought of that. The creature is so big we would have to fill the entire hide of a steer to stand the smallest chance of making it ill. Besides, it allows its prey to rot and become infested before it eats it. I think that any poison I can devise is as nothing compared to what Kukulkan feeds itself voluntarily. And remember, it has lived for many hundreds of years. It is a very healthy creature, that god."

"Except," I said, glancing from the burn cure to Mariquilla, to Hulda, "for a chronic case of heartburn and a badly inflamed throat."

The idea was, as Hulda said, a harebrained one, but it was the only thing we could think of that had a prayer of working. We had eliminated poison and knew from vast experience that guns and cannon didn't even seriously annoy the dragon, which was vastly superior in firepower. Ordinary fire didn't hurt it either. And on the whole, we felt we had nothing to lose. Even if Mariquilla's concoctions had no effect, we would have given the dragon a sacrifice and could then ask for something in return.

That was the main source of contention. What to ask. What we really wanted was for it to go away, but that was one request unlikely to be granted. Besides, even if it did leave, depending on where it went our wish could make matters worse. Hulda thought we ought to ask for something modest like rain and replenishment of the herds, but I reminded her that thus far at least, the dragon hadn't worked any such actual magic as producing cows from thin air—the herds would have to come from someplace. Gold, true love, and distant travel were other suggestions, followed closely by requests for the demise of Drake and Kruger. Hulda told everybody to hush and stop countin' their chickens before they were hatched—or they'd be stillborn, courtesy of Drake and Kruger. I just prayed Mariquilla's medicine wouldn't let us down.

While we gathered utensils and flour, chilis and glue, Drake and Kruger gathered men—scalphunters and army— to pursue Dolores on foot. Such a plan would have seemed foolhardy, except that they knew Dolores would be heading only one of two places—to the crater or the water hole. They counted on the tracks to make the correct choice for them. What they didn't count on was the sandstorm.

The men had scarcely stepped out the gate when it swept across the desert with the force and suddenness of a tidal wave.

"To the rear, men!" the lieutenant half-cried, half-coughed, his voice choking on the gritty wind. The cavalrymen slid back inside the gates on a gale of dust and sand. Drake and Kruger thought they knew where they were going, however. They had been in sandstorms before. The tracks led off in the direction of the crater, and that was where they were going. If the storm got too bad they would go to ground. But they had water and knew the desert like the back of their hands.

"That is the first time I ever knew Drake to do

somethin' actually stupid," Hulda said wonderingly. She, Mariquilla, Merenciana, and I stood in the kitchen watching waves of sand and dust whip in front of the door. Her voice was muffled in the fold of the shawl she wore over her nose and mouth. "By the time he finds her in all this, Dolores will have done whatever damage she's a-gonna do. Why don't he stay home till this blow is over?"

I shook my head. "No," I told her, "he can't. We can't." I had to strain my voice through my rebozo and project above the whistling, hissing wind. Mariquilla pushed us back into the pantry. Her black eyes blinked away grit and tears of irritation.

"You have had another dream?" she asked me.

"I have. Dolores still needs these"—I held up the ring and disk—"to make the sacrifice. Once Drake finds her and the dragon, he'll know about it. If he has the ritual jewels, Dolores, and somebody to sacrifice, he can get whatever he wants from Kukulkan."

"But he can't get 'em if you have 'em."

"Not until he finds me, at least," I said.

"Oh."

"We have to proceed with our plan."

"The chilis are strung into garlands and all is in readiness," Merenciana said, "but we cannot walk so far in this. We will be blown away. And once there, what of your plan? We can do no baking in this."

"Won't hurt to be loaded down anyway," Hulda said. "Keep the wind from blowin' us clear to Santa Fe. And maybe it'll let up by the time we get there. If we get there."

"I think maybe we should wait for the major to come from the fort," Mariquilla said. "If we die in the sandstorm, we will not have helped."

She had a good point. But if the major also decided that dragons were a matter for the immigration authorities and that jewelry found on Drake's land belonged to Drake, even if the dragon bestowed it elsewhere, all would be lost. I personally had no faith in bureaucratic decisions when it came to saving the world.

Too frustrated and restless to stay cornered in the kitchen, I braved the storm. I intended to head for my room, but the wind drove me toward the corral, the sand stinging my back, arms, and legs through my clothing, lashing my exposed cheeks and hands. I had the outdoors to myself. Both civilian and military sentries did their guarding from inside, out of the wind and over decks of cards.

Since the dragon had destroyed the storeroom, I could look right through the spot where the back wall of the dungeon collapsed and out across the ruins into the desert. Or where I knew the desert should be. A rippling wall of sand obscured every detail of the landscape. Every detail except . . . Were those lanterns, those specks of greenish light beckoning in the distance?

They were still there when I pulled Mariquilla, Merenciana, and Hulda from the kitchen long enough to see. "The dragon is sending for me," I told them. "It wants the regalia. Will you come? Shall we try the plan?"

"But the baking, the storm . . ." Merenciana protested, shouting in my ear.

"Kukulkan is the Wind-bringer," Mariquilla said, raking the snaking rags of hair from her face. "The storm will pass."

So we gathered up our provisions and water. No one poked his head out long enough to protest except E.F. Once he saw that Hulda was determined to go, although he thought she was crazy, he hoisted the flour sack on one shoulder and his rifle on the other and waited for the rest of us. Claytie, with a child's sixth sense for hearing things she's not supposed to, blew in looking for something to eat and caught us preparing to leave. She threatened to tell if we didn't take her along, and showed she was Drake's true kin when she further blackmailed E.F. into breaking down the tack-room door to free Felipa and the Indians.

Before anything else could happen, we plunged into

the storm, four women, two girls, one able-bodied and two injured Indian warriors, an elderly wrangler, five big mixing bowls, two skins of water, fifty pounds of flour, and assorted other ingredients. Then we had to stop and wait for Merenciana to run back to the bakery and pick up the sack of glue powder.

She tore toward us as if the dragon was after her. "I was seen—" she began.

Right behind her sailed Mrs. Jenkins, her lavender lace skirts billowing in the wind, a Chinese silk shawl wrapped around her head and shoulders.

"Yoo-hoo! Girls!" she called, the wind having no chance against her shrill whinny. "Do wait for me!"

I turned to run, but Hulda held my elbow tight. Lovanche Jenkins' drawl might still be as sugary and silly as ever but her face was determinedly grim when she joined us. I glared at her, but without another word she pulled a half-dozen wooden spoons from beneath her shawl and extended them to Hulda.

Hulda stared at her for a moment, then clapped her on the back. "You carry 'em, Lovanche. We all got our own load."

The green lights bounced up and down impatiently, closer now, and we headed toward them, each of us following on the heels of the last.

The wind pushed at our backs and the lights bobbed just ahead. I thought maybe it was the dragon, invisible except for its eyes, but I seemed to be wrong. We waded through the sandstorm for another hour that felt like days. Our feet were barely able to rise, and if someone fell, as each of us did at one time or another, the others had to dig him out of a drift before we could proceed. E.F. was carrying his lariat on his belt and took it off to tie us together. The sand stung us to bleeding, cutting across our cheeks like saws and ripping our clothing. I kept expecting to suddenly bump into Drake's party, huddled in the sand, but we must have passed them in the storm. If Drake's party saw our lights, they must have ignored them, but the globes guided us well. I panicked when they blinked out, but with the next footstep I walked out onto the trail leading to the crater. Ahead, the mountains rose sharply against the sky, the sunlit clouds almost painfully bright after the darkness of the storm. Behind, the wind howled and the whole eastern horizon was rosy-dun with blowing dust and red lightning. But the twin green lights had disappeared altogether.

The walk seemed to take forever, but along the Rio's bed some of the reeds and plants Mariquilla needed for her medicines hung on for dear life in that slightly damper and more shaded soil. Only the yucca, of all her ingredients, was truly plentiful. With fresh ingredients, the effectiveness of her medicines increased.

We smelled the canyon before we saw it this time, but the stench was a little fainter. By common agreement, we unloaded our burdens at the lower end, near the cave.

Mariquilla built her greasewood fire for stewing her weeds inside the cave, while Merenciana supervised the bread-dough-making. I divested myself of the *jalapeño* garlands I had worn around my waist and left them inside the cave.

The faint reverberation of a giant heartbeat vibrated off the floor and walls of the riverbed.

I hunkered down beside Hulda, Lovanche, Claytie, and Felipa, and we each took one of the bowls and slapped together a big hunk of gluey, thick dough under the supervision of Merenciana.

She officiated, but was herself busy weaving a loose superstructure of twigs into a four-legged big-bodied shape complete with head. When our dough was the proper consistency, she called Mariquilla and the two of them began shaping it, spreading it with their fingertips and the flats of their thumbs across the basketlike frame. Slowly the bread dough and twigs took on the shape of a rather odd-looking albino cow.

I watched for a long time, but gradually the rhythmic thrum of the earth under my feet demanded that I turn from the seemingly peaceful domestic activity toward the heartbeat and the dragon's stench.

E.F. looked down from the ridge on top of the cave, where he stood guard. I waved up to him briefly and he nodded down to me. "Duststorm's about blowed itself out," he said, and resumed his watch. For the first time since I arrived in the *despoblado*, I wished it were a little hotter, so Merenciana's creation would bake more quickly in the sun. If Drake's party had lost their way in the sandstorm, they'd find it quickly enough now. And then what would we do? Perhaps if they didn't understand the nature of our offering they'd allow us to make it anyway, but no—I would not give up the ring and disk so that they could sacrifice a human being. If they made the first offering, we would no longer be on speaking terms, I feared. If only we could have baked our creation back at the fort! But with the sandstorm, it would have been bread crumbs by the time we arrived.

The walk was longer than I remembered it, the boom of the dragon's heart louder, the stench less overwhelming. Perhaps I had finally grown used to it. I trod carefully, monitoring the heartbeats, measuring them against my own. I passed a hole in the canyon wall, just wide enough for a man, and felt my way past it to solid rock again. I was about a foot farther down the wall when I heard a hoarse hacking and a slimy projectile slapped the back of my head. I whirled. Purdy's camel regarded me with an expression similar to that I have seen on various churchwomen bent on wrecking one's reputation—sanctimonious malice.

When I resumed breathing, I stuck my tongue out at the beast and scuttled away from it, glancing back to make sure I was not attacked from the rear again, and wondering how much of a camel hide Mariquilla's potions would fill. That was how I fell over Purdy and Rain-in-the-Face before I saw them.

My foot caught the bend of Purdy's knee and he flopped over the chief as I landed with my knees in his stomach. Other than to "oof" slightly, neither man said a thing. I rolled off Purdy, then crawled over to take a closer look.

They were warm and their chests rose and fell, but when I thumbed open one of Purdy's eyelids, his eye was rolled up in his head. The chief was in the same condition. Both were deeply unconscious. Neither of them roused, or so much as flinched, when touched. They needed help, the sooner the better.

As I approached the cave again, I saw E.F. stand, gun in hand, and shade his eyes with the flat of his hand.

"Hey, Ma," he called down to Hulda, "how much longer you reckon this little biscuit of yours is goin' to take?"

"Quite a while. It's hollow, so it'll bake fast, but we have to get it hard enough to hold the fixin's."

"Blow on it some, then. I saw mirrors flashin' from the fort and over to the south. I'd say we ought to look for company before long."

"Foot!" Hulda swore.

By that time I was within range to add my own bit of news. E.F. climbed down, and he, Felipa, Claytie, and the Indian braves walked back up the canyon with me. When the braves saw Purdy and the chief, they backed away, shaking their heads and talking rapidly among themselves, refusing to touch the rainmakers.

"Their spirits have been stolen," Felipa said, nodding to the inert bodies on the ground.

"No," Dolores, approaching us from behind, corrected her. "Just borrowed." She turned to me. "You brought the ring and disk?" Her eyes were wide and moony.

"Yes, but I left them in my shawl back at the campsite," I lied.

"What did you do to Dr. Purdy and the chief, Dolores?" Claytie demanded. "I thought you liked them."

Dolores' voice was slow and quiet. "You needed guides through the sandstorm, did you not? Souls travel faster and burn brighter unencumbered by flesh. They will be restored."

For someone who had been so crazy about Purdy just the day before, she did not appear to be in much of a hurry. "We may need their help," I told her. "We brought a fresh offering for Kukulkan, but it isn't done yet, and Mr. Ledbetter believes Drake and Kruger are on their way." I tried to pierce her mooniness by speaking crisply and staring hard into her eyes. She blinked a little at the mention of Kruger and Drake. "You do understand what it will mean if they make the first sacrifice?" I asked.

"Sacrifice?" she echoed, her voice only partially her own. "Sacrifice?" Green mist rolled forward to envelop us all as Kukulkan slithered around the bend in the canyon. The dragon appeared slightly smaller than it had when last I saw it, but its eyes were no less large. Two green globes faded in and out of the mist around its feet.

Felipa made herself very small and Rabbit cringed back a pace. "Yes, a sacrifice, Wind-bringer," I said. "An offering we are making ourselves, but we fear it will not finish baking before—"

"Baking? Then it is a comestible but not flesh?"

"I'm afraid so," I apologized. "We're fresh out of animals for some reason."

"But that is wonderful. We are so weary of flesh. And it is your creation. This pleases us. This pleases us greatly. Be not disturbed over baking, child. We are the most skillful of bakers."

I believe it was E.F. who groaned. He slid down the cliff wall beside Purdy and the chief, his expression not all that dissimilar from theirs.

"But we wished to surprise you, Wind-bringer," I said. "Besides, your fire is so intense—"

"We have the most minute control over our flame and we will avert our eyes in order to preserve the surprise so that proper presentation may be made. Simply tell us when to bake."

"Uh . . . it would go faster returning to the offering if

Dr. Purdy and the chief could walk under their own power," I suggested, hope fairly bounding back into my breast again. Perhaps we would beat Drake and Kruger after all.

Dolores signed a complex pattern with her fingers and plunged them into the green mist. The globes detached themselves from the rest of the greenery. She wiped her fingers against first Purdy, then the chief. The globes followed her lead, hovering over the faces of the unconscious men, growing and shifting in shape, fitting themselves over the heads, shoulders, torsos, and limbs until each body was covered in a green glow, which gradually sank in. The men rose and stretched.

" 'Mornin', darlin'. 'Mornin', dragon," Purdy remarked, then took in all of us. "Is this a party or a lynchin'?"

"Ugh," Rain-in-the-Face said.

The girls darted ahead to tell everyone the dragon was coming. It circled above us until we came upon our campsite, and when Dolores called to it, it landed with its eyes closed a few feet from our anemic steer. Merenciana peered anxiously from the cave mouth, her fingers working rosary beads, her mouth mumbling prayers. Hulda, Lovanche, and Mariquilla clustered around her, as the dragon breathed a gentle, foul-smelling glow onto the doughy structure, crisping and hardening it to a golden brown crust.

"We deem it should be perfect and now depart to prepare ourselves to receive the offering. Attend us, jaguar woman." With a flick of its tail it slithered rather than flew back up the valley, Dolores behind it. I was relieved that she did not demand the regalia then and there. I wanted to hold onto it in case Drake arrived before we could present our offering. Rather than allowing the ring and disk to fall into his hands, I was prepared to fling them into the dragon's maw.

Merenciana walked around her creation, patting it in an awestruck sort of way.

Hulda helped Merenciana lug the kettle of burn cure out of the cave. "Mighty neighborly of a big shot like that to come over and bake its own cookie," she said. "Shame it has to go. 'Cept for it's kinda hard on the stock, I'd as soon have it around as Drake."

Lovanche sniffed. "Bubba means well, but he has fallen in with evil companions. That Mr. Kruger is no gentleman, I can tell you. But the dragon has been a deity for thousands of years. I always did say breeding tells."

E.F. chose that moment to inform us that the men with the mirrors were less than two miles away, signaling to another group close behind them.

"Hey, now, don't you worry 'bout that, Gramps," the chief said, loading Purdy's horse pistol. "I don't exactly know what the ladies are up to, but both them and the dragon seem to have their hearts set on it and if there's one thing I hates to see it's a disappointed dragon. Critter gave me the best night's sleep I've had since before the war. Me an' you an' Al an' these fine Comanche gentlemen here, if they've a mind to, will make sure the boys down yonder don't go interruptin' nothin'. Meanwhile, you ladies better go play tea party, if that's so all-fired important."

"If the dragon thinks it's important, it's important," Purdy said, loading the buffalo rifle. "I only hope we have enough ammunition to hold 'em off."

E.F. shook his head. "I'm pretty much usin' this rifle-gun for a walkin' stick now. But I got my rope. Reckon I can hang 'em if need be."

The men deployed themselves above the cave, seeking the advantage of high ground. Felipa and her Comanche friends took the top of the opposite canyon wall. They had no weapons but there were many large, hard rocks close to hand.

The rest of us turned our attention to the bread-dough steer. "It's light enough to carry the way it is," Hulda said. "But once we put the weeds in it we might break it movin' it. Still, I think it ought to be all ready by the time Mr. Lizard sees it so he don't go swallowin' the shell premature, before we've got the juice in."

"There's a bend in the canyon wall just before the hole," I said. "We can stop there and fill it."

Had the dragon not been so busy preparing for its own appearance at its first formal presentation, it would no doubt have enjoyed the sight of our shabby little religious-seeming procession as we paced solemnly up the canyon, trying to coordinate skirts, footing, and the fragile sculpture rising above us. I was guiltily reminded of Moses' children and the golden calf, but quickly amended my thinking. This particular gift was actually more in the nature of a Trojan horse.

The camel watched with a supercilious smirk as we passed. I wondered if the beast realized how fortunate it was that the dragon was looking forward to something other than flesh. Merenciana, Hulda, and I carried the bread-dough creature between us, while Claytie, Mariquilla, and Mrs. Jenkins brought up the rear with the pots of sleeping potion and burn cure. We set out burdens down a few yards beyond the cleft where the camel sheltered.

The dragon's heartbeat was loud enough now to serve as a metronome, coordinating our activities so that we moved in time with each other. The pulped weeds of the burn cure slid smoothly down into the hole, slopping over a little on the sides. The sleeping potion bubbled down afterward and we closed the hole with the slab of dough cut from the bread-dough body for that purpose. When Claytie looped the garlands of *jalapeños* around our albino offering's neck, it was ready.

I straightened my skirts, placed the golden ring on my finger, and pulled the golden disk from my pocket. The others bent to lift the bread-dough steer, when Hulda stopped them, had Mariquilla sling her black wool rebozo beneath the steer's belly horizontally, and borrowed Lovanche's Chinese silk shawl to sling it from head to tail, between the legs. Then, with Merenciana on the left, Mariquilla on the right, Hulda in front, and Lovanche and Claytie each holding up a side behind, we resumed our procession.

We rounded the bend, the steer's new innards sloshing from side to side. The tight spot between my shoulders had begun to unknot. The offering was ready in time, the dragon showed every promise of liking it a great deal—if only the medicine worked. If not, I still had a chance to ask it for a boon. Perhaps Kukulkan would find it necessary to pay attention to the conflicts of mortals after all if I requested that it accept no sacrifices from Drake or Kruger. Of course, that didn't necessarily preclude offerings from representatives thereof, and making the request too involved would perhaps be counterproductive. Still—

A gunshot cracked across my reverie, followed by another, accompanied by a shrill scream in my right ear. The bread-dough steer lurched backward as Lovanche dropped her end of the shawl, her hands flying to her face. "Mercy sakes alive, they're *shootin'* at one another!" she cried.

"That was the general idea of checkin' the ammunition, I s'pect," Hulda said evenly, though she too looked a little worried. "Coverin' folks is like that."

"But *Bubba!*" she said. "They're shootin' at Bubba—"

"Daddy!" Claytie yelled plaintively, now that Lovanche had communicated her unhelpful hysteria. "Flip!" I wished the girl would at least make up her mind whose side she was on.

"It is a judgment!" Merenciana cried. "A judgment against us for making worship to heathen gods!"

"Now, don't you go gettin' softheaded too," Hulda said. "It ain't no more worshipin' than snarin' rabbits is worshipin', and you know it. Have you all—"

But it was too late. All she, Mariquilla, and I could do was to let our edges of the shawl down slowly as Claytie and Lovanche dropped their end in the dust and ran back the way we'd come. Merenciana shrank back, muttering to herself.

"Come on back over here now," Hulda told her. "We need all four of us to tote this thing." But Merenciana, heretofore so staunch, had cracked, as her creation threatened to. She shook her head and backed off even farther. "Some females," Hulda snorted. "It's not like my man wasn't in danger too. But as a matter of fact, if we're stuck here, I think I'll run down and take a gander myself—"

Two more shots rang out and someone let out a cry.

"Well," I said, "I wish everyone had thought of this before we got this far."

Mariquilla shrugged. "Señora Ledbetter will return. I go now and bring Dolores. You coming?"

Another shot cracked and a scream died in the middle. From the direction of the crater emitted a modest roar of impatient inquiry. I had heard far worse, but that was enough for Merenciana. She took to her heels and bolted back down the canyon, straight into the gunfire.

"You can't do that!" I said, seeing my career as a dauntless leader of worthy undertakings crumble around me. At least perhaps I could keep the fool woman from getting shot. I galloped after her.

I was younger and a few pounds lighter than she, but she was hardened by a life of heavy labor and was more used to the climate. By the time I finally ran her down and bore her to the ground under my weight, we were well within range. A rifle shot snappped past my ear on its way up the ridge. My face was buried in Merenciana's hair but I heard a crumping noise at the same time something bit into my neck and I felt the warm ooze of blood run down my collarbone and across my breast. Turning my head slightly, I saw that a great boulder had split into several smaller pieces just past Merenciana's outstretched palm.

Merenciana wriggled. "Keep down," I snapped, and looked around for a safe place to drag her. Safe places were a thing of the past.

When the echoes of the last shot died away I heard something that sounded like a continuous throaty cough. About twenty yards to our right and in front of us, just inside the entrance to the cave, Hulda sat shaking over a crumpled form. Above her, the chief lay over the lip of the ledge and aimed the horse pistol across the riverbed at one of the scalphunters, who hugged the wall of the Comanche side of the canyon.

I took in as much of the situation as I could. Kruger and Drake's men had taken cover under the ledge where the Comanche were. I suppose they felt being brained with rocks was better than being shot. E.F. was down. I didn't see Rabbit or Growling Porcupine either, though Felipa and the other warrior lobbed the odd stone or two into the fray now and again. Purdy, holding what appeared to be E.F.'s rifle, lay belly-down not far from the chief. His eye was trained on Kruger, who skipped around Drake just as another shot rang out. Drake yelped, giving Felipa a chance to draw a bead on him with her latest boulder.

"Flip, don't!" Claytie yelled, and burst from the cave with Lovanche right behind her. "Daddy—you hurt, Daddy?"

"Get down, you fool ch—" The rest was drowned out in an ear-splitting roar from up the canyon.

Claytie froze. Lovanche froze. Kruger jumped and grabbed one of them under each arm. When the roar died away Kruger's chuckle replaced it. Of the two, it was the more unpleasant noise. "Reckon that's about it, folks. Put down that rock, squaw. You boys up on the ridge, come on down now or I'll blow holes clear through these nice ladies."

"Daddy?" Claytie asked. Drake said nothing.

"Shit," the chief said, and threw the pistol down.

"You get down here too," Kruger said. "Your partner too."

Purdy watched Kruger the whole way down, but no opportunities presented themselves.

"Now, then. You two women on the ground, up. You over there—housekeeper. You get up too. Where I can see your hands."

I rose, and Merenciana, crying now, lumbered to her feet, which seemed to have gone to sleep on her while I held her down. Kruger's scalphunters dipped and wove among us, picking up weapons and pointing them until we were all well-covered.

With two mighty claps the sky darkened. "It's the dragon! John, let Lovanche and Claytie go now—"

"Not just yet, Frank. Here now, Norwood, you cover the woman."

"That's not necessary, Norwood. The woman is my sister. I don't know what she's doing here, but she and my daughter are not to be harmed," Drake said.

Norwood looked back to Kruger, who shoved Lovanche toward him. As the woman fell forward, something glittered briefly in the opening of Kruger's shirt before the scalphunter renewed his grip on Claytie. Drake aimed at Norwood's head but Kruger jerked Claytie toward her father to show him the knife blade poised beneath her chin.

"Drop it, Frank."

The dragon winged toward us like Victory, circling and swooping, its wings like an oncoming thunderstorm, its odor gassing everyone with swirls and curls of green mist which settled down over our heads, covering the riverbed with the miasma. I noticed with a sort of strange detachment that the dragon seemed to be able to generate more or less of the smokescreen as it pleased. This time it produced it in great quantities, using it in the same way a stage magician might. When the mist settled below eye level, we all necessarily looked up to get our bearings. It would have been a good time to make a move, had there been a good one to make. But none of us could look in any other direction than the one we were meant to—up to the ridge above the cave, where the dragon sat like an armored fortress, its green eyes glaring at us. Dolores stood between its foreclaws.

The dragon must have spent the time during which we finished preparing our sacrifice mucking about under its landing platform again. Dolores no longer resembled a downtrodden peasant girl. She was every inch the high priestess. She wore a golden headdress crowned with a somewhat rumpled mess of blue-green feathers, golden bracelets on her arms and legs, a golden scapular upon her neck and chest. Around her shoulders, covering her to her feet, shimmered a cloak of glowing feathers of a thousand different hues.

A hush fell with the mist. The dragon's eyes were compelling. I looked into them, and wished I had not. The great Kukulkan was peeved.

Dolores opened her mouth and her voice rang out like a politician's on election day. "We, the Mighty and Magnificent Wind-bringer, the All-Knowing and All-Wise Kukulkan, Benefactor of the World, Bearer of Civilization, Engineer of Countless Blessings, demand that our pupils cease quarreling among themselves and attend us with the honor and tribute due us. We retire to our landing platform, where we will receive appropriate sacrificial offerings prior to cleansing this area with our flame. Cleansing will commence when the sun's shadow has extended itself one scale's length. All who wish to avoid being cleansed will be prompt."

And with thundering wings and just enough smoke to cover Dolores' departure, the dragon ascended and departed.

"You heard her," Kruger said, keeping his forearm under Claytie's throat while waving his knife at his men and pointing its tip at us. "Bind 'em up and tie 'em together. Drake too. Sorry, Frank, but I'm senior partner now."

The scalphunters were quick and efficient as butchers at binding our arms and stringing us together. The man who grabbed me could have been no more than nineteen years old, with a face bland as a baby's, but his hands were hard and his eyes snapped when he saw the gold sacrificial ring on my finger. He didn't know what it was, of course, except that it was gold. Had it not been too large for me and come off easily, I'm sure he would have had no compunctions about slicing off my finger to get it. I closed my eyes and cursed myself as he took it, all my brave resolutions about flinging the thing into the dragon's flames forgotten, replaced by the immediate sickening fear of being mutilated. The only bright spot was that he did not take the disk—I must have dropped it when I tackled Merenciana.

Roped together like a chain gang, we were herded up the canyon, Claytie and Felipa leading, followed by Lovanche, Hulda, myself, Purdy, the chief, Drake, and the one conscious Indian brave. Merenciana screamed, cried, tore her hair, and shouted imprecations until one of the scalphunters knocked her in the head with his rifle butt and slung her over his shoulder like a sack of flour. E.F., Rabbit, and Growling Porcupine were similarly manhandled. The ropes bound us so tightly that we could barely stumble in order, much less make a bid for freedom.

When we passed the hole where the camel was tethered, Kruger grabbed the reins and led the beast behind him. At first Colonel balked and stayed seated, but when Kruger lifted his knife, Purdy suddenly clucked a command and the camel rose and followed meekly as a dog.

Dolores waited beside the bread-dough steer, still standing with the shawls crossed beneath it beside the canyon wall.

"What the hell is that?" Kruger demanded, kicking sand toward our fragile offering.

She did not answer but led us quickly past it. If the situation of her former friends and coworkers concerned her, her expression and behavior did not indicate it. Under the mesmerizing influence of the gaze of Kukulkan, she seemed to have grown as indifferent as the dragon to human problems.

The earth pulsed loudly, quickly around us. We marched forward, our footsteps moving in double-quick time, toward the dragon. Hulda stumbled, her braids falling loose, and was carried forward by the momentum.

Kukulkan curled around the crater, green phosphorescence smoking up on all sides, as if the dragon sat atop an open fire. The great green eyes drank all of us in with every evidence of satisfaction.

Dolores halted. "Where is the sacrifice?" she demanded, though surely it was obvious.

"Here it is, honey," Kruger said. "We got a couple of virgins here, a couple of prime hussies, two nice fat old cows, and three men just to make it chewy. Ask the lizard if it wants all of 'em or if I should take their hearts out first."

She turned to face the dragon and must have relayed the question. Kukulkan considered the question. "Much as it distresses us," I read in his eyes, "hearts are the traditional offering. Have him remove them with this." A great claw lifted to reveal an obsidian knife with a golden handle in the shape of a serpent. Dolores bent and picked it up, extending it in both hands to Kruger, who slit the rope binding Claytie to Felipa and grabbed the blond younster by the hair.

"Wait!" Dolores said, and faced the dragon again. "Kukulkan will not receive your offering until I wear the ring of sacrifice and hold the disk of power."

She strode past the first few prisoners until she reached me. "You brought them?"

I had no chance to reply.

"Does she mean this ring, boss?" the baby-faced scalphunter asked. "Do I have to give it to her?"

Kruger smacked it out of his hand and presented it to Dolores, who turned back to me. "I lost it," I replied smugly. I had no intention of telling anyone how or where. Unfortunately, I had no choice. Dolores held my eyes and forced them to join the dragon's.

"Where, child? We have waited long for the honor due us. It must be properly done."

In our previous conversation I had worn the disk and ring and now I saw the power they had given me. Then I spoke with the dragon of my own free will. Now I was compelled to answer it. "In the lower part of the riverbed," I said, "where I caught Merenciana."

Kruger dispatched his men at once to find it. Dolores returned to the dragon and they both waited with seeming impassivity while this new obstacle was overcome.

Drake, watching his daughter struggle in Kruger's grasp, was less than impassive. "You're makin' a mistake, John," he said. "You'll never be able to handle the dragon alone. I built Fort Draco, I can build us something bigger. We need each other, John—"

"Huh. You need me to turn you loose so's you can sit back smokin' your handmade cigars, drinkin' your fine liquor, and humpin' your fancy women. You never built nothin', Frank. You got other folks to do it for you, and I can too, with that lizard's gold."

"John, for God's sake, we've been *amigos*. We hunted Comanche, Yaqui together. You ain't gonna turn on me now? There's plenty of gold to share—"

"Yeah, and if you're around you'll find a way to get most of it away from me," Kruger said.

Claytie wiggled in Kruger's grasp and he jabbed the knife under her ear. She sagged. Drake lunged forward, pulling us all with him, and one of the scalphunters hit him with a gun barrel. He reeled backward and fell to his knees. His eyes unfocused for a moment but he retained consciousness. "Kruger, for pity's sake, if you think you have to kill me to get what you want, then kill me and get it over with. But that's my little girl you have there, a little girl, dammit. She can't hurt you. Neither can Lovanche. Let them go—"

"*El patrón*, beggin' me? Well, this was worth holdin' things up for," Kruger said.

Drake faced Dolores and the dragon, and we all turned

our faces into the all-seeing greenness. "Stop him, dragon. Come on. You owe me. It was my cattle you ate. My horses. The house I built with my own hands you wrecked. My woman you have for a flunky. My customers you ran off. Everything I built you've got now. Don't eat my baby too—there'll be nothin' left, my whole life, all that work and nobody even to remember—"

"Aw, shut up, Drake, you're breakin' its heart," Kruger said. "Don't worry. I'll be quick. I know my business. Hair's a little lighter than usual but like you said to Miss Valentine there, I'm good at what I do. She won't suffer. Much."

"Please," Drake begged Kukulkan, but the green eyes failed to do so much as blink. Drake's shoulders shook silently. Claytie's face ran with tears and blood but she could not move enough to sob. Merenciana muttered to herself, Hulda stared dead ahead with dry eyes, and Lovanche sniffled. Purdy and the chief looked alert but resigned. Dolores watched us all without a hint of pity.

"Got it!" Kruger's men returned, one of them waving the disk in the air. Dolores took possession of it.

"We will now commence," she said, slipping the ring on her finger and inserting the disk, not on her clothing as I had thought, but straight through her lower lip, from which a trickle of blood ran. "Where is the first offering?" Her voice was garbled by blood and the weight of the disk in her lip.

"Right here, honey," Kruger said, shoving Claytie to her knees in front of the giant claws.

Kukulkan grunted and Dolores gazed into the lamping eyes again. "We, the Wind-bringer, will first receive the fleshless offering blessed with our own fire."

"Huh?" Kruger asked.

"Our bread-dough steer," I said triumphantly. "Kukulkan wants our bread-dough steer first. It knows we brought it—"

"Fetch it here then," Kruger ordered his henchmen.

"Careful," I called. "It's fragile. Kukulkan won't like it if you break it. Use the shawls—"

"Shut up," Kruger said. "Or are you buckin' to be first after Drake's brat?"

I shut up. Miraculously, the men hauled our steer forward, only slopping a little of the green juice over the side. Kruger cocked an eyebrow at Dolores and the dragon. "If he eats that thing first, does it mean whoever brought it gets first crack at the gold?"

Dolores nodded solemnly.

"What the hell then, I'll give it to him."

Dolores shook her head. "Kukulkan knows this is the gift of the women, the work of their own hands in loving supplication to him."

Kruger's wild eyes got wilder and he dropped Claytie onto the stone floor and grabbed the *jalapeño* garland on our steer.

"It's just *tortilla* dough and chilis, dragon. It ain't even real," he said, jerking angrily at the chilis.

I sought Kukulkan's eyes imploringly. The side of the steer's neck cracked and green stuffing began to ooze out. Kruger hefted the obsidian knife and snatched Claytie's hair again. "Look, this little virgin baby girl here and all these other folks are gonna be much more appetizin' than that thing. You just open up that golden cave and you can have 'em all. Never mind that thing."

The green mist heaved back and forth and the dragon's eyes blazed, the vapors intensifying.

"Kukulkan has spoken," Dolores said. "We will have the fleshless offering first. Submit yourself."

"Submit, shit!" he cried, and flung his arm back to plunge the knife into Claytie. When he did so, two things happened. He knocked the head off the steer and the glittering object I had glimpsed inside his shirt came loose, dangling at his chest. The dragon spread its wings and roared, flicking its tongue toward the steer. Kruger's knife descended, slicing across the tongue. The mirror bounded against the scalphunter's chest and the dragon pulled its tongue back, the *jalapeños* curled within it, ichor dripping from the cut.

It didn't even swallow the *jalapeños*. Its eyes were totally fixed on Kruger and his mirror. Kruger, rigid with shock, stared into the great face.

"It was an accident. I didn't know your tongue was there. I told you I was gettin' you somethin' ready and you didn't need to eat that . . ."

Kruger kept yelling at the dragon, not reading the message in its eyes. The dragon drew itself higher and higher, hovering above the crater, green foul-smelling smoke pouring from its nostrils. Kruger pawed the ground, trying to find Claytie, who had rolled aside, and I caught the reflection of the dragon's awful face, surrounded by its breath, on Kruger's chest.

Dolores flung her arms wide. "We know you, Smoking Mirror. No longer will you dominate the hearts of our people!"

"No!" Kruger cried, and leapt for Dolores. "Don't blame me. It ain't my fault . . ." The obsidian knife in his fist flashed.

The dragon's tail whipped forward, knocking Dolores aside. Kruger saw it coming for him and drew his gun, shooting into the open fangs. The dragon bellowed and a spot of green light no larger than a leaf stem shot past me, through the rope binding me to Hulda, to glimmer along the barrel of Kruger's gun. Before the scalphunter could drop it, the gun glowed with green light, tingeing the stock, the trigger, the fingers curled around it. Everywhere it touched, it ate through, gun, hand, and arm, before they could withdraw. Kruger arched away from me, his lips pulled back from his teeth in a soundless snarl, his hair already on fire, the mirror melting onto his chest. Then with one beat of Kukulkan's wings, the fire extinguished as quickly as it had spread and Kruger's remains lay at our feet.

Kukulkan's great eyes were half-veiled by lids projecting patterns of shock and terror. "Smoking Mirror, embodiment of destruction, is by us destroyed, but"—the unveiled half of the eyes searched the corpse—"Smoking Mirror was not this man, but the object on the chest of the man which is no more. The object a mirror—the reflection a mockery of ourself. What evil is this? What wickedness?"

I was dimly aware that around me men were swearing, men and women screaming, but the dragon's anguish filled my mind. My eyes never left Kukulkan's. The rope which had bound me to Hulda sizzled and curled, and I felt its heat reach my wrists and the knot that held them together. I snapped my arms sharply and the rope came apart.

I don't even recall the burns hurting as I bent over Dolores, removing the ring from her finger, unplugging the disk from her lip.

Strength flooded through me. "Calm yourself, Windbringer."

"But we, who value creation, have destroyed this man, this land, while building nothing."

"He contradicted you," I pointed out. "He would have kept you from the offering you helped us create for you and instead killed more people in your name."

"We are not appreciated here," Kukulkan complained. "We have not been appreciated for some time. People do not want civilization and organization—"

"People learned the lessons you and your kind taught in the past so well that they no longer need your guidance," I told it. "One of the saddest of those lessons is that sometimes things have to be destroyed so that other things can be built. Come on. Pull yourself together."

"We are weak," it said.

I gestured to the bread-dough steer, feeling like Lucrezia Borgia.

The dragon took two steps to it and licked the whole thing in, spilling little of the juice.

I think Hulda sighed.

"Delectable." The eyes beamed down at me. "You should not have—" It began the ritual acceptance. A bullet zinged past me, into its mouth. That was the third shot to pass its fangs. More ichor dripped from it, but the great eyes continued burning, switching from me to the onrush flooding toward us from the rear.

"*Aquí, comandante! Aquí, ándale!* My friends are being murdered—"

Mariquilla flew up the canyon, the cavalry, now more nearly infantry, behind her.

Bullets rang past my ears and the dragon pumped its wings and took flight, knocking anyone who was standing to the ground and the approaching soldiers backward several paces. The sky darkened with wingbeats and roiling clouds. Kukulkan shot a thin warning fork of fire, which was answered by another in the lower end of the valley.

"Get clear, ladies!" Lieutenant Dougherty barked, his voice swept away on the whipping wind which countered the dragon's wingbeats. "We've got dynamite here. We'll blow the thing to kingdom come!"

The dragon belched another gout of fire, but it didn't have the range it should have, fizzling yards short of the soldiers.

Dolores rolled over, groaning. "My children—"

"Get out of here!" I screamed at the dragon. "They're going to blow you up!"

"Clear the area!" Dougherty screamed again.

Kukulkan seemed to be having difficulty. The rising wind buffeted the great beast, sending it into a tailspin. It righted itself and hovered above the hole, shooting a lazy tongue of smoke at the lieutenant.

The officer cringed but did not sizzle. The burn cure was working. More ichor dribbled out the dragon's mouth, and its eyelids drooped three-quarters shut.

"Please, Wind-bringer," I pleaded. "Down your hole."

Lightning snapped behind the plumage of the left wing and the dragon spun toward it, its eyes veiling completely. The wing tipped downward and the huge tail struggled to right itself.

The lieutenant screamed at me again to get down,

and above all the storm and bellowing and screaming I heard the thin sizzle of fire on the fuse of a dynamite stick as it sailed toward us.

Leaping aside, I rolled toward the wall of the canyon, landing against Hulda and E.F. Rolling, I saw the dragon lurch backward. Rolling, the tail lashed up, knocking the two scalphunters onto the ledges above. Rolling, the wings scraped the sides of the canyon and there was a splitting sound of breaking plumage. Rolling, the huge eyes, now blinded with dreaming patterns, tipped into the crater— another roll, and the head, the wings, the body and tail were gone.

The dynamite, so much slower, plunged in afterward.

It could have fallen less than halfway down that endless tunnel before it exploded, the muffled boom rocking the valley, raining boulders down on top of our unprotected heads and splitting the earth beneath us. I think I heard another roar, but it could have been an echo.

Sometime later, I awakened, hacking up dust, huddled on the ground, my eyes burning, my mind reeling from being snatched so abruptly from contact with that larger mind. My head and shoulders were wet, my shawl soaked through. Men in wet blue uniforms hauled rocks out of the way and knelt beside groaning people.

Hulda smiled at me. E.F. grimaced ruefully, his hand holding a blood-soaked bandanna to his right shoulder.

Mariquilla bathed Dolores' face while Merenciana rocked Lovanche Jenkins in her arms and cried. Lovanche cried too. Felipa's co-tribesmen had somehow managed to vanish, but Felipa stood helplessly, touching Claytie's shoulder, while she knelt beside her father. Drake was half-sitting, supported by a cavalryman. Blood covered his head and neck, soaked through his shirt.

"Rain," he babbled. "The great Kukulkan has brought us rain. Blessed be his name . . ." He threw his arms up, knocking aside both Claytie and the soldier, and washed his head in the rain, arched his neck back and drank the rain, stripped off his clothing and danced in the rain, bowing to it.

Beside me on the other side Purdy snorted. "See what I told you? We do all the work and someone else always gets the credit."

We steamed in the cool wetness and soon those of us who could walk walked back to the fort. Those who couldn't were dragged on makeshift travois. We had to leave quickly, for sudden rains, as Mariquilla reminded me, brought flash floods. We were barely clear of the riverbed before it became a raging torrent. Drake capered and hollered half the way down, then collapsed from his head wound and had to be carried.

Afterword

I received a letter from Hulda Ledbetter yesterday. She sends greetings from E.F., Mariquilla, and old Benito, who is back out herding sheep and goats again since E.F. imported the new flock from Mexico.

It gets lonesome here sometimes. My Spanish never was very good and there's no Lovanche Jenkins to try to make everybody talk English. Guess I'll just have to learn sign language, like the Indians. The dry-goods store Lovanche and Claytie started with that gold is working out fine for them in San Antonio, or so Millard Jones said the last time the mule train run through here. They haven't heard ary a word from Drake since he took off for Mexico. I never could stand the man but it seems a shame that someone capable of buildin' a place like Fort Draco should stay plumb crazy in the head for so long after gettin' knocked on the noggin by a rock. He never has said one word that made sense to anybody since then. Just disappeared across the Rio without even a horse. Muttered something about Kukulkan's other worshipers never having any horses. Oh well, there's crazier than him runnin' around these parts, I guess.

They tried Kruger's men, but nobody could convince the judge that feeding people to a dragon was a hanging offense, so they had to be let go. Guess they'll go back to lifting hair in Mexico. Dolores was mighty upset when you took off with Purdy and the chief like that. I told her she couldn't blame Purdy none for not wanting a woman who couldn't be trusted not to run off with the first big lizard she met, and besides, her lip looked awful. Mariquilla fixed it right up, though. Sure am glad that girl had sense enough to hide out behind the camel and hightail it for the cavalry or I believe our bones would be bleaching alongside Kruger's now. Anyway, Dolores finally did perk up some when Growling Porcupine and Five Horses brought her a pair of wild kids. When poor little old Rabbit died of his wounds, the tribe decided them kids was bad medicine, same way you did. Besides, I think Porcupine talked them into it. He showed signs of bein' almost human, for a Comanche.

Lieutenant Dougherty's commander didn't think much of him losing the horses and coming back with what he thought was a cock-and-bull story, but Dougherty doesn't seem to mind much. He has been spending a lot of time making regular visits of inspection here, just to make sure E.F. and me are doing things proper on Claytie's behalf. Between you and me, the man's been spending a lot of time hanging around the kitchen when Dolores is slapping *tortillas* together. I hope he knows what he's getting into. E.F. says he for one agrees with Purdy that he wouldn't have no woman who could call a dragon on him if he riled her. I told him I don't need no dragons to make myself understood.

I worry about Felipa, what with the army cracking down on the Comanche and rounding them up for Oklahoma, but so far Five Horses' band has kept out of their way. She visited when Porcupine brought Dolores' children back, and tells us she's trying to help her folks find some ways to outsmart the white man without having to lift his hair. Porcupine introduced her to a young half-white warrior, Quanah Parker, and the two of them seem to be hitting it off. I sure do hope she doesn't get caught in the crossfire.

Claytie worries too, and I feel sorry for her, but she's enjoying her new school. Away from Felipa, she sort of takes after Lovanche some. For San Antonio society, she could take after worse. Last I heard, Lovanche had the local doctor, the bank president, and two mine owners after her. Be interesting to see what happens.

Meanwhile, we're all looking forward to that story of yours. E.F. has run pretty much through Drake's library now several times over. He says give his regards to Mr. Buntline.

There's a town springing up west of here. Lot of squatters these days, what with the rain brightening everything up so pretty, the travelers aren't much inclined to go on. We just welcome them all. This is a big old country and not near enough folks to visit with. Mariquilla's remedies are very popular and she shows no inclination to go elsewhere. She picks a lot of plants from up by the hole now. Says the ones from up there have stronger medicine. Last week she asked E.F. to ride up with her. Found some black stuff kind of oozing along those old cracks where the dragon disappeared, and got to wondering what it was. E.F. has sent to Kansas City for some experts, but I don't know. I'm inclined to want to leave that place be.

Hope to hear from you soon that maybe you've found a nice fellow to settle down with. You take care of yourself now, hear?

Your friend,
Mrs. E. F. Ledbetter

I was pleased to get the letter, but I have no mind to settle down for a while. Papa has, and it serves him right for all his years of debauchery that the widow is making him perfectly miserable. I do not live with them, but have taken a small apartment above the Chinese laundry run by Wy Mi's sister. The gold baubles Claytie insisted that I take will bring enough money to set me up until I begin to earn an income from the serialization of my story. Meanwhile, I'm very busy with obituaries and theater reviews. As for the Widow Higgenbotham, she does not trifle with me. A self-righteous harpy is hardly a challenge for one used to dealing with a dragon.

ABOUT THE AUTHOR

ELIZABETH SCARBOROUGH was born in Kansas City, KS. She served as a nurse in the U.S. Army for five years, including a year in Viet Nam. Her interests include weaving and spinning, and playing the guitar and dulcimer. She has previously published light verse as well as five other Bantam novels, *Song of Sorcery, Bronwyn's Bane, The Unicorn Creed, The Harem of Aman Akbar,* and *The Christening Quest.* She makes her home in Fairbanks, Alaska.